Honoré de Balzac

Fame and Sorrow

with Chabert, The atheists mass, La grande bretèche, The purse, La grenadière

Honoré de Balzac

Fame and Sorrow

with Chabert, The atheists mass, La grande bretèche, The purse, La grenadière

ISBN/EAN: 9783337221263

Printed in Europe, USA, Canada, Australia, Japan

Cover: Foto ©Andreas Hilbeck / pixelio.de

More available books at **www.hansebooks.com**

HONORÉ DE BALZAC

TRANSLATED BY

KATHARINE PRESCOTT WORMELEY

FAME AND SORROW

WITH

COLONEL CHABERT, THE ATHEIST'S MASS,
LA GRANDE BRETÈCHE, THE PURSE,
LA GRENADIÈRE

ROBERTS BROTHERS

3 SOMERSET STREET

BOSTON

1890

CONTENTS.

FAME AND SORROW.[1]

DEDICATED TO MADEMOISELLE MARIE DE MONTHEAU.

ABOUT the middle of the rue Saint-Denis, and near the corner of the rue du Petit-Lion, there stood, not very long ago, one of those precious houses which enable historians to reconstruct by analogy the Paris of former times. The frowning walls of this shabby building seemed to have been originally decorated by hieroglyphics. What other name could a passing observer give to the X's and the Y's traced upon them by the transversal or diagonal pieces of wood which showed under the stucco through a number of little parallel cracks? Evidently, the jar of each passing carriage shook the old joists in their plaster coatings.

---

[1] This was the title (*Gloire et Malheur*) under which the story was first published in 1830. The name was changed in 1842 to La Maison du Chat-qui-pelote. The awkwardness of the title in English (The House of the Cat-playing-ball) leads the translator to use the original name given by Balzac.

The venerable building was covered with a triangular roof, a shape of which no specimen will exist much longer in Paris. This roof, twisted out of line by the inclemencies of Parisian weather, overhung the street by about three feet, as much to protect the door-steps from the rain as to shelter the wall of the garret and its frameless window; for the upper storey was built of planks, nailed one above the other like slates, so as not to overweight the construction beneath it.

On a rainy morning in the month of March, a young man carefully wrapped in a cloak was standing beneath the awning of a shop directly opposite to the old building, which he examined with the enthusiasm of an archæologist; for, in truth, this relic of the bourgeoisie of the sixteenth century presented more than one problem to the mind of an intelligent observer. Each storey had its own peculiarity; on the first were four long, narrow windows very close to each other, with wooden squares in place of glass panes to the lower sash, so as to give the uncertain light by which a clever shopkeeper can make his goods match any color desired by a customer.

The young man seemed to disdain this important part of the house; in fact, his eyes had not even rested on it. The windows of the second floor, the raised outer blinds of which gave to sight through large panes of Bohemian glass small muslin curtains of a reddish tinge, seemed also not to interest him. His attention centred on the third storey, — on certain humble windows, the wooden frames of which deserved a place in the Conservatory of Arts and Manufactures as specimens of the earliest efforts of French joinery. These windows had little panes of so green a glass that had he not possessed an excellent pair of eyes the young man could not have seen the blue-checked curtains which hid the mysteries of the room from the gaze of the profane. Occasionally the watcher, as if tired of his abortive watch, or annoyed by the silence in which the house was buried, dropped his eyes to the lower regions. An involuntary smile would then flicker on his lips as he glanced at the shop, where, indeed, were certain things that were laughable enough.

A formidable beam of wood, resting horizontally on four pillars which appeared to bend under the weight of the decrepit house, had received as many and diverse coats of paint as the cheek of an old duchess. At the middle of this large beam, slightly carved, was an antique picture representing a cat playing ball. It was this work of art which made the young man smile ; and it must be owned that not the cleverest of modern painters could have invented a more comical design. The animal held in one of its fore-paws a racket as big as itself, and stood up on its hind paws to aim at an enormous ball which a gentleman in a brocaded coat was tossing to it. Design, colors, and accessories were all

treated in a way to inspire a belief that the artist meant
to make fun of both merchant and customers. Time,
by altering the crude colors, had made the picture still
more grotesque through certain bewildering changes,
which could not fail to trouble a conscientious observer.
For instance, the ringed tail of the cat was cut apart in
such a way that the end might be taken for an onlooker,
so thick, long, and well-covered were the tails of the
cats of our ancestors. To the right of the picture, on a
blue ground, which imperfectly concealed the rotten
wood, could be read the name " GUILLAUME," and to the
left the words " SUCCESSOR TO THE SIEUR CHEVREL."

Sun and rain had tarnished or washed off the greater
part of the gilding parsimoniously bestowed upon the
letters of this inscription, in which U's stood in place of
V's, and *vice versa*, according to the rules of our ancient
orthography. In order to bring down the pride of those
who think the world is daily growing cleverer and wit-
tier, and that modern claptrappery surpasses everything
that went before, it may be well to mention here that
such signs as these, the etymology of which seems fantastic to many Parisian merchants, are really the dead
pictures of once living realities by which our lively ancestors contrived to entice customers into their shops.
Thus, " The Sow a-Spinning," " The Green Monkey,"
and so forth, were live animals in cages, whose clever
tricks delighted the passers in the streets, and whose

training proved the patience of the shopkeepers of the fifteenth century. Such natural curiosities brought better profits to their fortunate possessors than the fine names, " Good Faith," " Providence," " The Grace of God," " The Decapitation of Saint John the Baptist," which are still to be seen in that same rue Saint-Denis.

However, our unknown young man was certainly not stationed there to admire the cat, which a moment's notice sufficed to fix in his memory. He too, had his peculiarities. His cloak, flung about him after the manner of antique drapery, left to sight the elegant shoes and white silk stockings on his feet, which were all the more noticeable in the midst of that Parisian mud, several spots of which seemed to prove the haste with which he had made his way there. No doubt he had just left a wedding or a ball, for at this early hour of the morning he held a pair of white gloves in his hand, and the curls of his black hair, now uncurled and tumbling on his shoulders, seemed to indicate a style of wearing it called " Caracalla," a fashion set by the painter David and his school, and followed with that devotion to Greek and Roman ideas and shapes which marked the earlier years of this century.

In spite of the noise made by a few belated kitchen-gardeners as they gallopped their cartloads of produce to the markets, the street was still hushed in that calm stillness the magic of which is known only to those who wander about a deserted Paris at the hour when its nightly uproar ceases for a moment, then reawakes and is heard in the distance like the voice of Ocean.

This singular young man must have seemed as odd to the shopkeepers of the Cat-playing-ball as the Cat-playing-ball seemed to him. A dazzling white cravat made his harassed white face even paler than it really was. The fire of his black eyes, that were sparkling and yet gloomy, harmonized with the eccentric outline of his face, and with his large, sinuous mouth, which contracted when he smiled. His forehead, wrinkling under any violent annoyance, had something fatal about it. The forehead is surely the most prophetic feature of the face. When that of this unknown young man expressed anger, the creases which immediately showed upon it excited a sort of terror, through the force of passion which brought them there; but the moment he recovered his calmness, so easily shaken, the brow shone with a luminous grace that embellished the whole countenance, where joy and grief, love, anger, and disdain flashed forth in so communicative a way that the coldest of men was inevitably impressed.

It chanced that the man was so annoyed at the moment when some one hastily opened the garret window, that he missed seeing three joyous faces, plump, and white, and rosy, but also as commonplace as those given to the statues of Commerce on public buildings. These three heads framed by the open window, recalled the puffy angel faces scattered among the clouds, which usually accompany the Eternal Father. The apprentices were inhaling the emanations from the street with an eagerness which showed how hot and mephitic the atmosphere of their garret must have been. The elder of the three clerks, after pointing out to his companions the stranger in the street, disappeared for a moment and then returned, holding in his hand an instrument whose inflexible metal has lately been replaced by supple leather. Thereupon a mischievous expression came upon all three faces as they looked at the singular watcher, while the elder proceeded to shower him with a fine white rain, the odor of which proved that three chins had just been shaved. Standing back in the room on tiptoe to enjoy their victim's rage, the clerks all stopped laughing when they saw the careless disdain with which the young man shook the drops from his mantle, and the profound contempt apparent on his face when he raised his eyes to the now vacant window.

Just then a delicate white hand lifted the lower part of one of the roughly made windows on the third floor by means of those old-fashioned grooves, whose pulleys so often let fall the heavy sashes they were intended to hold up. The watcher was rewarded for his long waiting. The face of a young girl, fresh as the white lilies that bloom on the surface of a lake, appeared, framed by a rumpled muslin cap, which gave a delightful look of innocence to the head. Her neck and shoulders, though covered with some brown stuff, were plainly seen through rifts in the garment opened by movements made in sleep. No sign of constraint marred the ingenuous expression of that face nor the calm of those eyes, immortalized already in the sublime conceptions of Raffaelle; here was the same grace, the same virgin tranquillity now become proverbial. A charming contrast was produced by the youth of the checks, on which sleep had thrown into relief a superabundance of life, and the age of the massive window, with its coarse frame now blackened by time. Like those day-blooming flowers which in the early morning have not as yet unfolded their tunics tightly closed against the chill of night, the young girl, scarcely awake, let her eyes wander across the neighboring roofs and upward to the sky; then she lowered them to the gloomy precincts of the street, where they at once encountered those of her adorer. No doubt her innate coquetry caused her a pang of mortification at being seen in such dishabille, for she quickly drew back, the worn-out sash-pulley turned, the window came down with a rapidity which has earned, in our day, an odious name for that naïve invention of our ancestors, and the vision disappeared. The brightest of the stars of the morning seemed to the young man to have passed suddenly under a cloud.

While these trifling events were occurring, the heavy inside shutters which protected the thin glass of the windows in the shop, called the House of the Cat-playing-ball, had been opened as if by magic. The door, with its old-fashioned knocker, was set back against the inner wall by a serving-man, who might have been contemporary with the sign itself, and whose shaking hand fastened to the picture a square bit of cloth, on which were embroidered in yellow silk the words, " Guillaume, successor to Chevrel." More than one pedestrian would have been unable to guess the business in which the said Guillaume was engaged. Through the heavy iron bars which protected the shop window on the outside, it was difficult to see the bales wrapped in brown linen, which were as numerous as a school of herrings on their way across the ocean. In spite of the apparent simplicity of this gothic façade, Monsieur Guillaume was among the best known drapers in Paris, one whose shop was always well supplied, whose business relations were widely extended, and whose commercial honor no one had ever doubted. If some of his fellow-tradesmen made contracts with the government without possessing cloth enough to fulfil them, he was always able and willing to lend them enough to make up deficiencies, however large the number contracted for might be. The shrewd dealer knew a hundred ways of drawing the lion's share of profits to himself without being forced, like the others, to beg for influence, or do base things, or give rich presents. If the tradesmen he thus assisted could not pay the loan except by long drafts on good security, he referred them to his notary, like an accommodating man, and managed to get a double profit out of the affair; an expedient which led to a remark, almost proverbial in the rue Saint-Denis, "God keep us from the notary of Monsieur Guillaume!"

The old dealer happened, as if by some miraculous chance, to be standing at the open door of his shop just as the servant, having finished that part of his morning duty, withdrew. Monsieur Guillaume looked up and down the rue Saint-Denis, then at the adjoining shops, and then at the weather, like a man landing at Havre who sees France again after a long voyage. Having fully convinced himself that nothing had changed since he went to sleep the night before, he now perceived the man doing sentry duty, who, on his side, was examining the patriarch of drapery very much as Humboldt must have examined the first electric eel which he saw in America.

Monsieur Guillaume wore wide breeches of black velvet, dyed stockings, and square shoes with silver buckles; his coat, made with square lappels, square skirts, and square collar, wrapped a figure, slightly bent, in its loose folds of greenish cloth, and was fastened with large, white, metal buttons tarnished from use ; his gray hair was so carefully combed and plastered to his yellow skull that the two presented somewhat the effect of a ploughed field ; his little green eyes, sharp as gimlets, glittered under lids whose pale red edges took the place of lashes. Care had furrowed his brow with as many horizontal lines as there were folds in his coat. The pallid face bespoke patience, commercial wisdom, and a species of sly cupidity acquired in business.

At the period of which we write it was less rare than it is now to meet with old commercial families who preserved as precious traditions the manners, customs, and characteristics of their particular callings ; and who remained, in the midst of the new civilization, as antediluvian as the fossils discovered by Cuvier in the quarries. The head of the Guillaume family was one of these noteworthy guardians of old customs ; he even regretted the provost-marshal of merchants, and never spoke of a decision in the court of commerce without calling it " the sentence of the consuls." Having risen, in accordance with these customs, the earliest in the house, he was now awaiting with a determined air the arrival of his three clerks, intending to scold them if a trifle late. Those heedless disciples of Mercury knew nothing more appalling than the silent observation with which the master scrutinized their faces and their movements of a Monday morning, searching for proofs or traces of their frolics. But, strange to say, just as they appeared, the old draper paid no attention to his apprentices ; he was engaged in finding a motive for the evident interest with which the young man in silk stockings and a cloak turned his eyes alternately on the pictured sign and then into the depths of the shop. The daylight, now increasing, showed the counting-room behind an iron railing covered by curtains of faded green silk, where Monsieur Guillaume kept his huge books, the mute oracles of his business. The too inquisitive stranger seemed to have an eye on them, and also to be scrutinizing the adjoining dining-room, where the family, when assembled for a meal, could see whatever happened at the entrance of the shop. So great an interest in his private premises seemed suspicious to the old merchant, who had lived under the law of the *maximum.* Consequently, Monsieur Guillaume supposed, not unnaturally, that the doubtful stranger had designs upon his strong-box.

The elder of the clerks, after discreetly enjoying the silent duel which was taking place between his master and the stranger, ventured to come out upon the step where stood Monsieur Guillaume, and there he observed that the young man was glancing furtively at the third-floor windows. The clerk made three steps into the street, looked up, and fancied he caught sight of Mademoiselle Augustine Guillaume hastily retiring. Displeased with this show of perspicacity on the part of his head-clerk, the draper looked askance at his subordinate. Then suddenly the mutual anxieties excited in the souls of lover and merchant were allayed, — the stranger hailed a passing hackney coach, and jumped into it with a deceitful air of indifference. His departure shed a sort of balm into the souls of the other clerks, who were somewhat uneasy at the presence of their victim.

"Well, gentlemen, what are you about, standing there with your arms crossed?" said Monsieur Guillaume to his three neophytes. "In my day, good faith, when I was under the Sieur Chevrel, I had examined two pieces of cloth before this time of day!"

"Then it must have been daylight earlier," said the second clerk, whose duty it was to examine the rolls.

The old dealer could not help smiling. Though two of the three clerks, consigned to his care by their fathers, rich manufacturers at Louviers and Sedan, had only to ask on the day they came of age for a hundred thousand francs, to have them, Guillaume believed it to be his duty to keep them under the iron rod of an old-fashioned despotism, wholly unknown in these days in our brilliant modern shops, where the clerks expect to be rich men at thirty, — he made them work like negro slaves. His three clerks did as much as would have tired out ten of the modern sybarites whose laziness swells the columns of a budget. No sound ever broke the stillness of that solemn establishment, where all hinges were oiled, and the smallest article of furniture was kept with a virtuous nicety which showed severe economy and the strictest order. Sometimes the giddiest of the three clerks ventured to scratch upon the rind of the Gruyère cheese, which was delivered to them at breakfast and scrupulously respected by them, the date of its first delivery. This prank, and a few others of a like kind, would occasionally bring a smile to the lips of Guillaume's youngest daughter, the pretty maiden who had just passed like a vision before the eyes of the enchanted watcher.

Though each of the apprentices paid a large sum for his board, not one of them would have dared to remain at table until the dessert was served. When Madame Guillaume made ready to mix the salad, the poor young fellows trembled to think with what parsimony that prudent hand would pour the oil. They were not allowed to pass a night off the premises without giving long notice and plausible reasons for the irregularity. Every Sunday two clerks, taking the honor by turns, accompanied the Guillaume family to mass and to vespers. Mesdemoiselles Virginie and Augustine, Gillaume's two daughters, modestly attired in printed cotton gowns, each took the arm of a clerk and walked in front, beneath the piercing eyes of their mother, who brought up the domestic procession with her husband, compelled by her to carry two large prayer-books bound in black morocco. The second clerk received no salary; as to the elder, whom twelve years of perseverance and discretion had initiated into the secrets of the establishment, he received twelve hundred francs a year in return for his services. On certain family fête-days a few gifts were bestowed upon him, the sole value of which lay in the labor of Madame Guillaume's lean and wrinkled hands, — knitted purses, which she took care to stuff with cotton wool to show their patterns, braces of the strongest construction, or silk stockings of the heaviest make. Sometimes, but rarely, this prime minister was allowed to share the enjoyments of the family when they spent a day in the country or, after months of deliberation, they decided to hire a box at the theatre, and use their right to demand some play of which Paris had long been weary.

As to the other clerks, the barrier of respect which formerly separated a master draper from his apprentices was so firmly fixed between them and the old merchant that they would have feared less to steal a piece of cloth than to break through that august etiquette. This deference may seem preposterous in our day, but these old houses were schools of commercial honesty and dignity. The masters adopted the apprentices; their linen was cared for, mended, and often renewed by the mistress of the house. If a clerk fell ill the attention he received was truly maternal; in case of danger the master spared no money and called in the best doctors, for he held himself answerable to the parents of these young men for their health as well as for their morals and their business training. If one of them, honorable by nature, was overtaken by some disaster, these old merchants knew how to appreciate the real intelligence such a youth had displayed, and often did not hesitate to trust the happiness of a daughter to one to whom they had already confided the care of their business. Guillaume was one of these old-fashioned business men; if he had their absurdities, he had also their fine qualities. Thus it was that Joseph Lebas, his head-clerk, an orphan without property, was, to his mind, a suitable husband for Virginie, his eldest daughter. But Joseph did not share these cut-and-dried opinions of his master, who, for an empire, would not have married his youngest daughter before the elder. The unfortunate clerk felt that his heart was given to Mademoiselle Augustine, the younger sister. To explain this passion, which had grown up secretly, we must look further into the system of autocratic government which ruled the house and home of the old merchant draper.

Guillaume had two daughters. The eldest, Mademoiselle Virginie, was a reproduction of her mother. Madame Guillaume, daughter of the Sieur Chevrel, sat

so firmly upright behind her counter that she had more
than once overheard bets as to her being impaled there.
Her long, thin face expressed a sanctimonious piety.
Madame Guillaume, devoid of all grace and without
amiability of manner, covered her sexagenary head with
a bonnet of invariable shape trimmed with long lappets
like those of a widow. The whole neighborhood called
her "the nun." Her words were few ; her gestures
sudden and jerky, like the action of a telegraph. Her
eyes, clear as those of a cat, seemed to dislike the
whole world because she herself was ugly. Mademoiselle Virginie, brought up, like her younger sister, under
the domestic rule of her mother, was now twenty-eight
years of age. Youth softened the ill-favored, awkward
air which her resemblance to her mother gave at times
to her appearance ; but maternal severity had bestowed
upon her two great qualities which counterbalanced the
rest of her inheritance, — she was gentle and patient.
Mademoiselle Augustine, now scarcely eighteen years
old, was like neither father nor mother. She was one
of those girls who, by the absence of all physical ties
to their parents, seem to justify the saying of prudes,
"God sends the children." Augustine was small, or,
to give a better idea of her, delicate. Graceful and full
of simplicity and candor, a man of the world could have
found no fault with the charming creature except that
her gestures were unmeaning and her attitudes occasion-

ally common, or even awkward. Her silent and quiescent face expressed the fleeting melancholy which fastens upon all young girls who are too feeble to dare resist the will of a domineering mother.

Always modestly dressed, the two sisters had no way of satisfying the innate coquetry of their woman's nature except by a luxury of cleanliness and neatness which became them wonderfully, and put them in keeping with the shining counters and shelves on which the old servant allowed not a speck of dust to settle, — in keeping, too, with the antique simplicity of everything about them. Forced by such a life to find the elements of happiness in regular occupation, Augustine and Virginie had up to this time given nothing but satisfaction to their mother, who secretly congratulated herself on the perfect characters of her two daughters. It is easy to imagine the results of such an education as they had received. Brought up in the midst of business, accustomed to hear arguments and calculations that were grievously mercantile, taught grammar, book-keeping, a little Jewish history, a little French history in La Ragois, and allowed to read no books but those their mother sanctioned, it is unnecessary to say that their ideas were limited; but they knew how to manage a household admirably; they understood the value and the cost of things; they appreciated the difficulties in the way of amassing money; they were economical and full of respect for the faculties and qualities of men of business. In spite of their father's wealth, they were as clever at darning as they were at embroidery; their mother talked of teaching them to cook, so that they might know how to order a dinner and scold the cook from actual experience.

These girls, who were ignorant of the pleasures of the world and saw only the peaceful current of their parents' exemplary lives, seldom cast their youthful eyes beyond the precincts of that old patrimonial house, which to their mother was the universe. The parties occasioned by certain family solemnities formed the whole horizon of their terrestrial joys. When the large salon on the second floor was thrown open to receive guests, — such as Madame Roguin, formerly Mademoiselle Chevrel, fifteen years younger than her cousin, and who wore diamonds; young Rabourdin, head-clerk at the ministry of Finance; Monsieur Cæsar Birotteau, the rich perfumer, and his wife, called Madame Cæsar; Monsieur Camusot, the richest silk merchant in the rue des Bourdonnais; his father-in-law, Monsieur Cardot; two or three old bankers, and certain irreproachable women, — then the preparations in getting out the silver plate, the Dresden china, the wax candles, the choice glass, all carefully packed away, were a diversion to the monotonous lives of the three women, who went and came, with as many steps and as much fuss as though they were nuns preparing for the reception of their bishop. Then, at night, when all three were tired out with the exertion of wiping, rubbing, unpacking, and putting in their places the ornaments of these festivals, and the young girls were helping their mother to go to bed, Madame Guillaume would say, "My dears, we have really accomplished nothing."

If, at these solemn assemblies, the pious creature allowed a little dancing, and kept the whist and the boston and the tric-trac players to the confines of her own bedroom, the concession was accepted as an unhoped-for felicity, and gave as much happiness as the two or three public balls to which Guillaume took his daughters during the carnival. Once a year the worthy draper himself gave an entertainment on which he spared no expense. However rich and elegant the invited guests might be, they took care not to miss that fête ; for the most important business houses in the city often had recourse to the vast credit, or the wealth, or the great experience of Monsieur Guillaume. The two daughters of the worthy merchant did not, however, profit as much as might be thought from the instructions which society offers to young minds. They wore at these entertainments (bills of exchange, as it were, upon futurity) wreaths and ornaments of so common a kind as to make them blush. Their style of dancing was not of the best, and maternal vigilance allowed them to say only "Yes" or "No" to their partners. Then the invariable domestic rule of the Cat-playing-ball obliged them to retire at eleven o'clock, just as the party was getting animated. So their pleasures, apparently conformable with their father's wealth, were really dull and insipid through circumstances derived from the habits and principles of their family.

As to their daily life, a single fact will suffice to paint it. Madame Guillaume required her daughters to dress for the day in the early morning, to come downstairs at precisely the same hour, and to arrange their occupations with monastic regularity. Yet, with all this, chance had bestowed upon Augustine a soul that was able to feel the void of such an existence. Sometimes those blue eyes were lifted for a moment as if to question the dark depths of the stairway or the damp shop. Listening to the cloistral silence her ears seemed to hear from afar confused revelations of the passionate life, which counts emotions as of more value than things. At such moments the girl's face glowed; her idle hands let fall the muslin on the polished oaken counter; but soon the mother's voice would say, in tones that were always sharp, even when she intended them to be gentle, "Augustine, my dear, what are you thinking about?"

Perhaps "Hippolyte, Earl of Douglas," and the "Comte de Comminges," two novels which Augustine had found in the closet of a cook dismissed by Madame Guillaume, may have contributed to develop the ideas of the young girl, who had stealthily devoured those productions during the long nights of the preceding winter. The unconscious expression of vague desire, the soft voice, the jasmine skin, and the blue eyes of Augustine Guillaume had lighted a flame in the soul of poor Lebas as violent as it was humble. By a caprice that is easy enough to understand, Augustine felt no inclination for Joseph; perhaps because she did not know he loved her. On the other hand, the long legs and chestnut hair, the strong hands and vigorous frame of the head-clerk excited the admiration of Mademoiselle Virginie, who had not yet been asked in marriage in spite of a dowry of a hundred and fifty thousand francs. What could be more natural than these inversed loves, born in the silence of that shop like violets in the depths of the woods? The mute contemplation which constantly drew the eyes of these young people together, through their violent need of some relief from the monotonous toil and the religious calm in which they lived, could not fail to excite, sooner or later, the emotions of love. The habit of looking into the face of another leads to an understanding of the noble qualities of the soul, and ends by obliterating all defects.

"At the rate that man carries things," thought Monsieur Guillaume when he read Napoleon's first decree on the classes for conscription, '' our daughters will have to go upon their knees for husbands.''

It was about that time that the old merchant, noticing that his eldest daughter was beginning to fade, bethought him that he himself had married Mademoiselle Chevrel under very much the same circumstances as those in which Virginie and Joseph Lebas stood to each other. What a fine thing it would be to marry his daughter and pay a sacred debt by returning to the orphaned young man the same benefaction that he himself had received from his predecessor in a like situation? Joseph Lebas, who was thirty-three years of age, was fully conscious of the obstacles that a difference of fifteen years in their ages placed between Augustine and himself. Too shrewd and intelligent not to fathom Monsieur Guillaume's intentions, he understood his master's inexorable principles far too well to suppose for a moment that the younger daughter could be married before the elder. The poor clerk, whose heart was as good as his legs were long and his shoulders high, suffered in silence.

Such was the state of things in this little republic of the rue Saint-Denis, which seemed in many ways like an annex to La Trappe. But to explain external events as we have now explained inward feelings, it is necessary to look back a few months before the little scene which began this history.

One evening at dusk a young man, happening to pass before the shop of the Cat-playing-ball, stopped to look at a scene within those precincts which all the painters of the world would have paused to contemplate. The shop, which was not yet lighted up, formed a dark vista through which the merchant's dining-room was seen. An astral lamp on the dinner-table shed that yellow light which gives such charm to the Dutch pictures. The white table-linen, the silver, the glass, were brilliant accessories, still further thrown into relief by the sharp contrasts of light and shadow. The figures of the father of the family and his wife, the faces of the clerks, and the pure lines of Augustine, near to whom stood a stout, chubby servant-girl, composed so remarkable a picture, the heads were so original, the expression of each character was so frank, it was so easy to imagine the peace, the silence, the modest life of the family, that to an artist accustomed to express nature there was something absolutely commanding in the desire to paint this accidental scene.

The pedestrian, thus arrested, was a young painter who, seven years earlier, had carried off the *prix de Rome*. He had lately returned from the Eternal City. His soul, fed on poesy, his eyes surfeited with Raffaelle and Michael-Angelo, were now athirst for simple nature after his long sojourn in the mighty land where art has reached its highest grandeur. True or false, such was his personal feeling. Carried away for years by the fire of Italian passions, his heart now sought a calm and modest virgin, known to him as yet only upon canvas. The first enthusiasm of his soul at the simple picture before his eyes passed naturally into a deep admiration for the principal figure. Augustine seemed thoughtful, and was eating nothing. By a chance arrangement of the lamp, the light fell full upon her face, and her bust appeared to move in a circle of flame, which threw into still brighter relief the outline of her head, illuminating it in a way that seemed half supernatural. The artist compared her involuntarily to an exiled angel remembering heaven. A mysterious feeling, almost unknown to him, a love limpid and bubbling overflowed his heart. After standing a moment as if paralyzed beneath the weight of these ideas, he tore himself away from his happiness and went home, unable either to eat or sleep.

The next day he entered his studio, and did not leave it again until he had placed on canvas the magic charm of a scene the mere recollection of which had, as it were, laid a spell upon him. But his happiness was incomplete so long as he did not possess a faithful portrait of his idol. Many a time he passed before the house of the Cat-playing-ball; he even entered the shop once or twice on some pretext to get a nearer view of the ravishing creature who was always covered by Madame

Guillaume's wing. For eight whole months, given up to his love and to his brushes, he was invisible to his friends, even to his intimates ; he forgot all, — poetry, the theatre, music, and his most cherished habits.

One morning Girodet the painter forced his way in, eluding all barriers as only artists can, and woke him up with the inquiry, " What are you going to send to the Salon?"

The artist seized his friend's arm, led him to the studio, uncovered a little easel picture, and also a portrait. After a slow and eager examination of the two masterpieces, Girodet threw his arms around his friend and kissed him, without finding words to speak. His feelings could only be uttered as he felt them, — soul to soul.

" You love her ! " he said at last.

Both knew that the noblest portraits of Titian, Raffaelle, and Leonardo da Vinci are due to exalted human feelings, which, under so many diverse conditions, have given birth to the masterpieces of art. For all answer the young painter bowed his head.

" How fortunate, how happy you are to be able to love here, in Paris, after leaving Italy. I can't advise you to send such works as those to the Salon," added the distinguished painter. " You see, such pictures cannot be felt there. Those absolutely true colors, that stupendous labor, will not be understood ; the public is no longer able to see into such depths. The pictures we paint now-a-days, dear friend, are mere screens for decoration. Better make verses, say I, and translate the ancients, — we shall get a truer fame that way than our miserable pictures will ever bring us."

But in spite of this friendly advice the two pictures were exhibited. That of the interior made almost a revolution in art. It gave birth to the fashion of *genre* pictures which since that time have so filled our exhibitions that one might almost believe they were produced by some mechanical process. As to the portrait, there are few living artists who do not cherish the memory of that breathing canvas on which the general public, occasionally just in its judgment, left the crown of praise which Girodet himself placed there.

The two pictures were surrounded by crowds. People killed themselves, as women say, to look at them. Speculators and great lords would have covered both canvases with double-napoleons, but the artist obstinately refused to sell them, declining also to make copies. He was offered an immense sum if he would allow them to be engraved ; but the dealers were no more successful than the amateurs. Though this affair engrossed the social world, it was not of a nature to penetrate the depths of Egyptian solitude in the rue Saint-Denis. It so chanced, however, that the wife of a notary, paying a visit to Madame Guillaume, spoke of the exhibition before Augustine, of whom she was very fond, and explained what it was. Madame Roguin's chatter naturally inspired Augustine with a desire to see the pictures, and with the boldness to secretly ask her cousin to take her to the Louvre. Madame Roguin succeeded in the negotiation she undertook with Madame Guillaume, and was allowed to take her little cousin from her daily tasks for the short space of two hours.

Thus it was that the young girl, passing through the crowd, stood before the famous picture. A quiver made her tremble like a birch-leaf when she recognized her own self. She was frightened, and looked about to rejoin Madame Roguin, from whom the crowd had parted her. At that instant her eyes encountered the flushed face of the young painter. She suddenly remembered a man who had frequently passed the shop and whom she had often remarked, thinking he was some new neighbor.

" You see there the inspiration of love," said the artist in a whisper to the timid creature, who was terrified by his words.

She summoned an almost supernatural courage to force her way through the crowd and rejoin her cousin.

" You will be suffocated," cried Augustine. " Do let us go ! "

But there are certain moments at the Salon when two women are not able to move freely through the galleries. Mademoiselle Guillaume and her cousin were blocked and pushed by the swaying crowd to within a few feet of the second picture. The exclamation of surprise uttered by Madame Roguin was lost in the noises of the room; but Augustine involuntarily wept as she looked at the marvellous scene. Then, with a feeling that is almost inexplicable, she put her finger on her lips as she saw the ecstatic face of the young artist within two feet of her. He replied with a motion of his head toward Madame Roguin, as if to show Augustine that he understood her. This pantomime threw a fire of burning coals into the being of the poor girl, who felt she was criminal in thus allowing a secret compact between herself and the unknown artist. The stifling heat, the sight of the brilliant dresses, a giddiness which the wonderful combinations of color produced in her, the multitude of figures, living and painted, which surrounded her, the profusion of gold frames, — all gave her a sense of intoxication which redoubled her terrors. She might have fainted if there had not welled up from the depths of her heart, in spite of this chaos of sensations, a mysterious joy which vivified her whole being. Still, she fancied she was under the dominion of that demon whose dreadful snares were threats held out to her by the thundered words of the preach-

ers. The moment seemed like one of actual madness
to her. She saw she was accompanied to her cousin's
carriage by the mysterious young man, resplendent
with love and happiness. A new and unknown excitement possessed her, an intoxication which delivered
her, as it were, into the hands of Nature; she listened
to the eloquent voice of her own heart, and looked at
the young painter several times, betraying as she did
so the agitation of her thoughts. Never had the carna-
tion of her cheeks formed a more charming contrast to
the whiteness of her skin. The artist then beheld that
beauty in its perfect flower, that virgin modesty in all
its glory.

Augustine became conscious of a sort of joy mingling
with her terror as she thought how her presence had
brought happiness to one whose name was on every lip
and whose talent had given immortality to a passing
scene. Yes, she was beloved! she could not doubt it!
When she ceased to see him, his words still sounded in
her ear: " You see the inspiration of love !" The pal-
pitations of her heart were painful, so violently did the
now ardent blood awaken unknown forces in her being.
She complained of a severe headache to avoid replying
to her cousin's questions about the pictures ; but when
they reached home, Madame Roguin could not refrain
from telling Madame Guillaume of the celebrity given to
the establishment of the Cat-playing-ball, and Augus-

tine trembled in every limb as she heard her mother
say she should go to the Salon and see her own house.
Again the young girl complained of her headache, and
received permission to go to bed.

"That's what you get by going to shows!" exclaimed Monsieur Guillaume. "Headaches! Is it so
very amusing to see a picture of what you see every
day in the street? Don't talk to me of artists; they are
like authors, — half-starved beggars. Why the devil
should that fellow choose my house to villify in his
picture?"

"Perhaps it will help to sell some of our cloth," said
Joseph Lebas.

That remark did not save art and literature from
being once more arraigned and condemned before the
tribunal of commerce. It will be readily believed that
such discourse brought little encouragement to Augustine, who gave herself up in the night-time to the first
revery of love. The events of the day were like those
of a dream which she delighted to reproduce in thought.
She learned the fears, the hopes, the remorse, all those
undulations of feeling which rock a heart as simple and
timid as hers. What a void she felt within that gloomy
house, what a treasure she found within her soul! To
be the wife of a man of talent, to share his fame!
Imagine the havoc such a thought would make in the
heart of a child brought up in the bosom of such a fam-

ily! What hopes would it not awaken in a girl who lived among the vulgarities of life, and yet longed for its elegancies. A beam of light had come into her prison. Augustine loved, loved suddenly. So many repressed feelings were gratified that she succumbed at once, without an instant's reflection. At eighteen love flings its prism between the world and the eyes of a maiden. Incapable of imagining the harsh experience which comes to every loving woman married to a man gifted with imagination, she fancied herself called to make the happiness of such a man, seeing no disparity between them. For her the present was the whole future.

When Monsieur and Madame Guillaume returned the next day from the Salon, their faces announced disappointment and annoyance. In the first place, the artist had withdrawn the picture; in the next, Madame Guillaume had lost her cashmere shawl. The news that the pictures had been withdrawn after her visit to the Salon was to Augustine the revelation of a delicacy of sentiment which all women appreciate, if only instinctively.

The morning on which, returning from a ball, Théodore de Sommervieux (such was the name which celebrity had now placed in Augustine's heart), was showered with soapy water by the clerks of the Cat-playing-ball, as he awaited the apparition of his innocent beauty, — who certainly did not know he was there, — was only the fourth occasion of their seeing each other since that first meeting at the Salon. The obstacles which the iron system of the house of Guillaume placed in the way of the ardent and impetuous nature of the artist, added a violence to his passion for Augustine, which will be readily understood. How approach a young girl seated behind a counter between two such women as Mademoiselle Virginie and Madame Guillaume? How was it possible to correspond with her if her mother never left her? Ready, like all lovers, to invent troubles for himself, Théodore selected a rival among the clerks, and suspected the others of being in their comrade's interests. If he escaped their Argus eyes he felt he should succumb to the stern glances of the old merchant or Madame Guillaume. Obstacles on all sides, despair on all sides! The very violence of his passion prevented the young man from inventing those clever expedients which, in lovers as well as in prisoners, seem to be crowning efforts of intellect roused either by a savage desire for liberty or by the ardor of love. Then Théodore would rush round the corner like a madman, as if movement alone could suggest a way out of the difficulty.

After allowing his imagination to torment him for weeks, it came into his head to bribe the chubby servant-girl. A few letters were thus exchanged during the fortnight which followed the unlucky morning when

Monsieur Guillaume and Théodore had first met. The loving pair had now agreed to see each other daily at a certain hour, and on Sunday at the church of Saint-Leu, during both mass and vespers. Augustine had sent her dear Théodore a list of the friends and relatives of the family to whom the young painter was to gain access. He was then to endeavor to interest in his loving cause some one of those money-making and commercial souls to whom a real passion would otherwise seem a monstrous and unheard-of speculation.

In other respects nothing happened and no change took place in the habits of the Cat-playing-ball. If Augustine was absent-minded; if, against every law of the domestic charter, she went up to her bedroom to make the signals under cover of the flower-pots; if she sighed, if she brooded, — no one, not even her mother, found it out. This may cause some surprise to those who have understood the spirit of the house-hold, where a single idea tinged with poetry would have contrasted sharply with the beings and with the things therein contained, and where no one was able to give a look or gesture that was not seen and analyzed. And yet, as it happened, nothing was really more natural. The tranquil vessel which navigated the seas of Parisian commerce under the flag of the Cat-playing-ball, was at this particular moment tossed about in one of those storms which may be called equinoctial, on account of their periodical return.

For the last fifteen days the five men of the establishment, with Madame Guillaume and Mademoiselle Virginie, had devoted themselves to that severe toil which goes by the name of " taking an inventory." All bales were undone, and the length of each piece of goods was measured, to learn the exact value of what remained on hand. The card attached to each piece was carefully examined to know how long the different goods had been in stock. New prices were affixed. Monsieur Guillaume, always standing up, yard-measure in hand, his pen behind his ear, was like a captain in command of a ship. His sharp voice, passing down a hatchway to the ware-rooms below, rang out that barbarous jargon of commerce expressed in enigmas: " How many H-N-Z?" "Take it away!" " How much left of Q-X?" "Two yards." " What price?" " Five-five-three." " Put at three A all J-J, all M-P, and the rest of V-D-O." A thousand other such phrases, all equally intelligible, resounded across the counters, like those verses of modern poetry which the romanticists recite to each other to keep up their enthusiasm for a favorite poet. At night Monsieur Guillaume locked himself and his head-clerk and his wife into the counting-room, went over the books, opened the new accounts, notified the dilatory debtors, and made out all bills.

The results of this immense toil, which could be noted down on one sheet of foolscap paper, proved to the house of Guillaume that it owned so much in money, so much in merchandise, so much in notes and cheques; also that it did not owe a sou, but that so many hundred thousand francs were owing to it; that its capital had increased; that its farms, houses, and stocks were to be enlarged, repaired, or doubled. Hence came a sense of the necessity of beginning once more with renewed ardor the accumulation of more money; though none of these brave ants ever thought of asking themselves, "What's the good of it?"

Thanks to this annual tumult, the happy Augustine was able to escape the observation of her Arguses. At last, one Saturday evening, the " taking of the inventory " was an accomplished fact. The figures of the total assets showed so many ciphers that in honor of the occasion Monsieur Guillaume removed the stern embargo which reigned throughout the year at dessert. The sly old draper rubbed his hands and told the clerks they might remain at table. They had hardly swallowed their little glass of a certain home-made liqueur, however, when carriage-wheels were heard in the street. The family were going to the Variétés to see " Cinderella," while the two younger clerks each received six francs and permission to go where they liked, provided they were at home by midnight.

The next morning, in spite of this debauch, the old merchant-draper shaved at six o'clock, put on his fine maroon coat, — the lustre of its cloth causing him, as usual, much satisfaction, — fastened his gold buckles to the knee-band of his ample silk breeches, and then, toward seven o'clock, while every one in the house was still asleep, he went to the little office adjoining the shop on the first floor. It was lighted by a window protected by thick iron bars, and looked out upon a little square court formed by walls so black that the place was like a well. The old merchant opened an inner blind that was clamped with iron, and raised a sash of the window. The chill air of the court cooled the hot atmosphere of the office, which exhaled an odor peculiar to all such places. Monsieur Guillaume remained standing, one hand resting on the greasy arm of a cane-chair covered with morocco, the primitive color of which was now effaced ; he seemed to hesitate to sit down. The old man glanced with a softened air at the tall double desk, where his wife's seat was arranged exactly opposite to his own, in a little arched alcove made in the wall. He looked at the numbered paper-boxes, the twine, the various utensils, the irons with which they marked the cloth, the safe, — all objects of immemorial origin, — and he fancied himself standing before the evoked shade of the late Chevrel. He pulled out the very stool on which he formerly sat in presence of his now defunct master. That stool, covered with black leather, from which the horsehair had long oozed at the corners (but without falling out), he now placed with a trembling hand on the particular spot where his predecessor had once placed it; then, with an agitation difficult to describe, he pulled a bell which rang at the bed's head of Joseph Lebas. When that decisive deed was done, the old man, to whom these memories may have been oppressive, took out three or four bills of exchange which had been presented to him the day before, and was looking them over, but without seeing them, when Joseph Lebas entered the office.

"Sit there," said Monsieur Guillaume, pointing to the stool.

As the old master-draper had never before allowed a clerk to sit in his presence, Joseph trembled.

"What do you think of these drafts?" asked Guillaume.

"They will not be paid."

"Why not?"

"I heard yesterday that Étienne and Company were making their payments in gold."

"Ho! ho!" cried the draper. "They must be very ill to show their bile. Let us talk of something else, Joseph; the inventory is finished?"

"Yes, monsieur, and the dividend is the finest you have ever had."

"Pray don't use those new-fangled words. Say 'proceeds,' Joseph. Do you know, my boy, that we owe that result partly to you? Therefore, I do not wish you to have a salary any longer. Madame Guillaume has put it into my head to offer you a share in the business. Hey, Joseph, what do you say? 'Guillaume and Lebas,'— don't the names make a fine partnership? and we can add 'and Company' to complete the signature."

Tears came into Joseph's eyes, though he tried to hide them. "Ah, Monsieur Guillaume," he said, "how have I deserved such goodness? I have only done my duty. It was enough that you should even take an interest in a poor orph — "

He brushed the cuff of his left sleeve with his right sleeve, and dared not look at the old man, who smiled as he thought that this modest young fellow no doubt needed, as he himself once needed, to be helped and encouraged to make the explanation complete.

"It is true, Joseph," said Virginie's father, "that you do not quite deserve that favor. You do not put as much confidence in me as I do in you" (here the clerk looked up hurriedly). "You know my secrets. For the last two years I have told you all about the business. I have sent you travelling to the manufactories. I have nothing to reproach myself with as to you. But you! You have a liking in your mind, and you have never said a word to me about it" (Joseph colored). "Ha! ha!" cried Guillaume, "so you thought you could deceive an old fox like me? Me! when you know how I predicted the Lecocq failure!"

"Oh, monsieur!" replied Joseph Lebas, examining his master as attentively as his master examined him, "is it possible that you know whom I love?"

"I know all, you good-for-nothing fellow," said the worthy and astute old dealer, twisting the lobe of the young man's ear; "and I forgive it, for I did as much myself."

"Will you give her to me?"

"Yes, with a hundred and fifty thousand francs, and I will leave you as much more; and we will meet our new expenses under the new firm name. Yes, boy, we will stir up the business finely and put new life into it," cried the old merchant, rising and gesticulating with his arms. "There is nothing like business, son-in-law. Those who sneer and ask what pleasures can be found in it are simply fools. To have the cue of money-matters, to know how to govern the market, to wait with the anxiety of gamblers till Étienne and Company fail, to see a regiment of Guards go by with our cloth on their backs, to trip up a neighbor, — honestly, of course, — to manufacture at a lower price than others, to follow up an affair when we've planned it, to watch it begin, increase, totter, and succeed, to understand, like the minister of police, all the ways and means of all the commercial houses so as to make no false step, to stand up straight when others are wrecked and ruined, to have friends and correspondents in all the manufacturing towns and cities — Ha, Joseph! is n't that perpetual pleasure? I call that living! Yes, and I shall die in that bustle like old Chevrel himself."

In the heat of his allocution Père Guillaume scarcely looked at his clerk, who was weeping hot tears; when he did so he exclaimed, "Hey, Joseph, my poor boy, what is the matter?"

"Ah! I love her so, Monsieur Guillaume, that my heart fails me, I believe."

"Well, my boy," said the old man, quite moved, "you are happier than you think you are; for, by the powers, she loves you. I know it; yes, I do!"

And he winked his two little green eyes as he looked at Joseph.

"Mademoiselle Augustine! Mademoiselle Augustine!" cried Joseph Lebas in his excitement. He was about to rush out of the office when he felt himself grasped by an iron arm, and his astonished master pulled him vigorously in front of him.

"What has Augustine got to do with it?" asked Guillaume, in a voice that froze the unfortunate young man.

"It is she — whom — I love," stammered the clerk.

Disconcerted at his own lack of perspicacity, Guillaume sat down and put his pointed head into his two hands to reflect upon the queer position in which he found himself. Joseph Lebas, ashamed, mortified, and despairing, stood before him.

" Joseph," said the merchant, with cold dignity, " I was speaking to you of Virginie. Love is not to be commanded; I know that. I trust your discretion; we will forget the whole matter. I shall never allow Augustine to be married before Virginie. Your interest in the business will be ten per cent."

The head-clerk, in whom love inspired a mysterious degree of courage and eloquence, clasped his hands, opened his lips, and spoke to Guillaume for fifteen minutes with such ardor and deep feeling that the situation changed. If the matter had concerned some business affair the old man would have had a fixed rule by which to settle it; but suddenly cast upon the sea of feelings, a thousand miles from business and without a compass, he floated irresolutely before the wind of an event so " out of the way," as he kept saying to himself. Influenced by his natural paternal kindness, he was at the mercy of the waves.

" Hey, the deuce, Joseph, you know of course that my two children came with ten years between them. Mademoiselle Chevrel was not handsome, no; but I never gave her any reason to complain of me. Do as

I did. Come, don't fret,—what a goose you are! Perhaps we can manage it; I'll try. There's always some way to do a thing. We men are not exactly Celadons to our wives,—you understand, don't you? Madame Guillaume is pious, and— There, there, my boy, you may give Augustine your arm this morning when we go to mass."

Such were the sentences which Père Guillaume scattered at random. The last of them filled the lover's soul with joy. He was already thinking of a friend who would do for Mademoiselle Virginie as he left the smoky office, after pressing the hand of his future father-in-law and saying, in a confidential way, that it would all come right.

"What will Madame Guillaume say?" That idea was terribly harrassing to the worthy merchant when he found himself alone.

At breakfast, Madame Guillaume and Virginie, whom the draper had left, provisionally, in ignorance of her disappointment, looked at Joseph with so much meaning that he became greatly embarrassed. His modesty won him the good-will of his future mother-in-law. The matron grew so lively that she looked at Monsieur Guillaume with a smile, and allowed herself a few little harmless pleasantries customary from time immemorial in such innocent families. She discussed the relative heights of Joseph and Virginie, and placed them side

by side to be measured. These little follies brought a
cloud to the paternal brow; in fact, the head of the
family manifested such a sense of decorum that he
ordered Augustine to take the arm of his head-clerk on
their way to church. Madame Guillaume, surprised at
so much masculine delicacy, honored her husband's act
with an approving nod. The procession left the house
in an order that suggested no gossipping constructions
to the neighbors.

"Do you not think, Mademoiselle Augustine," said
the head-clerk in a trembling voice, "that the wife of a
merchant in high standing, like Monsieur Guillaume
for example, ought to amuse herself rather more than
— than your mother amuses herself? She ought surely
to wear diamonds, and have a carriage. As for me, if
I should ever marry I should want to take all the cares
myself, and see my wife happy; I should not let her sit
at any counter of mine. You see, women are no longer
as much needed as they used to be in draper's shops.
Monsieur Guillaume was quite right to do as he did, and
besides, Madame likes it. But if a wife knows how to
help in making up the accounts at times, and looking
over the correspondence; if she can have an eye to a
few details and to the orders, and manage her household,
so as not to be idle, that's enough. As for me, I should
always wish to amuse her after seven o'clock, when the
shop is closed. I should take her to the theatre and

the picture galleries, and into society, — but you are not listening to me."

"Oh, yes I am, Monsieur Joseph. What were you saying about painters? It is a noble art."

" Yes, I know one, a master painter, Monsieur Lourdois; he makes money."

Thus conversing, the family reached Saint-Leu; there, Madame Guillaume recovered her rights. She made Augustine, for the first time, sit beside her; and Virginie took the fourth chair, next to that of Lebas. During the sermon all went well with Augustine and with Théodore, who stood behind a column and prayed to his madonna with great fervor; but when the Host was raised, Madame Guillaume perceived, somewhat tardily, that her daughter Augustine was holding her prayerbook upside down. She was about to scold her vigorously when, suddenly raising her veil, she postponed her lecture and looked in the direction which her daughter's eyes had taken. With the help of her spectacles, she then and there beheld the young artist, whose fashionable clothes bespoke an officer of the army on furlough rather than a merchant belonging to the neighborhood. It is difficult to imagine the wrath of Madame Guillaume, who flattered herself she had brought up her daughters in perfect propriety, on detecting this clandestine love in Augustine's heart, the evils of which she magnified out of ignorance and prudery. She concluded instantly that her daughter was rotten to the core.

"In the first place, hold your book straight, mademoiselle," she said in a low voice, but trembling with anger; then she snatched the tell-tale prayer-book, and turned it the right way. "Don't dare to raise your eyes off those prayers," she added; "otherwise you will answer for it to me. After service, your father and I will have something to say to you."

These words were like a thunderbolt to poor Augustine. She felt like fainting; but between the misery she endured and the fear of creating a disturbance in church, she gathered enough courage to hide her suffering. Yet it was easy enough to guess the commotion of her mind by the way the book shook in her hands and by the tears which fell on the pages as she turned them. The artist saw, from the incensed look which Madame Guillaume flung at him, the perils which threatened his love, and he left the church with rage in his heart, determined to dare all.

"Go to your room, mademoiselle!" said Madame Guillaume when they reached home. "Don't dare to leave it; you will be called when we want you."

The conference of husband and wife was held in secret, and at first nothing transpired. But after a while Virginie, who had comforted her sister with many tender suggestions, carried her kindness so far as to slip down to the door of her mother's bedroom, where the discussion was taking place, hoping to over-hear a few sentences. At her first trip from the third to the second floor she heard her father exclaim, "Madame, do you wish to kill your daughter?"

" My poor dear," said Virginie, running back to her disconsolate sister, " papa is defending you ! "

" What will they do to Théodore ? " asked the inno-cent little thing.

Virginie went down again ; but this time she stayed longer ; she heard that Lebas loved Augustine.

It was decreed that on this memorable day that usually calm house should become a hell. Monsieur Guillaume brought Joseph Lebas to the verge of de-spair by informing him of Augustine's attachment to the artist. Lebas, who by that time had met his friend and advised him to ask for Mademoiselle Virginie in marriage, saw all his hopes overthrown. Virginie, overcome by the discovery that Joseph had, as it were, refused her, was taken with a violent headache. And finally, the jar between husband and wife, result-ing from the explanation they had together, when for the third time only in their lives they held different opinions, made itself felt in a really dreadful manner. At last, about four o'clock in the afternoon Augus-tine, pale, trembling, and with red eyes, was brought before her father and mother. The poor child related artlessly the too brief story of her love. Reassured by her father, who promised to hear her through in silence, she gathered enough courage to utter the name of her dear Théodore de Sommervieux, dwelling with some diplomacy on the aristocratic particle. As she yielded to the hitherto unknown delight of speaking out her feelings, she found courage to say with innocent boldness that she loved Monsieur de Sommervieux and had written to him, adding, with tears in her eyes: "It would make me unhappy for life to sacrifice me to any one else."

"But Augustine, you do not know what a painter is," cried her mother, in horror.

"Madame Guillaume!" said the old father, imposing silence on his wife — "Augustine," he went on, "artists are generally poor, half-starved creatures. They squander what they have, and are always worthless. I know, for the late Monsieur Joseph Vernet, the late Monsieur Lekain, and the late Monsieur Noverre were customers of mine. My dear, if you knew the tricks that very Monsieur Noverre, and Monsieur le chevalier de Saint-Georges, and above all, Monsieur Philidor played upon my predecessor Père Chevrel! They are queer fellows, very queer. They all have a glib way of talking and fine manners. Now your Monsieur Sumer — Som — "

"De Sommervieux, papa."

"Well, so be it, — de Sommervieux, he never could

be as charming with you as Monsieur le chevalier de Saint-Georges was with me the day I obtained a consular sentence against him. That's how it was with people of good-breeding in those days."

"But papa, Monsieur Théodore is a nobleman, and he writes me that he is rich; his father was called the Chevalier de Sommervieux before the Revolution."

At these words Monsieur Guillaume looked at his terrible better-half, who was tapping her foot and keeping a dead silence with the air of a thwarted woman; she would not even cast her indignant eyes at Augustine, and seemed determined to leave the whole responsibility of the misguided affair to Monsieur Guillaume, inasmuch as her advice was not listened to. However, in spite of her apparent phlegm, she could not refrain from exclaiming, when she saw her husband playing such a gentle part in a catastrophe that was not commercial: "Really, monsieur, you are as weak as your daughter, but —"

The noise of a carriage stopping before the door interrupted the reprimand which the old merchant was dreading. A moment more, and Madame Roguin was in the middle of the room looking at the three actors in the domestic drama.

"I know all, cousin," she said, with a patronizing air.

If Madame Roguin had a fault, it was that of thinking that the wife of a Parisian notary could play the part of a 'great lady.

" I know all," she repeated, " and I come to Noah's Ark like the dove, with an olive-branch, — I read that allegory in the ' Genius of Christianity,' " she remarked, turning to Madame Guillaume ; " therefore the comparison ought to please you.   Let me tell you," she added, smiling at Augustine, " that Monsieur de Sommervieux is a charming man.   He brought me this morning a portrait of myself, done with a masterly hand.   It is worth at least six thousand francs."

At these words she tapped lightly on Monsieur Guillaume's arm.   The old merchant could not refrain from pushing out his lips in a manner that was peculiar to him.

" I know Monsieur de Sommervieux very well," continued the dove.   " For the last fortnight he has attended my parties, and he is the present attraction of them.   He told me all his troubles, and I am here on his behalf.   I know that he adores Augustine, and is determined to have her.   Ah ! my dear cousin, don't shake your head.   Let me tell you that he is about to be made a baron, and that the Emperor himself, on the occasion of his visit to the Salon, made him a chevalier of the Legion of honor.   Roguin is now his notary and knows all his affairs.   Well, I can assure you that Monsieur de Sommervieux has good, sound property which brings him in twelve thousand a year. Now, the father-in-law of a man in his position might count on becoming something of importance, — mayor of the arrondissement, for instance. Don't you remember how Monsieur Dupont was made count of the Empire and senator merely because, as mayor, it was his duty to congratulate the Emperor on his entrance to Vienna? Yes, yes, this marriage must take place. I adore the young man, myself. His behavior to Augustine is hardly met with now-a-days outside of a novel. Don't fret, my dear child, you will be happy, and everybody will envy you. There 's the Duchesse de Carigliano, she comes to my parties and delights in Monsieur de Sommervieux. Gossiping tongues do say she comes to my house only to meet him, — just as if a duchess of yesterday was out of place in the salon of a Chevrel whose family can show a hundred years of good, sound bourgeoisie behind it. Augustine," added Madame Roguin, after a slight pause, " I have seen the portrait. Heavens! it is lovely. Did you know the Emperor had asked to see it? He said, laughing, to the vice-chamberlain, that if he had many women like that at his court so many kings would flock there that he could easily keep the peace of Europe. Was n't that flattering? "

The domestic storms with which the day began were something like those of nature, for they were followed by calm and serene weather. Madame Roguin's arguments were so seductive, she managed to pull so many cords in the withered hearts of Monsieur and Madame Guillaume that she at least found one which enabled her to carry the day. At this singular period of our national history, commerce and finance were to a greater degree than ever before possessed with an insane desire to ally themselves with the nobility, and the generals of the Empire profited immensely by this sentiment. Monsieur Guillaume, however, was remarkable for his opposition to this curious passion. His favorite axioms were that if a woman wanted happiness she ought to marry a man of her own class; that persons were always sooner or later punished for trying to climb too high ; that love could ill endure the petty annoyances of home-life, and that persons should look only for solid virtues in each other; that neither of the married pair should know more than the other, because the first requisite was complete mutual understanding; and that a husband who spoke Greek and a wife who spoke Latin would be certain to die of hunger. He promulgated that last remark as a sort of proverb. He compared marriages thus made to those old-fashioned stuffs of silk and wool in which the silk always ended by wearing out the wool. And yet, there was so much vanity at the bottom of his heart that the prudence of the pilot who had guided with such wisdom the affairs of the

Cat-playing-ball succumbed to the aggressive volubil-
ity of Madame Roguin. The stern Madame Guillaume
was the first to derogate from her principles and to find
in her daughter's inclinations an excuse for so doing.
She consented to receive Monsieur de Sommervieux at
her house, resolving in her own mind to examine him
rigorously.

The old merchant went at once to find Joseph Lebas
and explain to him the situation of things. At half-
past six that evening the dining-room immortalized by
the painter contained under its skylight Monsieur and
Madame Roguin, the young artist and his charming
Augustine, Joseph Lebas, who found his comfort in sub-
mission, and Mademoiselle Virginie, whose headache
had disappeared. Monsieur and Madame Guillaume
beheld in perspective the establishment of both their
daughters, and the certainty that the fortunes of the
Cat-playing-ball were likely to pass into good hands.
Their satisfaction was at its height when, at dessert,
Théodore presented to them the marvellous picture,
representing the interior of the old shop (which they
had not yet seen), to which was due the happiness of
all present.

" Is n't it pretty ! " cried Monsieur Guillaume ; " and
they give you thirty thousand francs for it ? "

" Why, there are my lappets ! " exclaimed Madame
Guillaume.

"And the goods unfolded!" added Lebas; "you might take them in your hand."

"All kinds of stuffs are good to paint," replied the painter. "We should be only too happy, we modern artists, if we could approach the perfection of ancient draperies."

"Ha! so you like drapery?" cried Père Guillaume. "Shake hands, my young friend. If you value commerce we shall soon understand each other. Why, indeed, should persons despise it? The world began with trade, for did n't Adam sell Paradise for an apple? It did not turn out a very good speculation, by the bye!"

And the old merchant burst into a hearty laugh, excited by the champagne which he was circulating liberally. The bandage over the eyes of the young lover was so thick that he thought his new parents very agreeable. He was not above amusing them with a few little caricatures, all in good taste. He pleased every one. Later, when the party had dispersed, and the salon, furnished in a way that was "rich and warm," to use the draper's own expression, was deserted, and while Madame Guillaume was going about from table to table and from candelabra to candlestick, hastily blowing out the lights, the worthy merchant who could see clearly enough when it was a question of money or of business, called his daughter Augustine, and, placing her on his knee, made her the following harangue : —

"My dear child, you shall marry your Sommervieux since you wish it; I give you permission to risk your capital of happiness. But I am not taken in by those thirty thousand francs, said to be earned by spoiling good canvas. Money that comes so quickly goes as quickly. Didn't I hear that young scatterbrain say this very evening that if money was coined round it was meant to roll? Ha! if it is round for spendthrifts, it is flat for economical folks who pile it up. Now, my child, your handsome youth talks of giving you carriages and diamonds. If he has money and chooses to spend it on you, *bene sit ;* I have nothing to say. But as to what I shall give you, I don't choose that any of my hard-earned money shall go for carriages and trumpery. He who spends too much is never rich. Your dowry of three hundred thousand francs won't buy all Paris, let me tell you ; and you need n't reckon on a few hundred thousand more, for I 'll make you wait for them a long time yet, God willing ! So I took your lover into a corner and talked to him ; and a man who manœuvred the failure of Lecocq did n't have much trouble in getting an artist to agree that his wife's property should be settled on herself. I shall have an eye to the contract and see that he makes the proper settlements upon you. Now, my dear, I hope you 'll make me a grandfather, and for that reason, faith, I 'm beginning to think about my grandchildren. Swear to me, therefore, that you will not sign any paper about money without first consulting me ; and if I should go to rejoin Père Chevrel too soon, promise me to consult Lebas, who is to be your brother-in-law. Will you promise and swear these two things?"

"Oh, yes, papa, I swear it."

At the words, uttered in a tender voice, the old man kissed his daughter on both cheeks. That night all the lovers slept as peacefully as Monsieur and Madame Guillaume.

A few months after that memorable Sunday the high altar of Saint-Leu witnessed two marriages very unlike each other. Augustine and Théodore approached it beaming with happiness, their eyes full of love, elegantly attired, and attended by a brilliant company. Virginie, leaning on the arm of her father, followed her young sister in humbler guise, like a shadow needed for the harmony of the picture. Monsieur Guillaume had taken infinite pains to so arrange the wedding that Virginie's marriage should take precedence of Augustine's ; but he had the grief of seeing that the higher and lesser clergy one and all addressed the younger and more elegant of the brides first. He overheard some of his neighbors highly commending Mademoiselle

Virginie's good sense in making, as they said, a solid marriage and remaining faithful to " the quarter ; " and he also overheard a few sneers, prompted by envy, about Augustine who had chosen to marry an artist, a nobleman, coupled with a pretended fear that if the Guillaumes were becoming ambitious the draper's trade was ruined. When an old dealer in fans declared that the young spendthrift would soon bring his wife to poverty, Monsieur Guillaume congratulated himself *in petto* for his prudence as to the marriage settlements.

That night, after an elegant ball followed by one of those sumptuous suppers that are almost forgotten by the present generation, Monsieur and Madame Guillaume remained at a house belonging to them in the rue du Colombier, where the wedding party took place, and where they intended to live in future ; Monsieur and Madame Lebas returned in a hired coach to the rue Saint-Denis and took the helm of the Cat-playing-ball ; while the artist, intoxicated with his happiness, caught his dear Augustine in his arms as their coupé reached the rue des Trois-Frères, and carried her to an apartment decorated with the treasures of all the arts.

The raptures of passion to which Théodore now delivered himself up carried the young household through one whole year without a single cloud to dim the blue of the sky beneath which they lived. To such lovers existence brought no burden ; each day some new and

exquisite *floriture* of pleasure were evolved by Théodore, who delighted in varying the transports of love
with the soft languor of those moments of repose when
souls float upward into ecstasy and there forget cor-
poreal union. Augustine, wholly incapable of reflection, gave herself up to the undulating current of her
happiness; she felt she could not yield too much to
the sanctioned and sacred love of marriage; simple
and artless, she knew nothing of the coquetry of denial,
still less of the ascendency a young girl of rank obtains
over a husband by clever caprices; she loved too well
to calculate the future, and never once imagined that
so enchanting a life could come to an end. Happy in
being all the life and all the joy of her husband, she
believed his inextinguishable love would forever crown
her with the noblest of wreaths, just as her devotion
and her obedience would remain a perpetual attraction.
In fact, the felicity of love had made her so brilliant that
her beauty filled her with pride and inspired her with a
sense that she could always reign over a man so easy
to impassion as Monsieur de Sommervieux. Thus her
womanhood gave her no other instructions than those
of love. In the bosom of her happiness she was still
the ignorant little girl who lived obscurely in the rue
Saint-Denis, with no thought of acquiring the manners,
or the education, or the tone of the world in which she
was to live. Her words were the words of love, and

there, indeed, she did display a certain suppleness of mind and delicacy of expression; but she was using a language common to all womankind when plunged into a passion which seems their element. If, by chance, Augustine gave utterance to some idea that jarred with those of Théodore, the artist laughed, just as we laugh at the first mistakes of a stranger speaking our language, though they weary us if not corrected.

In spite of all this ardent love, Sommervieux felt, at the end of a year as enchanting as it had been rapid, the need of going back to his work and his old habits. Moreover, his wife was *enceinte.* He renewed his relations with his friends. During the long year of physical suffering, when, for the first time, a young wife carries and nurses an infant, he worked, no doubt, with ardor; but occasionally he returned for some amusement to the distractions of society. The house to which he preferred to go was that of the Duchesse de Carigliano, who had finally attracted the now celebrated artist to her parties.

When Augustine recovered, and her son no longer required assiduous cares which kept his mother from social life, Théodore had reached a point where self-love roused in him a desire to appear before the world with a beautiful woman whom all men should envy and admire. The delight of showing herself in fashionable salons decked with the fame she derived from her husband, was to Augustine a new harvest of pleasures, but it was also the last that conjugal happiness was to bring her.

She began by offending her husband's vanity; for, in spite of all his efforts, her ignorance, the incorrectness of her language, and the narrowness of her ideas, viewed from the standpoint of her present surroundings, were manifest. The character of de Sommervieux, held in check for nearly two years and a half by the first transports of love, now took, under the calm of a possession no longer fresh, its natural bent, and he returned to the habits which had for a time been diverted from their course. Poetry, painting, and the exquisite enjoyments of the imagination possess inalienable rights over minds that can rise to them. These needs had not been balked in Théodore during those two and a half years; they had simply found another nourishment. When the fields of love were explored, when the artist, like the children, had gathered the roses and the wake-robins with such eagerness that he did not notice his hands were full, the scene changed. It now happened that when the artist showed his wife a sketch of his most beautiful compositions, he took notice that she answered, in the tone of Monsieur Guillaume, " Oh, how pretty ! " Such admiration, without the slightest warmth, did not come, he felt, from an inward feeling, it was the expression of blind love. Augustine preferred a glance of love to the noblest work of art. The only sublimity she was able to perceive was that in her own heart.

At last Théodore could not blind himself to the evidence of a bitter truth; his wife had no feeling for poetry; she could not live in his sphere of thought; she could not follow in the flight of his caprices, his impulses, his joys, his sorrows; she walked the earth in a real world, while his head sought the heavens. Ordinary minds cannot appreciate the ever-springing sufferings of one who, being united to another by the closest of all ties, is compelled to drive back within his own soul the precious overflow of his thoughts, and to crush into nothingness the images which some magic force compels him to create. To such a one the torture is the more cruel when his feeling for his companion commands him, as his first duty, to keep nothing from her, neither the outcome of his thoughts nor the effusions of his soul. The will of nature is not to be evaded; it is inexorable, like necessity, which is, as it were, a sort of social law. Sommervieux took refuge in the silence and solitude of his studio, hoping that the habit of living among artists might train his wife and develop the benumbed germs of mind which all superior souls believe to exist in other souls.

But, alas, Augustine was too sincerely religious not to be frightened at the tone of the artist-world. At the first dinner given by Théodore, a young painter said to her, with a juvenile light-heartedness she was unable to understand, but which really absolves all jests about religion: "Why, madame, your paradise is not as glorious as Raffaelle's Transfiguration, but I get a little tired of looking even at that." Augustine, consequently, met this brilliant and artistic society in a spirit of disapproval, which was at once perceived. She became a constraint upon it. When artists are constrained they are pitiless; they either fly, or they stay and scoff.

Madame Guillaume had, among other absurdities, that of magnifying the dignity she considered to be an appanage of a married woman; and though Augustine had often laughed about it she was unable to keep herself from a slight imitation of the maternal prudery. This exaggeration of purity, which virtuous women do not always escape, gave rise to a few harmless caricatures and epigrams, innocent nonsense in good taste, with which de Sommervieux could scarcely be angry. In fact, such jests were only reprisals on the part of his friends. Still, nothing could be really a jest to a soul so ready as that of Théodore to receive impressions from without. Thus he was led, perhaps insensibly, to a coldness of feeling which went on increasing. Whoso desires to reach perfect conjugal happiness must climb a mountain along a narrow way close to a sharp and slippery precipice; down that precipice the artist's love now slid. He believed his wife incapable of understanding the moral considerations which justified, to his mind, the course he now adopted towards her; and he thought himself innocent in hiding thoughts she could not comprehend, and in doing acts which could never be justified before the tribunal of her commonplace conscience.

Augustine retired into gloomy and silent sorrow. These secret feelings drew a veil between the married pair which grew thicker day by day. Though her husband did not cease his attentions to her, Augustine could not keep from trembling when she saw him reserving for society the treasures of mind and charm which he had hitherto bestowed on her. Soon she took fatally to heart the lively talk she heard in the world about man's inconstancy. She made no complaint, but her whole bearing was equivalent to a reproach. Three years after her marriage this young and pretty woman, who seemed so brilliant in her brilliant equipage, who lived in a sphere of fame and wealth, always envied by careless and unobserving people who never rightly estimate the situations of life, was a prey to bitter grief; her color faded; she reflected, she compared; and then, at last, sorrow revealed to her the axioms of experience.

She resolved to maintain herself courageously within the circle of her duty, hoping that such generous conduct would, sooner or later, win back her husband's love; but it was not to be. When Sommervieux, tired of work, left his studio, Augustine never hid her work so quickly that the artist did not see her mending the household linen or his own with the minute care of a good housekeeper. She supplied, generously and without a word, the money required for her husband's extravagances; but in her desire to save her dear Théodore's own fortune she was too economical on herself and on certain details of the housekeeping. Such conduct is incompatible with the free and easy ways of artists, who, when they reach the end of their tether, have enjoyed life so much that they never ask the reason of their ruin.

It is useless to note each lowered tone of color through which the brilliancy of their honeymoon faded and then expired, leaving them in deep darkness. One evening poor Augustine, who had lately heard her husband speaking with enthusiasm of the Duchesse de Carigliano, received some ill-natured information on the nature of de Sommervieux's attachment to that celebrated coquette of the imperial court. At twenty-one, in the glow of youth and beauty, Augustine learned she was betrayed for a woman of thirty-six. Feeling herself wretched in the midst of society and of *fêtes* that were now a desert to her, the poor little creature no longer noticed the admiration she excited nor the envy she inspired. Her face took another expression. Sorrow laid upon each feature the gentleness of resignation and the pallor of rejected love. It was not long before men, known for their seductive powers, courted her; but she remained solitary and virtuous. A few contemptuous words which escaped her husband brought her to intolerable despair. Fatal gleams of light now showed her the points where, through the pettiness of her education, complete union between her soul and that of Théodore had been prevented; and her love was great enough to absolve him and blame herself. She wept tears of blood as she saw, too late, that there are ill-assorted marriages of minds as well as of habits and of ranks.

Thinking over the spring-tide happiness of their union, she comprehended the fulness of her past joys, and admitted to her own soul that so rich a harvest of love was indeed a lifetime which might well be paid for by her present sorrow. And yet she loved with too single a mind to lose all hope; and she was brave enough at one-and-twenty to endeavor to educate herself and make her imagination more worthy of the one she so admired. "If I am not a poet," she said in her heart, "at least I will understand poetry." Employing that force of will and energy which all women possess when they love, Madame de Sommervieux attempted to change her nature, her habits, and her ideas; but though she read many volumes and studied with the utmost courage, she only succeeded in making herself less ignorant. Quickness of mind and the charms of conversation are gifts of nature or the fruits of an education begun in the cradle. She could appreciate music and enjoy it, but she could not sing with taste. She understood literature and even the beauties of poetry, but it was too late to train her rebellious memory. She listened with interest to conversation in society, but she contributed nothing to it. Her religious ideas and the prejudices of her early youth prevented the complete emancipation of her mind. And besides all this, a bias against her which she could not conquer had, little by little, glided into her husband's mind. The artist laughed in his heart at those who praised his wife to him, and his laughter was not unfounded. Embarrassed by her strong desire to please him, she felt her mind and her knowledge melt away in his presence. Even her fidelity displeased the unfaithful husband; it seemed as though he would fain see her guilty of wrong when he complained of her virtue as unfeeling. Augustine struggled hard to abdicate her reason, to yield and bend to the fancies and caprices of her husband, and to devote her whole life to soothe the egotism of his vanity, — she never gathered the fruit of her sacrifices. Perhaps they had each let the moment go by when souls can comprehend each other. The day came when the too-sensitive heart of the young wife received a blow, — one of those shocks which strain the ties of feeling so far that it seems as though they snapped. At first she isolated herself. But soon the fatal thought entered her mind to seek advice and consolation from her own family.

Accordingly, one morning early, she drove to the grotesque entrance of the silent and gloomy house in which her childhood had been passed. She sighed as she looked at the window from which she had sent a first kiss to him who had filled her life with fame and sorrow. Nothing was changed in those cavernous precincts, except that the business had taken a new lease of life. Augustine's sister sat behind the counter in her mother's old place. The poor afflicted woman met her brother-in-law with a pen behind his ear, and he hardly listened to her, so busy was he. The alarming signs of an approaching "inventory" were evident, and in a few moments he left her, asking to be excused.

Her sister received her rather coldly, and showed some ill-will. In fact, Augustine in her palmy days, brilliant in happiness and driving about in a pretty equipage, had never come to see her sister except in passing. The wife of the prudent Lebas now imagined that money was the cause of this early visit, and she assumed a reserved tone, which made Augustine smile. The artist's wife saw that her mother had a counterpart (except for the lappets of her cap) who would keep up the antique dignity of the Cat-playing-ball. At breakfast, however, she noticed certain changes which did honor to the good sense of Joseph Lebas, — the clerks no longer rose and went away at dessert; they were allowed to use their faculty of speech, and the abundance on the table showed ease and comfort, without luxury. The young woman of society noticed the coupons of a box at the Français, where she remembered having seen her sister from time to time. Madame Lebas wore a cashmere shawl over her shoulders, the elegance of which was a sign of the generosity with which her husband treated her. In short, the pair were advancing with their century.

Augustine was deeply moved to see, during the course of the day, many signs of a calm and equable happiness enjoyed by this well-assorted couple, — a happiness without exaltation, it was true, but also without peril. They had taken life as a commercial enterprise, in which their first duty was to honor their business. Not finding in her husband any great warmth of love, Virginie had set to work to produce it. Led insensibly to respect and to cherish his wife, the time it took for their wedded happiness to blossom now seemed to Joseph Lebas as a pledge of its duration; so, when the sorrowful Augustine told her tale of trouble, she was forced to endure a deluge of the commonplace ideas which the ethics of the rue Saint-Denis suggested to Virginie.

"The evil is done, wife," said Joseph Lebas; "we must now try to give our sister the best advice." Whereupon, the able man of business ponderously explained the relief that the laws and established customs might give to Augustine, and so enable her to surmount her troubles. He numbered, if we may so express it, all the considerations; ranged them in categories, as though they were goods of different qualities; then he put them in the scales, weighed them, and finally came to the conclusion that necessity required his sister-in-law to take a firm stand, — a decision which did not satisfy the love she still felt for her husband, a feeling that was reawakened in full force when she heard Lebas discussing judicial methods of asserting her rights. Augustine thanked her two friends and returned home, more undecided than before she consulted them.

The next day she ventured to the house in the rue du Colombier, intending to confide her sorrows to her father and mother, for she was like those hopelessly ill persons who try all remedies in sheer despair, even the recipes of old women. Monsieur and Madame Guillaume received their daughter with a warmth that touched her; the visit brought an interest which, to them, was a treasure. For four years they had floated

on the sea of life like navigators without chart or compass.   Sitting in their chimney-corner, they told each
other again and again the disasters of the *maximum ;*
the story of their first purchases of cloth, the manner in
which they escaped bankruptcy, and above all, the tale
of the famous Lecocq failure, old Guillaume's battle of
Marengo.   Then, when these stock stories were exhausted, they recapitulated the profits of their most
productive years, or reminded each other of the gossip
of the Saint-Denis quarter.   At two o'clock Père Guillaume invariably went out to give an eye to the establishment of the Cat-playing-ball; on his way back he
stopped at all the shops which were formerly his rivals,
whose young proprietors now endeavored to inveigle
the old merchant into speculative investments which,
according to his usual custom, he never positively de-
clined.   Two good Norman horses were dying of pleth-
ora in the stable, but Madame Guillaume never used
them except to be conveyed on Sundays to high mass
at the parish church.   Three times a week the worthy
couple kept open table.

Thanks to the influence of his son-in-law, de Sommervieux, Père Guillaume had been appointed member
of the advisory committee on the equipment of troops.
Ever since her husband had held that high post under
government, Madame Guillaume had felt it her duty to
maintain its dignity; her rooms were therefore encum-

bered with so many ornaments of gold and silver, so much tasteless though costly furniture, that the simplest of them looked like a tawdry chapel. Economy and prodigality seemed fighting for precedence in all the accessories of the house. It really looked as if old Guillaume had considered the purchase of everything in it, down to a candlestick, as an investment. In the midst of this bazaar, de Sommervieux's famous picture held the place of honor, and was a source of consolation to Monsieur and Madame Guillaume, who turned their spectacled eyes twenty times a day on that transcript of their old life, to them so active and so exciting.

The appearance of the house and of these rooms where all things had an odor of old age and mediocrity, the spectacle of the two old people stranded on a rock far from the real world and the ideas that move it, surprised and affected Augustine; she recognized the second half of the picture which had struck her so forcibly at the house of Joseph Lebas, — that of an active life without movement, a sort of mechanical and instinctive existence, like that of rolling on castors; and there came into her mind a sense of pride in her sorrows as she remembered how they sprang from a happiness of eighteen months duration, worth more to her than a thousand existences like this, the void of which now seemed to her horrible. But she hid the rather unkindly thought, and displayed her new qualities of mind to her old parents and the endearing tenderness which love had taught her, hoping to win them to listen favorably to her matrimonial trials.

Old people delight in such confidences. Madame Guillaume wished to hear the minutest particulars of that strange life which, to her, was almost fabulous. "The Travels of the Baron de La Houtan," which she had begun many times and never finished, had revealed to her nothing more inconceivable among the savages of Canada.

"But, my dear child," she said, "do you mean to say that your husband shuts himself up with naked women, and you are simple enough to believe he paints them?" With these words she laid her spectacles on a work-table, shook out her petticoats, and laid her clasped hands on her knees, raised by a foot-warmer, — her favorite attitude.

"But, my dear mother, all painters are obliged to employ models."

"He took care not to tell us *that* when he asked you in marriage. If I had known it I would never have given my daughter to a man with such a trade. Religion forbids such horrors; they are immoral. What time of night do you say he comes home?"

"Oh, at one o'clock, — or two, perhaps."

The old people looked at each other in amazement.

"Then he gambles," said Monsieur Guillaume. "In my day it was only gamblers who stayed out so late."

Augustine made a little face to deny the accusation.

"You must suffer dreadfully waiting for him," said Madame Guillaume. "But no, you go to bed, I hope, — don't you? Then when he has gambled away all his money, the monster comes home and wakes you up?"

"No, mother; on the contrary, he is sometimes very gay; indeed, when the weather is fine, he often asks me to get up and go into the woods with him."

"Into the woods! — at that hour? Your house must be very small if he has n't room enough in it to stretch his legs! No, no, it is to give you cold that the villain makes such proposals as that; he wants to get rid of you. Did any one ever know a decent man with a home of his own and a steady business galloping round like a were-wolf!"

"But, my dear mother, you don't understand that he needs excitements to develop his genius. He loves the scenes which —"

"Scenes! I 'd make him fine scenes, I would," cried Madame Guillaume, interrupting her daughter. "How can you keep on any terms at all with such a man? And I don't like that idea of his drinking nothing but water. It is n't wholesome. Why does he dislike to see women eat? what a strange notion! He 's a mad- man, that 's what he is. All that you say of him proves it. No sane man leaves his home without a word, and stays away ten days. He told you he went to Dieppe to paint the sea! How can any one paint the sea? He told you such nonsense to blind you."

Augustine opened her lips to defend her husband, but Madame Guillaume silenced her with a motion of her hand which the old habit of obedience led her to obey, and the old woman continued, in a sharp voice: "Don't talk to me of that man. He never set foot in a church except to marry you. Persons who have no religion are capable of anything. Did your father ever venture to hide anything from me, or keep silent three days without saying boo to me, and then begin to chatter like a blind magpie? No!"

"My dear mother, you judge superior men too severely. If they had ideas like other people they would not be men of genius."

"Well! then men of genius should keep to themselves and not marry. Do you mean to tell me that a man can make his wife miserable, and if he has got genius it is all right? Genius! I don't see much genius in saying a thing is black and white in the same breath, and ramming people's words down their throats, and lording it over his family, and never letting his wife know how to take him, and forbidding her to amuse herself unless monsieur, forsooth, is gay, and forcing her to be gloomy as soon as he is — "

"But, my dear mother, the reason for all such imaginations — "

"What do you mean by all such imaginations?" cried Madame Guillaume, again interrupting her daughter. "He has fine ones, faith! What sort of man is he who takes a notion, without consulting a doctor, to eat nothing but vegetables? If he did it out of piety, such a diet might do him some good; but he has no more religion than a Huguenot. Who ever saw a man in his senses love a horse better than he loves his neighbor, and have his hair curled like a pagan image, and cover his statues with muslin, and shut up the windows in the daytime to work by lamplight? Come, come, don't talk to me; if he were not so grossly immoral he ought to be put in the insane asylum. You had better consult Monsieur Loraux, the vicar of Saint-Sulpice; ask him what he thinks of all this. He'll tell you that your husband does n't behave like a Christian man."

"Oh! mother, how can you think — "

"Think! yes I do think it! You used to love him and therefore you don't see these things. But I remember how I saw him, not long after your marriage, in the Champs-Élysées. He was on horseback. Well, he galloped at full speed for a little distance, then he stopped and went at a snail's pace. I said to myself then, 'There 's a man who has no sense.'"

"Ah!" cried Monsieur Guillaume, rubbing his hands,

"what a good thing it is I had your property settled on yourself."

After Augustine had the imprudence to explain her real causes of complaint against her husband the two old people were silent with indignation. Madame Guillaume uttered the word " divorce." It seemed to awaken the now inactive old business-man. Moved by his love for his daughter and also by the excitement such a step would give to his eventless life, Père Guillaume roused himself to action. He demanded divorce, talked of managing it, argued the pros and cons, and promised his daughter to pay all the costs, engage the lawyers, see the judges, and move heaven and earth. Madame de Sommervieux, much alarmed, refused his services declaring she would not separate from her husband were she ten times more unhappy than she was, and saying no more about her sorrows. After the old people had endeavored, but in vain, to soothe her with many little silent and consoling attentions, Augustine went home feeling the impossibility of getting narrow minds to take a just view of superior men. She learned then that a wife should hide from all the world, even from her parents, the sorrows for which it is so difficult to obtain true sympathy. The storms and the sufferings of the higher spheres of human existence are comprehended only by the noble minds which inhabit them. In all things, we can be justly judged only by our equals.

Thus poor Augustine found herself once more in the cold atmosphere of her home, cast back into the horrors of her lonely meditations. Study no longer availed her, for study had not restored her husband's heart. Initiated into the secrets of those souls of fire but deprived of their resources, she entered deeply into their trials without sharing their joys. She became disgusted with the world, which seemed to her small and petty indeed in presence of events born of passion. In short, life to her was a failure.

One evening a thought came into her mind which illuminated the dark regions of her grief with a gleam of celestial light. Such a thought could have smiled into no heart that was less pure and guileless than hers. She resolved to go to the Duchesse de Carigliano, not to ask for the heart of her husband, but to learn from that great lady the arts which had taken him from her ; to interest that proud woman of the world in the mother of her friend's children ; to soften her, to make her the accomplice of her future peace, just as she was now the instrument of her present sorrow.

So, one day, the timid Augustine, armed with supernatural courage, got into her carriage about two o'clock in the afternoon, intending to make her way into the boudoir of the celebrated lady, who was never visible until that time of day.

Madame de Sommervieux had never yet seen any of

the old and sumptuous mansions of the faubourg Saint-
Germain. When she passed through the majestic ves-
tibule, the noble stairways, the vast salons, filled with
flowers in spite of the inclemencies of the season, and
decorated with the natural taste of women born to opu-
lence or to the elegant habits of the aristocracy, Augustine was conscious of a terrible constriction of her heart.
She envied the secrets of an elegance of which till then
she had had no idea ; she inhaled a breath of grandeur
which explained to her the charm that house possessed
over her husband.

When she reached the private apartments of the
duchess she felt both jealousy and despair as she noted
the voluptuous arrangement of the furniture, the draperies, the hangings upon the walls. There, disorder
was a grace ; there, luxury affected disdain of mere
richness. The perfume of this soft atmosphere pleased
the senses without annoying them. The accessories of
these rooms harmonized with the vista of gardens and
a lawn planted with trees seen through the windows.
All was seductive, and yet no calculated seduction was
felt. The genius of the mistress of these apartments
pervaded the salon in which Augustine now awaited her.
Madame de Sommervieux endeavored to guess the
character of her rival from the objects about the room ;
but there was something impenetrable in its disorder as
in its symmetry, and to the guileless Augustine it was

a sealed book. All that she could really make out was that the duchess was a superior woman *as woman.* The discovery brought her a painful thought.

"Alas! can it be true," she said to herself, "that a simple and loving heart does not suffice an artist? and to balance the weight of their strong souls must they be joined to feminine souls whose force is equal to their own? If I had been brought up like this siren our weapons at least would have been matched for the struggle."

"But I am not at home!" The curt, sharp words, though said in a low voice in the adjoining boudoir, were overheard by Augustine, whose heart throbbed.

"The lady is here," said the waiting-woman.

"You are crazy! Show her in," added the duchess, changing her voice to a cordially polite tone. Evidently she expected then to be overheard.

Augustine advanced timidly. At the farther end of the cool boudoir she saw the duchess luxuriously reclining on a brown-velvet ottoman placed in the centre of a species of half-circle formed by folds of muslin draped over a yellow ground. Ornaments of gilded bronze, arranged with exquisite taste, heightened still further the effect of the dais under which the duchess posed like an antique statue. The dark color of the velvet enabled her to lose no means of seduction. A soft chiaro-scuro, favorable to her beauty, seemed more a reflection than a light. A few choice flowers lifted their fragrant heads from the Sèvres vases. As this scene caught the eye of the astonished Augustine she came forward so quickly and softly that she surprised a glance from the eyes of the enchantress. That glance seemed to say to a person whom at first the painter's wife could not see: "Wait; you shall see a pretty woman, and help me to put up with a tiresome visit."

As Augustine advanced the duchess rose, and made her sit beside her.

"To what do I owe the pleasure of this visit, madame?" she said, with a smile full of charm.

"Why so false?" thought Augustine, who merely bowed her head.

Silence was a necessity; for the young woman now saw a witness to the interview in the person of an officer of the army,— the youngest, and most elegant and dashing of the colonels. His clothes, which were those of a civilian, set off the graces of his person. . His face, full of life and youth and very expressive, was still further enlivened by small moustachios, black as jet and waxed to a point, by a well-trimmed imperial, carefully combed whiskers and a forest of black hair which was somewhat in disorder. He played with a riding-whip and showed an ease and freedom of manner which agreed well with the satisfied expression of his face and the elegance of his dress; the ribbons in his buttonhole were carelessly knotted and he seemed more vain of his appearance than of his courage. Augustine looked at the Duchesse de Carigliano, with a glance at the colonel in which many prayers were included.

"Well, adieu, Monsieur d'Aiglemont; we shall meet in the Bois de Boulogne," said the siren, in a tone as if the words were the result of some agreement made before Augustine entered the room; she accompanied them with a threatening glance, which the officer deserved, perhaps, for the undisguised admiration with which he looked at the modest flower who contrasted so admirably with the haughty duchess. The young dandy bowed in silence, turned on the heels of his boots, and gracefully left the room. At that moment Augustine, watching her rival whose eyes followed the brilliant officer, caught sight of a sentiment the fugitive expressions of which are known to every woman. She saw with bitter sorrow that her visit would be useless; the artful duchess was too eager for homage not to have a pitiless heart.

"Madame," said Augustine, in a broken voice, "the step I now take will seem very strange to you; but despair has its madness, and that is my excuse. I can now understand only too well why Théodore prefers your house to mine, and how it is that your mind should exercise so great an empire over him. Alas!

I have but to look within myself to find reasons that are more than sufficient. But I adore my husband, madame. Two years of sorrow have not changed the love of my heart, though I have lost his. In my madness I have dared to believe that I might struggle against you; I have come to you to be told by what means I can triumph over you. Oh, madame!" cried the young woman, seizing the hand which her rival allowed her to take, " never will I pray God for my own happiness with such fervor as I will pray to him for yours, if you will help me to recover, I will not say the love, but the friendship of my husband. I have no longer any hope except in you. Ah! tell me how it is you have won him, and made him forget the early days of—"

At these words Augustine, choking with her sobs, was compelled to pause. Ashamed of her weakness, she covered her face with a handkerchief that was wet with tears.

" Ah, what a child you are, my dear little lady!" said the duchess, fascinated by the novelty of the scene and touched in spite of herself at receiving such homage from as perfect a virtue as there was in Paris, taking the young wife's handkerchief and herself drying her tears and soothing her with a few murmured monosyllables of graceful pity.

After a moment's silence the accomplished coquette,

clasping poor Augustine's pretty hands in her own,
which had a rare character of noble beauty and power,
said, in a gentle and even affectionate voice : " My first
advice will be not to weep ; tears are unbecoming. We
must learn how to conquer sorrows which make us ill,
for love will not stay long on a bed of pain. Sadness
may at first bestow a certain charm which pleases a
man, but it ends by sharpening the features and
fading the color of the sweetest face. And remember,
our tyrants have the self-love to require that their
slaves shall be always gay."

" Ah, madame ! is it within my power to cease feeling? How is it possible not to die a thousand deaths
when we see a face which once shone for us with love
and joy, now harsh, and cold, and indifferent? No, I
cannot control my heart."

" So much the worse for you, my poor dear. But I
think I already know your history. In the first place,
be very sure that if your husband has been unfaithful
to you, I am not his accomplice. If I made a point of
attracting him to my salon, it was, I freely confess, out
of vanity ; he was famous, and he went nowhere. I
like you too well already to tell you all the follies he has
committed for me. • But I shall reveal one of them because it may perhaps help us to bring him back to you,
and to punish him for the audacity he has lately shown
in his proceedings toward me. He will end by com-

promising me. I know the world too well, my dear, to put myself at the mercy of a superior man. Believe me, it is very well to let them court us, but to marry them is a blunder. ·We women should admire men of genius, enjoy them as we would a play, but live with them — never! No, no! it is like going behind the scenes and seeing the machinery, instead of sitting in our boxes and enjoying the illusions. But with you, my poor child, the harm is done, is it not? Well, then, you must try to arm yourself against tyranny."

" Ah, madame, as I entered this house and before I saw you I became aware of certain arts that I never suspected."

" Well, come and see me sometimes, and you will soon learn the science of such trifles, — really important, however, in their effects. External things are to fools more than one half of life ; and for that reason more than one man of talent is a fool in spite of his superiority. I will venture to lay a wager that you have never refused anything to Théodore."

" How can we refuse anything to those we love? "

" Poor, innocent child ! I adore your folly. Let me tell you that the more we love the less we should let a man, specially a husband, see the extent of our passion. Whoever loves the most is certain to be the one that is tyrannized over, and, worse than all, deserted sooner or later. Whoever desires to reign must — "

"Oh, madame, must we all dissimulate, calculate, be false at heart, make ourselves an artificial nature, and forever? Oh, who could live thus? Could you — "

She hesitated; the duchess smiled.

"My dear," resumed the great lady in a grave tone, "conjugal happiness has been from time immemorial a speculation, a matter which required particular study. If you persist in talking passion while I am talking marriage we shall never understand each other. Listen to me," she continued, in a confidential tone. "I have been in the way of seeing many of the superior men of our day. Those of them who married chose, with few exceptions, women who were ciphers. Well, those women have governed them just as the Emperor governs us, and they have been, if not beloved, at least always respected by them. I am fond of secrets, especially those that concern our sex, and to amuse myself I have sought the key to that riddle. Well, my dear little angel, it is this, — those good women knew enough to analyze the characters of their husbands; without being frightened, as you have been, at their superiority, they have cleverly discovered the qualities those men lacked, and whether they themselves had them or only feigned to have them, they found means to make such a show of those very qualities before the eyes of their husbands that they ended by mastering them. Remember one thing more: those souls which seem so great all have a little grain of folly in them, and it is our business to make the most of it. If we set our wills to rule them and let nothing deter us, but concentrate all our actions, our ideas, our fascinations upon that, we can master those eminently capricious minds, — for the very inconstancy of their thoughts gives us the means of influencing them."

"Oh!" cried the young wife, horror-struck, "can that be life? Then it is a battle — "

" — in which whoso would win must threaten," said the duchess laughing. "Our power is artificial. Consequently we should never let a man despise us; we can never rise after such a fall except through vile manœuvres. Come," she added, "I will give you the means to hold your husband in chains."

She rose, and guided her young and innocent pupil in conjugal wiles through the labyrinths of her little palace. They came presently to a private staircase which communicated with the state apartments. When the duchess touched the secret lock of the door she stopped, looked at Augustine with an inimitable air of wiliness and grace, and said, smiling: "My dear, the Duc de Carigliano adores me, — well, he would not dare to enter this door without my permission. Yet he is a man who has the habit of command over thousands of soldiers. He can face a battery, but in my presence — he is afraid."

Augustine sighed. They reached a noble gallery, where the duchess led the painter's wife before the portrait Théodore had once made of Mademoiselle Guillaume. At sight of it Augustine uttered a cry.

"I knew it was no longer in the house," she said, "but—here!"

"My dear child, I exacted it only to see how far the folly of a man of genius would go. I intended to return it to you sooner or later; for I did not expect the pleasure of seeing the original standing before the copy. I will have the picture taken to your carriage while we finish our conversation. If, armed with that talisman, you are not mistress of your husband during the next hundred years, you are not a woman and you deserve your fate."

Augustine kissed the hand of the great lady, who pressed her to her heart with all the more tenderness because she was certain to have forgotten her on the morrow. This scene might have destroyed forever the purity and candor of a less virtuous woman than Augustine, to whom the secrets revealed by the duchess could have been either salutary or fatal; but the astute policy of the higher social spheres suited Augustine as little as the narrow reasoning of Joseph Lebas or the silly morality of Madame Guillaume. Strange result of the false positions into which we are thrown by the even trivial mistakes we make in life! Augustine was like an Alpine herdsman overtaken by an avalanche; if he hesitates, or listens to the cries of his comrades, he is lost. In these great crises the heart either breaks or hardens.

Madame de Sommervieux returned home a prey to an agitation it is difficult to describe. Her conversation with the duchess had roused a thousand contradictory ideas in her mind. Like the sheep of the fable, full of courage when the wolf was away, she preached to herself and laid down admirable lines of conduct; she imagined stratagems of coquetry; she talked to her husband, he being absent, with all the resources of that eloquence which never leaves a woman; then, remembering the glance of Théodore's fixed, light eyes, she trembled with fear. When she asked if Monsieur were at home, her voice failed her. Hearing that he would not be at home to dinner, she was conscious of a feeling of inexplicable relief. Like a criminal who appeals against a death-sentence, the delay, however short, seemed to her a lifetime.

She placed the portrait in her bedroom, and awaited her husband in all the agonies of hope. Too well she knew that this attempt would decide her whole future, and she trembled at every sound, even at the ticking of her clock, which seemed to increase her fears by measuring them. She tried to cheat time; the idea occurred to her to dress in a manner that made her still more like the portrait. Then, knowing her husband's uneasy nature, she caused her rooms to be lighted up with unusual brilliancy, certain that curiosity would bring him to her as soon as he came in. Midnight sounded, and at the groom's cry the gates opened and the painter's carriage rolled into the silent courtyard.

"What is the meaning of all this illumination?" asked Théodore, gayly, as he entered his wife's room.

Augustine took advantage of so favorable a moment and threw herself into his arms as she pointed to the portrait. The artist stood still; immovable as a rock, gazing alternately at Augustine and at the tell-tale canvas. The timid wife, half-dead with fear, watched the changing brow, that terrible brow, and saw the cruel wrinkles gathering like clouds; then the blood seemed to curdle in her veins when, with a flaming eye and a husky voice, he began to question her.

"Where did you get that picture?"

"The Duchesse de Carigliano returned it to me."

"Did you ask her for it?"

"I did not know she had it."

The softness, or rather the enchanting melody of that angel voice might have turned the heart of cannibals, but not that of an artist in the tortures of wounded vanity.

"It is worthy of her!" cried the artist, in a voice of thunder. "I will be revenged!" he said, striding up and down the room. " She shall die of shame; I will paint her, — yes, I will exhibit her in the character of Messalina leaving Claudius' palace by night."

" Théodore ! " said a faint voice.

" I will kill her ! "

" My husband ! "

" She loves that little cavalry colonel, because he rides well ! "

" Théodore ! "

" Let me alone ! " said the painter to his wife, in a voice that was almost a roar.

The scene is too repulsive to depict here; the rage of the artist led him, before it ended, to words and acts which a woman less young and timid than Augustine would have ascribed to insanity.

About eight o'clock on the following morning Madame Guillaume found her daughter pale, with red eyes and her hair in disorder, gazing on the fragments of a painted canvas and the pieces of a broken frame which lay scattered on the floor. Augustine, almost unconscious with grief, pointed to the wreck with a gesture of despair.

" It is not such a very great loss," cried the old woman. " It was very like you, that's true; but I 'm told there is a man on the boulevard who paints charming portraits for a hundred and fifty francs."

" Ah, mother ! "

" Poor dear ! well, you are right," answered Madame Guillaume, mistaking the meaning of the look her daughter gave her; " there is nothing so tender as a mother's love. My dearest, I can guess it all; tell me your troubles and I 'll comfort you. Your maid has told me dreadful things ; I always said your husband was a madman, — why, he 's a monster ! "

Augustine put her finger on her pallid lips as if to implore silence. During that terrible night sorrow had brought her the patient resignation which, in mothers and in loving women, surpasses in its effects all other human forces, and reveals, perhaps, the existence of certain fibres in the hearts of women which God has denied to those of men.

An inscription engraved on a broken column in the cemetery of Montmartre states that Madame de Sommervieux died at twenty-seven years of age. Between the simple lines of her epitaph a friend of the timid creature reads the last scenes of a drama. Every year, on the solemn second of November, as he passes before that early grave he never fails to ask himself if stronger women than Augustine are not needed for the powerful clasp of genius.

" The modest, humble flower, blooming in the valley dies," he thought, " if transplanted nearer to heaven, to the regions where the storms gather and the sun wilts."

COLONEL CHABERT.

To Madame la Comtesse Ida de Bocarmé
née du Chasteler.

"There's our old top-coat again!"

This exclamation came from the lips of a clerk of the species called in Parisian law-offices "gutter-jumpers," who was at the moment munching with a very good appetite a slice of bread. He took a little of the crumb and made a pellet, which he flung, with a laugh, through the blinds of the window against which he was leaning. Well-aimed, the pellet rebounded nearly to the height of the window after hitting the hat of a stranger who was crossing the courtyard of a house in the rue Vivienne, where Maître Derville, the lawyer, resided.

"Come, come, Simonnin, don't play tricks, or I'll turn you off. No matter how poor a client may be, he is a man, the devil take you!" said the head-clerk, pausing as he added up a bill of costs.

The gutter-jumper is usually, like Simonnin, a lad of thirteen or fourteen years of age, who in all law-offices is under the particular supervision of the head-clerk, whose errands he does, and whose love-letters he carries, together with the writs of the courts and the petitions entered. He belongs to the *gamin de Paris* through his ethics, and to the pettifogging side of law through fate. The lad is usually pitiless, undisciplined, totally without reverence, a scoffer, a writer of epigrams, lazy, and also greedy. Nevertheless, all such little fellows have an old mother living on some fifth story, with whom they share the thirty or forty francs they earn monthly."

" If it is a man, why do you call him an ' old topcoat,'" said Simonnin, in the tone of a scholar who detects his master in a mistake.

Thereupon he returned to the munching of his bread with a bit of cheese, leaning his shoulder against the window-frame; for he took his rest standing, like the horses of the hackney-coaches, with one leg raised and supported against the other.

" Couldn't we play that old guy some trick?" said the third clerk, Godeschal, in a low voice, stopping in the middle of a legal document he was dictating to be engrossed by the fourth clerk and copied by two neophytes from the provinces. Having made the above suggestion, he went on with his dictation: " *But in his gracious and benevolent wisdom His Majesty Louis the Eighteenth,* — Write all the letters, hi, there! Desroches the learned! — *so soon as he recovered the reins of power, understood* — What did that fat joker understand, I 'd like to know ? — *the high mission to which Divine Providence had called him!* . . . . . . Put an exclamation mark and six dots; they are pious enough at the Palais to let 'em pass — *and his first thought was, as is proved by the date of the ordinance herein named, to repair evils caused by the frightful and lamentable disasters of the revolutionary period by restoring to his faithful and numerous adherents* — 'Numerous' is a bit of flattery which ought to please the court — *all their unsold property wheresoever situate, whether in the public domain or the ordinary and extraordinary crown domains, or in the endowments of public institutions ; for we contend and hold ourselves able to maintain that such is the spirit and the meaning of the gracious ordinance, rendered in* — "

" Stop, stop," said Godeschal to the three clerks; " that rascally sentence has come to the end of my paper and is n't done yet. Well," he added, stopping to wet the back of the cahier with his tongue to turn the thick page of his stamped paper, " if you want to play the old top-coat a trick tell him that the master is so busy he can talk to clients only between two and three o'clock in the morning; we 'll see if he comes then, the old villain!" and Godeschal returned to his dictation: "*gracious ordinance rendered in*— Have you got that down?"

"Yes," cried the three copyists.

"*Rendered in*— Hi, papa Boucard, what 's the date of that ordinance? Dot your i's, *unam et omnes*— it fills up."

"*Omnes*," repeated one of the clerks before Boucard, the head-clerk, could answer.

"Good heavens! you have n't written that, have you?" cried Godeschal, looking at the provincial new-comer with a truculent air.

"Yes, he has," said Desroches, the fourth clerk, leaning over to look at his neighbor's copy, "he has written, "Dot your i's, and he spells it e-y-e-s."

All the clerks burst into a roar of laughter.

"Do you call that a law-term, Monsieur Huré?" cried Simonnin, "and you say you come from Mortagne!"

"Scratch it out carefully," said the head-clerk. "If one of the judges were to get hold of the petition and see that, the master would never hear the last of it. Come, no more such blunders, Monsieur Huré; a Norman ought to know better than to write a petition carelessly; it 's the ' Shoulder-arms!' of the legal guild."

Rendered in—*in*—" went on Godeschal. "Do tell me when, Boucard?"

" June, 1814," replied the head-clerk, without raising his head from his work.

A knock at the door interrupted the next sentence of the prolix petition. Five grinning clerks, with lively, satirical eyes and curly heads, turned their noses towards the door, having all shouted with one voice, " Come in ! " Boucard remained with his head buried in a mound of deeds, and went on making out the bill of costs on which he was employed.

The office was a large room, furnished with the classic stove that adorns all other pettifogging precincts. The pipes went diagonally across the room and entered the chimney, on the marble mantel-shelf of which were diverse bits of bread, triangles of Brie cheese, fresh pork-chops, glasses, bottles, and a cup of chocolate for the head-clerk. The smell of these comestibles amalgamated so well with the offensive odor of the over-heated stove and the peculiar exhalations of desks and papers that the stench of a fox would hardly have been perceived. The floor was covered with mud and snow brought in by the clerks. Near the window stood the rolling-top desk of the head-clerk, and next to it the little table of the second clerk. The latter was now on duty in the courts, where he usually went between eight and nine o'clock in the morning. The sole decorations of the office were the well-known large yellow posters which announce attachments on property, mortgagee-

7

sales, litigations between guardians and minors, and auctions, final or postponed, the glory of legal offices.

Behind the head-clerk, and covering the wall from top to bottom, was a case with an enormous number of pigeon-holes, each stuffed with bundles of papers, from which hung innumerable tags and those bits of red tape which give special character to legal documents. The lower shelves of the case were filled with pasteboard boxes, yellowed by time and edged with blue paper, on which could be read the names of the more distinguished clients whose affairs were cooking at the present time. The dirty window-panes let in but a small amount of light; besides, in the month of February there are very few law-offices in Paris where the clerks can write without a lamp before ten o'clock in the day. Such offices are invariably neglected, and for the reason that while every one goes there nobody stays; no personal interest attaches to so mean a spot; neither the lawyers, nor the clients, nor the clerks, care for the appearance of the place which is to the latter a school, to the clients a means, to the master a laboratory. The greasy furniture is transmitted from lawyer to lawyer with such scrupulous exactness that certain offices still possess boxes of " residues," parchments engrossed in black-letter, and bags, which have descended from the solicitors of the " Chlet," an abbreviation of the word " Châtelet," an institution which represented under the old order of things what a court of common pleas is in our day.

This dark office, choked with dust and dirt, was therefore, like all such offices, repulsive to clients, and one of the ugly monstrosities of Paris. Certainly, if the damp sacristies where prayers are weighed and paid for like spices, if the second-hand shops, where flutter rags which blight the illusions of life by revealing to us the end of our festive arrays, if these two sewers of poesy did not exist, a lawyer's office would be the most horrible of all social dens. But the same characteristic may be seen in gambling-houses, in court-rooms, in the lottery bureaus, and in evil resorts. Why? Perhaps because the drama played in such places within the soul renders men indifferent to externals, — a thought which likewise explains the simplicity of great thinkers and men of great ambitions.

"Where 's my penknife?"

"I shall eat my breakfast."

"Look out! there 's a blot on the petition."

"Hush, gentlemen!"

These various exclamations went off all at once just as the old client entered and closed the door, with the sort of humility which gives an unnatural air to the movements of a poverty-stricken man. The stranger tried to smile, but the muscles of his face relaxed when he had vainly looked for symptoms of civility on the inexorably indifferent faces of the six clerks. Accustomed, no doubt, to judge men, he addressed himself politely to the gutter-jumper, hoping that the office drudge might answer him civilly : —

" Monsieur, can I see your master?"

The mischievous youngster replied by tapping his ear with the fingers of his left hand, as much as to say, " I am deaf."

" What is it you want, monsieur?" asked Godeschal swallowing an enormous mouthful as he asked the question, — brandishing his knife and crossing his legs till the foot of the upper one came on a line with his nose.

" I have called five times, monsieur," replied the visitor ; " I wish to speak to Monsieur Derville."

" On business?"

" Yes ; but I can explain my business only to him."

" He 's asleep ; if you wish to consult him you 'll have to come at night ; he never gets to work before midnight.　But if you will explain the matter to us we can perhaps do as well — "

The stranger was impassive.　He looked humbly about him like a dog slipping into a strange kitchen and afraid of kicks.　Thanks to their general condition, law-clerks are not afraid of thieves ; so they felt no suspicion of the top-coat, but allowed him to look round in search of a seat, for he was evidently fatigued.

It is a matter of calculation with lawyers: to have few chairs in their offices. The common client, weary of standing, goes away grumbling.

"Monsieur," replied the stranger, "I have already had the honor of telling you that I can explain my business to no one but Monsieur Derville. I will wait until he is up."

Boucard had now finished his accounts. He smelt the fumes of his chocolate, left his cane chair, came up to the chimney, looked the old man over from head to foot, gazed at the top-coat and made an indescribable grimace. He probably thought that no matter how long they kept this client on the rack not a penny could be got out of him; and he now interposed, meaning with a few curt words to rid the office of an unprofitable client.

"They tell you the truth, monsieur," he said; "Monsieur Derville works only at night. If your business is important I advise you to come back here at one or two in the morning."

The client looked at the head-clerk with a stupid air, and remained for an instant motionless. Accustomed to see many changes of countenance, and many singular expressions produced by the hesitation and the dreaminess which characterize persons who go to law, the clerks took no notice of the old man, but continued to eat their breakfasts with as much noise of their jaws as if they were horses at a manger.

"Monsieur. I shall return to-night," said the visitor, who, with the tenacity of an unhappy man, was determined to put his tormentors in the wrong.

The only retaliation granted to poverty is that of forcing justice and benevolence to unjust refusals. When unhappy souls have convicted society of falsehood then they fling themselves the more ardently upon the bosom of God.

"Did you ever see such a skull?" cried Simonnin, without waiting till the door had closed on the old man.

"He looks as if he had been buried and dug up again," said one.

"He's some colonel who wants his back-pay," said the head-clerk.

"No, he's an old porter."

"Who'll bet he's a nobleman?" cried Boucard.

"I'll bet he has been a porter," said Godeschal. "None but porters are gifted by nature with top-coats as greasy and ragged round the bottom as that old fellow's. Did n't you notice his cracked boots which let in water, and that cravat in place of a shirt? That man slept last night under a bridge."

"He may be a nobleman and have burnt his candle at both ends, — that's nothing new!" cried Desroches.

"No," replied Boucard, in the midst of much laughter, "I maintain he was a brewer in 1789 and a colonel under the Republic."

" Ha! I 'll bet tickets for a play all round that he never was a soldier," said Godeschal.

" Done," said Boucard.

" Monsieur, monsieur!" called the gutter-jumper, opening the window.

" What are you doing, Simonnin?" asked Boucard.

" I 'm calling him back to know if he is a colonel or a porter, — he ought to know, himself."

" What shall we say to him?" exclaimed Godeschal.

" Leave it to me," said Boucard.

The poor man re-entered timidly, with his eyes lowered, perhaps not to show his hunger by looking too eagerly at the food.

" Monsieur," said Boucard, " will you have the kindness to give us your name, so that Monsieur Derville may — "

" Chabert."

" The colonel who was killed at Eylau?" asked Huré, who had not yet spoken, but was anxious to get in his joke like the rest.

" The same, monsieur," answered the old man, with classic simplicity. Then he left the room.

" Thunder ! "

" Sold ! "

" Puff ! "

" Oh ! "

" Ah ! "

“ Boum ! ”

“ The old oddity ! ”

“ Done for ! ”

“ Monsieur Desroches, you and I will go to the theatre for nothing ! ” cried Huré to the fourth clerk, with a rap on the shoulders fit to have killed a rhinoceros.

Then followed a chorus of shouts, laughs, and exclamations, to describe which we should have to use all the onomatopœias of the language.

“ Which theatre shall we choose ? ”

“ The Opera,” said the head-clerk.

“ In the first place,” said Godeschal, “ I never said theatre at all.   I can take you, if I choose, to Madame Saqui.”

“ Madame Saqui is not a play,” said Desroches.

“ What ’s a play ? ” retorted Godeschal.   “ Let ’s first establish the fact.   What did I bet, gentlemen ? tickets for a play.   What ’s a play ? a thing we go to see — ”

“ If that ’s so, you can take us to see the water running under the Pont Neuf,” interrupted Simonnin.

“ — see for money,” went on Godeschal.

“ But you can see a great many things for money that are not plays.   The definition is not exact,” said Desroches.

“ But just listen to me — ”

“ You are talking nonsense, my dear fellow,” said Boucard.

" Do you call Curtius a play ? " asked Godeschal.

" No," said the head-clerk, " I call it a gallery of wax figures."

" I 'll bet a hundred francs to a sou," retorted Godeschal, " that Curtius's gallery constitutes a collection of things which may legally be called a play. They combine into one thing which can be seen at different prices according to the seats you occupy — "

" You can't get out of it ! " said Simonnin.

" Take care I don't box your ears ! " said Godeschal. The clerks all shrugged their shoulders.

" Besides, we don't know that that old baboon wasn't making fun of us," he continued, changing his argument amid roars of laughter. " The fact is, Colonel Chabert is as dead as a door-nail; his widow married Comte Ferraud, councillor of state. Madame Ferraud is one of our clients."

" The cause stands over for to-morrow," said Boucard. " Come, get to work, gentlemen. Heavens and earth ! nothing ever gets done here. Finish with that petition, — it has to be sent in before the session of the fourth court which meets to-day. Come, to work ! "

" If it was really Colonel Chabert, would n't he have kicked that little Simonnin when he pretended to be deaf ? " said the provincial Huré, considering that observation quite as conclusive as those of Godeschal.

" Nothing is decided," said Boucard. " Let us agree

to accept the second tier of boxes at the Français and see Talma in Nero. Simonnin can sit in the pit."

Thereupon the head-clerk sat down at his desk, and the others followed his example.

" *Rendered June one thousand eight hundred and fourteen —* Write it in letters, mind," said Godeschal. " Have you written it?"

" Yes," replied the copyists and the engrosser, whose pens began to squeak along the stamped paper with a noise, well known in all law-offices, like that of scores of cockchafers tied by schoolboys in a paper bag.

" *And we pray that the gentlemen of this tribunal —* Hold on ! let me read that sentence over to myself; I don't know what I 'm about."

" Forty-six — should think that often happened — and three, forty-nine," said Boucard.

" *We pray,*" resumed Godeschal, having re-read his clause, " *that the gentlemen of this tribunal will not show less magnanimity than the august author of the ordinance, and that they will deny the miserable pretensions of the administration of the grand chancellor of the Legion of honor by determining the jurisprudence of this matter in the broad sense in which we have established it here —* "

" Monsieur Godeschal, don't you want a glass of water?" said the gutter-jumper.

" That imp of a Simonnin ! " said Boucard. " Come

here, saddle your double-soled horses, and take this package and skip over to the Invalides."

"*Which we have established it here —*" went on Godeschal. "Did you get to that? Well, then add *in the interests of Madame* (full length) *la Vicomtesse de Grandlieu —*"

"What's that?" cried the head clerk, "the idea of petitioning in that affair! Vicomtesse de Grandlieu against the Legion of honor! Ah! you must be a fool! Have the goodness to put away your copies and your minute, — they'll answer for the Navarreins affair against the monasteries. It's late, and I must be off with the other petitions; I'll attend to that myself at the Palais."

Towards one o'clock in the morning the individual calling himself Colonel Chabert knocked at the door of Maître Derville, solicitor in the court of common pleas for the department of the Seine. The porter told him that Monsieur Derville had not yet come in. The old man declared he had an appointment and passed up to the rooms of the celebrated lawyer, who, young as he was, was even then considered one of the best legal heads in France. Having rung and been admitted, the persistent client was not a little astonished to find the head-clerk laying out on a table in the dining-room a number of documents relating to affairs which were to come up on the morrow. The clerk, not less astonished at the apparition of the old man, bowed to the colonel and asked him to sit down, which he did.

"Upon my word, monsieur, I thought you were joking when you named such a singular hour for a consultation," said the old man, with the factitious liveliness of a ruined man who tries to smile.

"The clerks were joking and telling the truth also," said the head-clerk, going on with his work. "Monsieur Derville selects this hour to examine his causes, give directions for the suits, and plan his defences. His extraordinary intellect works freer at this hour, the only one in which he can get the silence and tranquillity he requires to evolve his ideas. You are the third person only who has been admitted here for a consultation at this time of night. After Monsieur Derville comes in he will talk over each affair, read everything connected with it, and spend perhaps five or six hours at his work; then he rings for me, and explains his intentions. In the morning, from ten to two, he listens to his clients; the rest of the day he passes in visiting. In the evening he goes about in society to keep up his relations with the great world. He has no other time than at night to delve into his cases, rummage the arsenals of the Code, make his plans of campaign. He is determined, out of love for his profession, not to lose a single case. And for that reason he won't take all that are brought to him, as other lawyers do. That's his life; it's extraordinarily active. He makes a lot of money."

The old man was silent as he listened to this explanation, and his singular face assumed a look so devoid of all intelligence that the clerk after glancing at him once or twice took no further notice of him. A few moments later Derville arrived, in evening dress; his head-clerk opened the door to him and then went back to the papers. The young lawyer looked amazed when he saw in the dim light the strange client who awaited him. Colonel Chabert was as motionless as the wax figures of Curtius's gallery where Godeschal proposed to take his comrades. This immovability might have been less noticeable than it was, if it had not, as it were, completed the supernatural impression conveyed by the whole appearance of the man. The old soldier was lean and shrunken. The concealment of his forehead, which was carefully hidden beneath a wig brushed smoothly over it, gave a mysterious expression to his person. The eyes seemed covered with a film; you might have thought them bits of dirty mother-of-pearl, their bluish reflections quivering in the candle-light. The pale, livid, hatchet face, if I may borrow that term, seemed dead. An old black-silk stock was fastened round the neck. The shadow of the room hid the body so effectually below the dark line of the ragged article that a man of vivid imagination might have taken that old head for a sketch drawn at random on the wall or for a portrait by Rembrandt without its frame. The brim of the hat worn by the strange old man cast a black line across the upper part of his face. This odd effect, though perfectly natural, brought out in abrupt contrast the white wrinkles, the stiffened lines, the unnatural hue of that cadaverous countenance. The absence of all motion in the body, all warmth in the glance, combined with a certain expression of mental alienation, and with the degrading symptoms which characterize idiocy, to give that face a nameless horror which no words can describe.

But an observer, and especially a lawyer, would have seen in that blasted man the signs of some deep anguish, indications of a misery that degraded that face as the drops of rain falling from the heavens on pure marble gradually disfigure it. A doctor, an author, a magistrate would have felt intuitively a whole drama as they looked at this sublime wreck, whose least merit was a resemblance to those fantastic sketches drawn by artists on the margins of their lithographic stones as they sit conversing with their friends.

When the stranger saw the lawyer he shuddered with the convulsive movement which seizes a poet when a sudden noise recalls him from some fecund revery amid the silence of the night. The old man rose quickly and took off his hat to the young lawyer. The leather that lined it was no doubt damp with grease, for his wig stuck to it without his knowledge and exposed his skull, horribly mutilated and disfigured by a scar running from the crown of his head to the angle of his right eye and forming a raised welt. The sudden removal of that dirty wig, worn by the poor soul to conceal his wound, caused no desire to laugh in the minds of the two young men ; so awful was the sight of that skull. "The mind fled through it!" was the first thought suggested to them as they saw that wound.

"If he is not Colonel Chabert he is some bold trooper," thought Boucard.

"Monsieur," said Derville, "to whom have I the honor of speaking?"

"To Colonel Chabert."

"Which one?"

"The one who was killed at Eylau," replied the old man.

Hearing those extraordinary words the clerk and the lawyer looked at each other as if to say, "He is mad."

"Monsieur," said the colonel, "I desire to confide my secrets to you in private."

The intrepidity which characterizes lawyers is worthy of remark. Whether from their habit of receiving great numbers of persons, whether from an abiding sense of the protection of the law, or from perfect confidence in their ministry, certain it is they go everywhere and take all risks, like priests and doctors. Derville made a sign to Boucard, who left the room.

" Monsieur," said the lawyer, " during the day I am not very chary of my time; but in the middle of the night every moment is precious to me. Therefore, be brief and concise. Tell your facts without digression; I will ask you any explanations I may find necessary. Go on."

Bidding his strange client be seated, the young man sat down before the table, and while listening to the tale of the late colonel he turned over the pages of a brief.

" Monsieur," said the deceased, " perhaps you know that I commanded a regiment of cavalry at Eylau. I was the chief cause of the success of Murat's famous charge which won the day. Unhappily for me, my death is given as an historic fact in ' Victories and Conquests' where all the particulars are related. We cut the three Russian lines in two; then they closed behind us and we were obliged to cut our way back again. Just before we reached the Emperor, having dispersed the Russians, a troop of the enemy's cavalry met us. I flung myself upon them. Two Russian officers, actual giants, attacked me together. One of them cut me over the head with his sabre, which went through everything, even to the silk cap which I wore, and laid my skull open. I fell from my horse. Murat came up to support us, and he and his whole party, fifteen hundred men, rode over me. They reported my death to the Emperor, who sent (for he loved me a little, the master!) to see if there were no hope of saving a man to whom he owed the vigor of our attack. He despatched two surgeons to find me and bring me in to the ambulances, saying — perhaps too hurriedly, for he had work to attend to — ' Go and see if my poor Chabert is still living.' Those cursed saw-bones had just seen me trampled under the hoofs of two regiments ; no doubt they never took the trouble to feel my pulse, but reported me as dead. The certificate of my death was doubtless drawn up in due form of military law."

Gradually, as he listened to his client, who expressed himself with perfect clearness, and related facts that were quite possible, though somewhat strange, the young lawyer pushed away his papers, rested his left elbow on the table, put his head on his hand, and looked fixedly at the colonel.

" Are you aware, monsieur," he said, " that I am the solicitor of the Countess Ferraud, widow of Colonel Chabert? "

" Of my wife? Yes, monsieur. And therefore, after many fruitless efforts to obtain a hearing from lawyers, who all thought me mad, I determined to come to you. I shall speak of my sorrows later. Allow me now to

state the facts, and explain to you how they probably
happened, rather than how they actually did happen.
Certain circumstances, which can never be known except to God Almighty, oblige me to relate much in the
form of hypotheses. I must tell you, for instance, that
the wounds I received probably produced something
like lockjaw, or threw me into a state analogous to a
disease called, I believe, catalepsy. Otherwise, how
can I suppose that I was stripped of my clothing and
flung into a common grave, according to the customs of
war, by the men whose business it was to bury the
dead? Here let me state a circumstance which I only
knew much later than the event which I am forced to
call my death. In 1814 I met in Stuttgard an old cavalry sergeant of my regiment. That dear man — the
only human being willing to recognize me, of whom I
will presently speak to you — explained to me the extraordinary circumstances of my preservation. He said
that my horse received a bullet in the body at the same
moment when I myself was wounded. Horse and rider
were therefore knocked over together like a stand of
muskets. In turning, either to the right or to the
left, I had doubtless been protected by the body of
my horse which saved me from being crushed by the
riders or hit by bullets."

The old man paused for a moment as if to collect
himself and then resumed : —

" When I came to myself, monsieur, I was in a place and in an · atmosphere of which I could give you no idea, even if I talked for days. The air I breathed was mephitic. I tried to move but I found no space. My eyes were open but I saw nothing. The want of air was the worst sign, and it showed me the dangers of my position. I felt I was in some place where the atmosphere was stagnant, and that I should die of it. This thought overcame the sense of extreme pain which had brought me to my senses. My ears hummed violently. I heard, or thought I heard (for I can affirm nothing), groans from the heap of dead bodies among whom I lay. Though the recollection of those moments is dark, though my memory is confused, and in spite of still greater sufferings which I experienced later and which have bewildered my ideas, there are nights, even now, when I think I hear those smothered moans. But there was something more horrible than even those cries, — a silence that I have never known elsewhere, the silence of the grave. At last, raising my hands and feeling for the dead, I found a void between my head and the human carrion about me. I could even measure the space thus left to me by some mere chance, the cause of which I did not know. It seemed as if, thanks to the carelessness or to the haste with which we had been flung pell-mell into the trench, that two dead bodies had fallen across each other above me, so as to form an angle like that of two cards which children lay together to make houses. Quickly feeling in all directions, — for I had no time to idle, — I happily came across an arm, the arm of a Hercules, detached from its body ; and those good bones saved me ! Without that unlooked-for succor I must have perished. But now, with a fury you will readily understand, I began to work my way upward through the bodies which separated me from the layer of earth hastily flung over us, — I say ' us,' as though there were others living. I worked with a will, monsieur, for here I am ! Still, I don't know to-day how it was that I managed to tear through the covering of flesh that lay between me and life. I had, as it were, three arms. That Herculean crow-bar, which I used carefully, brought me a little air confined among the bodies which it helped me to displace, and I economized my breathing. At last I saw daylight, but through the snow, monsieur ! Just then I noticed for the first time that my head was cut open. Happily, my blood — that of my comrades, possibly, how should I know? or the bleeding flesh of my horse — had co-agulated on my wound and formed a natural plaster. But in spite of that scab I fainted when my head came in contact with the snow. The little heat still left in my body melted the snow about me, and when I came to myself my head was in the middle of a little opening, through which I shouted as long as I was able. But

the sun had risen and I was little likely to be heard.
People seemed already in the fields. I raised myself to
my feet, making stepping-stones of the dead whose
thighs were solid, — for it was n't the moment to stop
and say, ' Honor to heroes ! '

" In short, monsieur," continued the old man, who
had stopped speaking for a moment, " after going
through the anguish — if that word describes the rage —
of seeing those cursed Germans, ay, many of them,
run away when they heard the voice of a man they
could not see, I was at last taken from my living grave
by a woman, daring enough or inquisitive enough to
come close to my head, which seemed to grow from the
ground like a mushroom. The woman fetched her husband, and together they took me to their poor hovel.
It seems that there I had a return of catalepsy, — allow
me that term with which to describe a state of which I
have no idea, but which I judge, from what my hosts
told me, must have been an effect of that disease. I lay
for six months between life and death, not speaking,
or wandering in mind when I did speak. At last my
benefactors placed me in the hospital at Heilsberg. Of
course you understand, monsieur, that I issued from
my grave as naked as I came from my mother's womb ;
so that when, many months later, I remembered that I
was Colonel Chabert, and endeavored to make my
nurses treat me with more respect than if I were a

poor devil of a private, all the men in the ward laughed. Happily for me, the surgeon made it a point of honor or vanity to cure me; and he naturally became interested in his patient. When I spoke to him in a connected manner of my former life, that good man (his name was Sparchmann) had my statements recorded in the legal forms of his country, also a statement of the miraculous manner in which I had escaped from the trench, and the day and hour my benefactress and her husband had rescued me, together with the nature and exact position of my wounds and a careful description of my person. Well, monsieur, I do not possess a single one of those important papers, nor the declaration I made before a notary at Heilsberg to establish my identity. The events of the war drove us from the town, and from that day I have wandered like a vagabond, begging my bread, treated as a lunatic when I told my story, unable to earn a single sou that would enable me to send for those papers, which alone can prove the truth of what I say and restore me to my social status. Often my physical sufferings have kept me for weeks and months in some obscure country town, where the greatest kindness has been shown to the sick Frenchman, but where they laughed in his face when he asserted he was Colonel Chabert. For a long while such doubts and laughter made me furious, and that injured my cause, and once I was shut up as a madman at Stuttgard. You can imagine, from what I have told you, that there were reasons to lock me up. After two years in a madhouse, where I was forced to hear my keepers say: ' This poor man fancies he was once Colonel Chabert,' to visitors, who replied compassionately, ' Ah, poor man ! ' I myself was convinced of the impossibility of my story being true ; I grew sad, resigned, tranquil, and I ceased to call myself Colonel Chabert, so as to get my release and return to France. Oh, monsieur ! to see Paris once more ! it was a joy I — "

With those unfinished words Colonel Chabert sank into a revery, which the lawyer did not disturb.

" Monsieur," resumed the client presently, " one fine day, a spring day, they gave me my freedom and ten thalers, on the ground that I talked sensibly on all subjects and had given up calling myself Colonel Chabert ; and, God knows, at that time my name was disagreeable to me, and has been at intervals ever since. I would like not to be myself; the sense of my rights kills me. If my illness had only taken from me forever the remembrance of my past existence, I might be happy. I might have re-entered the service under some other name ; and, who knows? perhaps I should have ended as a Russian or an Austrian field-marshal."

" Monsieur," said the lawyer, " you have upset all my ideas ; I fancy I dream as I listen to you. Let us pause here for a moment, I beg of you."

"You are the only person," said the colonel sadly, "who have ever listened to me patiently. No lawyer has been willing to lend me ten napoleons, that I might send to Germany for the papers necessary for my suit."

"What suit?" asked the lawyer, who had forgotten the unfortunate present position of his client, as he listened to the recital of his past misery.

"Why, monsieur, you are well aware that the Comtesse Ferraud is my wife. She possesses an income of thirty thousand francs which belongs to me, and she refuses to give me one penny of it. When I tell this to lawyers and to men of common-sense, when I, a beggar, propose to sue a count and countess, when I, risen from the dead, deny the proofs of my death, they put me off, — they refuse to listen to me, either with that coldly polite air with which you lawyers know so well how to rid yourselves of hapless creatures, or brutally, as men do when they think they are dealing with a swindler or a madman. I have been buried beneath the dead, but now I am buried beneath the living, — beneath facts, beneath records, beneath society itself, which seeks to thrust me back underground!"

"Monsieur, have the goodness to sue, to prosecute now," said the lawyer.

"Have the goodness! Ah!" exclaimed the unfortunate old man, taking the hand of the young lawyer; "that is the first polite word I have heard since —"

He wept. Gratitude stifled his voice. The all-penetrative, indescribable eloquence of look, gesture, — even silence, — clinched Derville's conviction, and touched him keenly.

" Listen to me, monsieur," he said. " I won three hundred francs at cards to-night ; I can surely afford to give half that sum to procure the happiness of a man. I will make all the investigations and orders necessary to obtain the papers you mention ; and, until their arrival, I will allow you five francs a day. If you are Colonel Chabert, you will know how to pardon the smallness of the loan offered by a young man who has his fortune to make. Continue."

The self-styled colonel remained for an instant motionless, and as if stupefied ; his great misfortunes had, perhaps, destroyed his powers of belief. If he were seeking to recover his illustrious military fame, his home, his fortune, — himself, in short, — it may have been only in obedience to that inexplicable feeling, that germ in the hearts of all men, to which we owe the researches of the alchemists, the passion for glory, the discoveries of astronomy and of physics, — all that urges a man to magnify himself by the magnitude of the facts or the ideas that are a part of him. The *ego* was now but a secondary consideration to his mind, just as the vanity of triumph or the satisfaction of gain are dearer to a man who bets than the object of his wager. The words of the young lawyer came, therefore, like a miracle to this man, repudiated for the last ten years by wife, by justice, by the whole social creation. To receive from a lawyer those ten gold pieces so long denied him, by so many persons, in so many ways! The colonel was like the lady who had been ill so long, that when she was cured she thought she was suffering from a new malady. There are joys in which we no longer believe; they come, and we find them thunderbolts, — they blast us. So now the poor man's gratitude was so deep that he could not utter it. He might have seemed cold to a superficial mind, but Derville saw integrity in that very stupor. A swindler would have spoken.

" Where was I?" said the colonel, with the guilelessness of a child or a soldier; for there is much of the child in the true soldier, and nearly always something of a soldier in a child, especially in France.

" At Stuttgard ; they had set you at liberty."

" You know my wife?" asked the colonel.

" Yes," replied Derville, with a nod of his head.

" How is she?"

" Always fascinating."

The old man made a gesture with his hand, and seemed to conquer some secret pang with the grave and solemn resignation that characterizes men who have been tried in the fire and blood of battle-fields.

" Monsieur," he said, with a sort of gayety; for he breathed anew, poor soul; he had issued a second time from the grave; he had broken through a crust of ice and snow harder to melt than that which once had frozen his wounded head; he inhaled the air as though he were just issuing from a dungeon. "Monsieur," he said, "if I were a handsome fellow I should n't be where I am now. Women believe men when they lard their sentences with words of love. Then they'll fetch and carry, and come and go, and do anything to serve you. They'll intrigue; they'll swear to facts; they'll play the devil for the man they love. But how could I make a woman listen to one like me? With a face like a death's head, and clothed like a sans-culotte, I was more of an Esquimau than a Frenchman, — I, who in 1799 was the finest coxcomb in the service! — I, Chabert, count of the Empire! At last the day came when I knew I was an outcast on the streets, like a pariah dog. That day I met the sergeant I told you of; his name was Boutin. That poor devil and I made the finest pair of broken-down old brutes I have ever seen. I met him, and recognized him; but he couldn't even guess who I was. We went into a tavern. When I told him my name his mouth split open with a roar of laughter like a burst mortar. Monsieur, that laugh is among the bitterest of my sorrows. It revealed, without disguise, the changes there were in me. I saw myself unrecognizable, even to the humblest and most grateful of my friends; for I had once saved Boutin's life, though that was a return for something I owed him. I need n't tell you the whole story; the thing happened in Italy, at Ravenna. The house where Boutin saved me from being stabbed was none too decent. At that time I was not colonel, only a trooper, like Boutin. Happily, there were circumstances in the affair known only to him and me; when I reminded him of them, his incredulity lessened. Then I told him the story of my extraordinary fate. Though my eyes and my voice were, he told me, strangely altered; though I had neither hair, nor teeth, nor eyebrows, and was as white as an albino, he did finally recognize his old colonel in the beggar before him, after putting a vast number of questions to which I answered triumphantly.

"Ah!" went on the old soldier, after a moment's pause, "he told me his adventures too, and they were hardly less extraordinary than mine. He was just back from the borders of China, to which he had escaped from Siberia. He told me of the disasters of the Russian campaign and Napoleon's first abdication; that news was another of my worst pangs. We were two strange wrecks drifting over the globe, as the storms of ocean drift the pebbles from shore to shore. We had each seen Egypt, Syria, Spain, Russia, Holland, Germany, Italy, Dalmatia, England, China, Tartary, Siberia; nothing was left for us to know but the Indies and America. Boutin, who was more active on his legs than I, agreed to go to Paris as quickly as he could, and tell my wife the state in which I was. I wrote a long and detailed letter to Madame Chabert; it was the fourth I had written her. Monsieur, if I had had relatives of my own, the thing could not have happened; but, I must tell you plainly, I was a foundling, a soldier whose patrimony was his courage, the world his family, France his country, God his sole protector, — no! I am wrong; I had a father, — the Emperor! Ah! if he, dear man, were still among us; if he saw 'his Chabert,' as he called me, in such a plight, he would be furious. But what's to be done? our sun has set; we are all left out in the cold! After all, political events might be the reason of my wife's silence; at least I thought so. Boutin departed. He was lucky, *he* was, poor fellow! he had two white bears who danced and kept him in food. I could not accompany him; my pains were so great I could not go long distances. I wept when we parted, having walked as far as I had strength with the bears and him. At Carlsruhe I was taken with neuralgia in my head, and lay six weeks in the straw of an inn barn.

"Ah! monsieur," continued the unhappy man, "there is no end to what I might tell you of my miserable life. Moral anguish, before which all physical sufferings are as nought, excites less pity because it is not seen. I remember weeping before a mansion in Strasburg where I once gave a ball, and where they now refused me a crust of bread. Having agreed with Boutin as to the road I should follow, I went to every post-office on my way expecting to find a letter and some money. I reached Paris at last without a line. Despair was in my heart! Boutin must be dead, I thought; and I was right; the poor fellow died at Waterloo, as I heard later and accidentally. His errand to my wife was no doubt fruitless. Well, I reached Paris just as the Cossacks entered it. To me, that was grief upon grief. When I saw those Russians in France I no longer remembered that I had neither shoes on my feet nor money in my pocket. Yes, monsieur, my clothes were literally in shreds. The evening of my arrival I was forced to bivouac in the woods of Claye. The chilliness of the night gave me a sort of illness, I hardly know what it was, which seized me as I was crossing the faubourg Saint-Martin. I fell, half-unconscious, close by the door of an ironmonger. When I came to my senses I was in a bed at the Hôtel-Dieu. There I stayed a month in some comfort; then I was discharged. I had no money, but I was cured and I had my feet on the blessed pavements of Paris. With what joy and speed I made my way to the rue du Mont-Blanc, where I supposed my wife was living in my house.　Bah! the rue du Mont-Blanc had become the rue de la Chaussée-d'Antin.　My house was no longer standing; it was pulled down.　Speculators had built houses in my gardens.　Not knowing that my wife had married Monsieur Ferraud, I could hear nothing of her. At last I went to an old lawyer who formerly took charge of my affairs.　The good man was dead, and his office had passed into the hands of a younger man.　The latter informed me, to my great astonishment, of the settlement of my estate, the marriage of my wife, and the birth of her two children.　When I told him that I was Colonel Chabert, he laughed so loudly in my face that I turned and left him without a word.　My detention at Stuttgart made me mindful of Charenton, and I resolved to act prudently.　Then, monsieur, knowing where my wife lived, I made my way to the house — Ah!" cried the colonel, with a gesture of intense anger, "I was not received when I gave a borrowed name, but when I sent in my own I was turned out of the house! I have stood night after night leaning against the buttress of her porte-cochère to see her returning from a ball or from the theatre.　I have plunged my eyes into that carriage where I could see the woman who is mine and who is not mine!　Oh! from that day I have lived for vengeance," cried the old man, in a hollow voice, standing suddenly erect in front of Derville.　" She knows I am living; she has received three letters which

I have written to her since my return. She loves me no longer! I—I don't know if I love her or if I hate her; I long for her and I curse her by turns! She owes her prosperity and all her happiness to me, and she denies me even the meanest succor! Sometimes I don't know where to turn!"

The old man fell back into a chair, motionless and silent. Derville too was silent, contemplating his client.

"The matter is serious," he said at last in a mechanical way. "Even admitting the authenticity of the papers which ought to be found at Heilsberg, it is not clear that we can establish our case,—certainly not at once. The suit will have to go before three courts. I must reflect at my leisure over such a case. It is exceptional."

"Oh!" replied the colonel, coldly, lifting his head with a proud gesture, "if I am compelled to succumb, I can die,—but not alone."

With the words the old man seemed to vanish; the eyes of the man of energy shone with the fires of desire and vengeance.

"Perhaps we shall have to compromise," said the lawyer.

"Compromise!" repeated Colonel Chabert. "Am I dead, or am I living?"

"Monsieur," said the lawyer, "you will, I hope,

follow my advice. Your cause shall be my cause. You will soon, I trust, see the true interest I take in your situation, which is almost without precedent in legal annals. Meantime let me give you an order on my notary, who will remit you fifty francs every ten days on your receipt. It is not desirable that you should come here for this money. If you are Colonel Chabert you ought not to be beholden to any one. I shall make these advances in the form of a loan. You have property to recover; you are a rich man."

This last delicate consideration for his feelings brought tears from the old man's eyes. Derville rose abruptly, for assuredly it is not the thing for a lawyer to show feeling; he went into his private study and returned presently with an unsealed letter, which he gave to Colonel Chabert. When the old man took it he felt two gold pieces within the paper.

"Tell me precisely what the papers are; give me the exact name of the town and kingdom," said the lawyer.

The colonel dictated the necessary information and corrected the spelling of the names. Then he took his hat in one hand, looked at Derville, offered him the other hand, a horny hand, and said in a simple way, —

"After the Emperor you are the man to whom I owe most. You are a noble man."

The lawyer clasped the colonel's hand, and went with him to the stairway to light him down.

"Boucard," said the lawyer to his head-clerk, whom he summoned, "I have just heard a tale which may cost me some money. If I am deceived I shall never regret what I pay, for I shall have seen the greatest comedian of our time."

"When the colonel reached the street, he stopped under a lamp, drew the two pieces of twenty francs each from the letter which the lawyer had given him, and looked at them for a moment in the dim light. He saw gold for the first time in nine years.

"I can smoke cigars," he said to himself.

About three months after the nocturnal consultation of Colonel Chabert with Derville, the notary whom the latter had directed to pay the stipend he allowed to his singular client went to the lawyer's office one day to confer on some important matter, and opened the conversation by asking for the six hundred francs he had already paid to the old soldier.

"Do you find it amusing to support the old army?" said the notary, laughing. His name was Crottat, — a young man who had just bought a practice in which he was head-clerk, the master of which, a certain Roguin, had lately absconded after a frightful failure.

"Thank you, my dear fellow, for reminding me of

that affair," replied Derville. "My philanthropy does not go beyond twenty-five louis; I fear I have been the dupe of my patriotism."

As Derville uttered the words his eyes lighted on a packet of papers the head-clerk had laid upon his desk. His attention was drawn to one of the letters by the postmarks, oblong, square, and triangular, and red and blue stamped upon it in the Prussian, Austrian, Bavarian, and French post-offices.

"Ah!" said he, laughing, "here's the conclusion of the comedy; now we shall see if I have been taken in."

He took up the letter and opened it, but was unable to read a word, for it was in German.

"Boucard!" he called, opening the door and holding out the letter to his head-clerk, "go yourself and get that letter translated, and come back with it as fast as you can."

The Berlin notary to whom Derville had written now replied by informing the latter that the papers he had asked for would reach him a few days after this letter of advice. They were all, he said, perfectly regular, and were fully certified with the necessary legal forms. He added, moreover, that nearly all the witnesses to the facts were still living, and that the woman to whom Monsieur le Comte Chabert owed his life could be found in a certain suburb of Heilsberg.

"It is getting serious," said Derville, when Boucard

had told him the substance of the letter. "But see here, my dear fellow, I want some information which I am sure you must have in your office. When that old swindler of a Roguin —"

"We say 'the unfortunate Roguin,'" said Crottat, laughing, as he interrupted Derville.

"Well — when that unfortunate Roguin ran off with eight hundred thousand francs of his clients' money and reduced many families to pauperism, what was done about the Chabert property? It seems to me I have seen something about it among our Ferraud papers."

"Yes," replied Crottat, "I was third clerk at the time, and I remember copying and studying the documents. Rose Chapotel, wife and widow of Hyacinthe, called Chabert, count of the Empire, grand officer of the Legion of honor. They had married without a contract and therefore they held their property in common. As far as I can recollect, the assets amounted to about six hundred thousand francs. Before his marriage Comte Chabert had made a will leaving one fourth of the property of which he might die possessed to the Parisian hospitals ; the State inherited another fourth. There was an auction sale and a distribution of the property, for the lawyers made good speed with the affair. Upon the settlement of the estate the monster who then ruled France made a decree restoring the amount which had gone to the Treasury to the colonel's widow."

" So that Comte Chabert's individual property," said Derville, " does not amount to more than three hundred thousand francs? "

" Just that, old man," said Crottat ; " you solicitors do occasionally get things right, — though some people accuse you of arguing just as well against as for the truth."

Comte Chabert, whose address was written at the foot of the first receipt he had given to the notary, lived in the faubourg Saint-Marceau, rue du Petit-Banquier, with an old sergeant of the Imperial Guard named Vergniaud, now a cow-keeper. When Derville reached the place he was obliged to go on foot to find his client, for his groom positively refused to drive through an unpaved street the ruts of which were deep enough to break the wheels of a cabriolet. Looking about him on all sides, the lawyer at length discovered at the end of the street nearest to the boulevard and between two walls built of bones and mud, two shabby rough stone pillars, much defaced by wheels in spite of wooden posts placed in front of them. These pillars supported a beam covered with a tiled hood, on which, painted red, were the words, " VERGNIAUD, COW-KEEPER." To the right of the name was a cow, and to the left eggs, all painted white. The gate was open.

At the farther end of a good-sized yard and opposite to the gate stood the house, if indeed that name rightfully belongs to one of those hovels built in the suburbs of Paris, the squalor of which cannot be matched elsewhere, not even in the most wretched of country huts; for they have all the poverty of the latter without their poetry. In fact, a cabin in the open country has the charm that pure air, verdure, the meadow vistas, a hill, a winding road, creepers, evergreen hedges, a mossy roof and rural implements can give to it; but in Paris poverty is heightened only by horrors. Though recently built, the house seemed tumbling to ruins. None of its materials were originally destined for it; they came from the "demolitions" which are daily events in Paris. On a shutter made of an old sign Derville read the words " Fancy-articles." No two of the windows were alike, and all were placed hap-hazard. The ground-floor, which seemed to be the habitable part of the hovel, was raised from the earth on one side, while on the other the rooms were sunk below a bank. Between the gate and the house was a slough of manure, into which flowed the rain-water and the drainage from the house. The wall upon which this rickety building rested was surrounded by hutches in which rabbits brought forth their numerous young. To the right of the gate was the cow-shed, which communicated with the house through a dairy, and over it the hay-loft.

To the left was a poultry-yard, a stable, and a pig-sty, all of which were finished off, like the house, with shabby planks of white-wood nailed one above the other and filled in with rushes. Like most of the purlieus whence the elements of the grand dinners daily eaten in Paris are derived, the yard in which Derville now stood showed signs of the haste required for the prompt filling of orders. The great tin cans in which the milk was carried, the smaller cans with their linen stoppers which contained the cream, were tossed higgledy-piggledy in front of the dairy. The rags used to wipe them out were hanging in the sun to dry, on lines fastened to hooks. The steady horse, of a race extinct except among milk-dealers, had walked a few steps away from the cart and stood in front of the stable, the door of which was locked. A goat browsed upon the spindling, powdery vine-shoots which crept along the cracked and yellow walls of the house. A cat was creeping among the cream-cans and licking the outside of them. The hens, scared at Derville's advent, scuttled away cackling, and the watch-dog barked.

"The man who decided the victory of Eylau lives here!" thought Derville, taking in at a glance the whole of this squalid scene.

The house seemed to be under the guardianship of three little ragamuffins. One, who had clambered to the top of a cart laden with green fodder, was throwing

stones down the chimney of the next house, probably
hoping that they would fall into the saucepans below;
another was trying to lead a pig up the floor of a tip-
cart, one end of which touched the ground, while the
third, hanging on to the other end, was waiting till the
pig was fairly in to tip the cart up again. When Derville asked if that was where Monsieur Chabert lived
none of them answered ; and all three gazed at him
with lively stupidity, — if it is allowable to unite those
words.   Derville repeated his question without result.
Provoked at the saucy air of the little scamps, he spoke
sharply, in a tone which young men think they can use
to children, and the boys broke silence with a roar of
laughter.   Derville was angry. The colonel, who heard
the noise, came out of a little room near the dairy and
stood on the sill of his door with the imperturbable
phlegm of a military training. In his mouth was a
pipe in process of being " colored," — one of those
humble pipes of white clay with short stems called
" muzzle-scorchers." He raised the peak of a cap
which was horribly greasy, saw Derville, and came
across the manure heap in haste to meet his benefactor, calling out in a friendly tone to the boys,
"Silence, in the ranks!" The children became instantly and respectfully silent, showing the power the
old soldier had over them.

   " Why haven't you written to me?" he said to Derville. " Go along by the cow-house ; see, the yard is paved on that side," he cried, noticing the hesitation of the young lawyer, who did not care to set his feet in the wet manure.

Jumping from stone to stone, Derville at last reached the door through which the colonel had issued. Chabert seemed annoyed at the necessity of receiving him in the room he was occupying. In fact, there was only one chair. The colonel's bed was merely a few bundles of straw on which his landlady had spread some ragged bits of old carpet, such as milk-women lay upon the seats of their wagons, and pick up, heaven knows where. The floor was neither more nor less than the earth beaten hard. Such dampness exuded from the nitrified walls, greenish in color and full of cracks, that the side where the colonel slept had been covered with a mat made of reeds. The top-coat was hanging to a nail. Two pairs of broken boots lay in a corner. Not a vestige of under-clothing was seen. The " Bulletins of the Grand Army," reprinted by Plancher, was lying open on a mouldy table, as if constantly read by the colonel, whose face was calm and serene in the midst of this direful poverty. His visit to Derville seemed to have changed the very character of his features, on which the lawyer now saw traces of happy thought, the special gleam which hope had cast.

" Does the smoke of a pipe annoy you?" he asked,

offering the one chair, and that half-denuded of straw.

"But colonel, you are shockingly ill-lodged here!"

The words were wrung from Derville by the natural distrust of lawyers, caused by the deplorable experience that comes to them so soon from the dreadful, mysterious dramas in which they are called professionally to take part.

"That man," thought Derville to himself, "has no doubt spent my money in gratifying the three cardinal virtues of a trooper, — wine, women, and cards.

"True enough, monsieur; we don't abound in luxury. It is a bivouac, tempered, as you may say, by friendship; but" (here the soldier cast a searching look at the lawyer) "I have done wrong to no man, I have repulsed no man, and I sleep in peace."

Derville felt there would be a want of delicacy in asking his client to account for his use of the money he had lent him, so he merely said: "Why don't you come into Paris, where you could live just as cheaply as you do here, and be much better off?"

"Because," replied the colonel, "the good, kind people I am with took me in and fed me gratis for a year, and how could I desert them the moment I got a little money? Besides, the father of these young scamps is an Egyptian."

"An Egyptian?"

"That's what we call the troopers who returned from the expedition to Egypt, in which I took part. Not only are we all brothers in heart, but Vergniaud was in my regiment; he and I shared the water of the desert. Besides, I want to finish teaching those little monkeys to read."

"He might give you a better room for your money," said the lawyer.

"Bah!" said the colonel, "the children sleep as I do on straw. He and his wife have no better bed themselves. They are very poor, you see; they have more of an establishment here than they can manage. But if I get back my fortune — Well, enough!"

"Colonel, I expect to receive your papers from Heilsberg to-morrow; your benefactress is still living."

"Oh! cursed money! to think I have n't any!" cried the colonel, flinging down his pipe.

A "colored" pipe is a precious pipe to a smoker; but the action was so natural and so generous that all smokers would have forgiven him that act of leze-tobacco; the angels might have picked up the pieces.

"Colonel, your affair is very complicated," said Derville, leaving the room to walk up and down in the sun before the house.

"It seems to me," said the soldier, "perfectly simple. They thought me dead, and here I am! Give me back my wife and my property; give me the rank of general, — to which I have a right, for I had passed colonel in the Imperial Guard the night before the battle of Eylau."

"Matters are not managed that way in law," said Derville. "Listen to me. You are Comte Chabert, — I'll admit that; but the thing is to prove it legally against those persons whose interest it is to deny your existence. All your papers and documents will be disputed; and the very first discussions will open a dozen or more preliminary questions. Every step will be fought over up to the supreme court. All that will involve expensive suits, which will drag along, no matter how much energy I put into them. Your adversaries will demand an inquiry, which we cannot refuse, and which will perhaps necessitate sending a commission to Prussia. But suppose all went well, and you were promptly and legally recognized as Colonel Chabert, what then? Do we know how the question of Madame Ferraud's innocent bigamy would be decided ? Here's a case where the question of rights is outside of the Code, and can be decided by the judges only under the laws of conscience, as a jury does in many delicate cases which social perversities bring up in criminal courts. Now, here's a point: you had no children by your marriage, and Monsieur Ferraud has two; the judges may annul the marriage where the ties are weakest, in favor of a marriage which involves the well-being of children, admitting that the parents married in good faith. Would it be a fine or moral position for you, at your age, and under these circumstances, to insist on having — will ye, nill ye — a wife who no longer loves you? You would have against you a husband and wife who are powerful and able to bring influence upon the judges. The case has many elements of duration in it. You may spend years and grow an old man still struggling with the sharpest grief and anxiety."

" But my property? "

" You think you have a large fortune? "

" I had an income of thirty thousand francs."

" My dear colonel, in 1799, before your marriage, you made a will leaving a quarter of your whole property to the hospitals."

" That is true."

" Well, you were supposed to be dead; then of course an inventory of your property was made and the whole wound up in order to give that fourth part to the said hospitals. Your wife had no scruples about cheating the poor. The inventory, in which she took care not to mention the cash on hand or her jewelry, or the full amount of the silver, and in which the furniture was appraised at two-thirds below its real value (either to please her or to lessen the treasury tax, for appraisers are liable for the amount of their valuations), —

this inventory, I say, gave your property as amounting to six hundred thousand francs. Your widow had a legal right to half. Everything was sold and bought in by her; she gained on the whole transaction, and the hospitals got their seventy-five thousand francs. Then, as the Treasury inherited the rest of your property (for you had not mentioned your wife in your will), the Emperor made a decree returning the portion which reverted to the Treasury to your widow. Now, then, the question is, to what have you any legal right? — to three hundred thousand francs only, less costs."

"You call that justice?" said the colonel, thunder-struck.

"Of course."

"Fine justice!"

"It is always so, my poor colonel. You see now that what you thought so easy is not easy at all. Madame Ferraud may also try to keep the portion the Emperor returned to her."

"But she was not a widow, and therefore the decree was null."

"I admit that. But everything can be argued. Listen to me. Under these circumstances, I think a compromise is the best thing both for you and for her. You could get a larger sum that way than by asserting your rights."

"It would be selling my wife!"

“ With an income of twenty-four thousand francs
you would be in a position to find another who would
suit you better and make you happier. I intend to go
and see the Comtesse Ferraud to-day, and find out how
the land lies ; but I did not wish to take that step without letting you know.”

“ We will go together.”

“ Dressed as you are ? ” said the lawyer. “ No, no,
colonel, no ! You might lose your case.”

“ Can I win it ? ”

“ Yes, under all aspects,” answered Derville. “ But
my dear Colonel Chabert, there is one thing you pay
no heed to. I am not rich, and my practice is not
yet wholly paid for. If the courts should be willing
to grant you a provisional maintenance they will only
do so after recognizing your claims as Colonel Chabert,
grand officer of the Legion of honor.”

“ So I am ! ” said the old man, naïvely, “ grand officer
of the Legion of honor, — I had forgotten that.”

“ Well, as I was saying,” resumed Derville, “ till
then you will have to bring suits, pay lawyers, serve
writs, employ sheriffs, and live. The cost of those
preliminary steps will amount to more than twelve or
even fifteen thousand francs. I can’t lend you the
money for I am crushed by the enormous interest I
am forced to pay to those who lent me money to buy
my practice. Where, then, can you get it ? ”

Big tears fell from the faded eyes of the old soldier and rolled down his cheeks. The sight of these difficulties discouraged him. The social and judicial world lay upon his breast like a nightmare.

" I will go to the column of the place Vêndome," he said, " and cry aloud, ' I am Colonel Chabert, who broke the Russian square at Eylau ! ' The man of iron up there — ah ! he 'll recognize me ! "

" They would put you in Charenton."

At that dreaded name the soldier's courage fell.

" Perhaps I should have a better chance at the ministry of war," he said.

" In a government office? Well, try it," said Derville. " But you must take with you a legal judgment declaring your death disproved. The government would prefer to get rid of the Empire people."

The colonel remained for a moment speechless, motionless, gazing before him and seeing nothing, plunged in a bottomless despair. Military justice is prompt and straight-forward ; it decides peremptorily, and is generally fair ; this was the only justice Chabert knew. Seeing the labyrinth of difficulty which lay before him, and knowing that he had no money with which to enter it, the poor soldier was mortally wounded in that particular power of human nature which we call *will*. He felt it was impossible for him to live in a legal struggle ; far easier to his nature was it to stay poor and a beggar, or to enlist in some cavalry regiment if they would still take him. Physical and mental suffering had vitiated his body in some of its important organs. He was approaching one of those diseases for which the science of medicine has no name, the seat of which is, in a way, movable (like the nervous system which is the part of our machinery most frequently attacked), an affection which we must fain call "the spleen of sorrow." However serious this invisible but most real disease might be, it was still curable by a happy termination of his griefs. To completely unhinge and destroy that vigorous organization some final blow was needed, some unexpected shock which might break the weakened springs and produce those strange hesitations, those vague, incomplete, and inconsequent actions which physiologists notice in all persons wrecked by grief.

Observing symptoms of deep depression in his client, Derville hastened to say: "Take courage; the issue of the affair must be favorable to you in some way or other. Only, examine your own mind and see if you can place implicit trust in me, and accept blindly the course that I shall think best for you."

"Do what you will," said Chabert.

"Yes, but will you surrender yourself to me completely, like a man marching to his death?"

"Am I to live without a status and without a name? Is that bearable?"

"I don't mean that," said the lawyer. "We will bring an amicable suit to annul the record of your decease, and also your marriage; then you will resume your rights. You could even be, through Comte Ferraud's influence, restored to the army with the rank of general, and you would certainly obtain a pension."

"Well, go on, then," replied Chabert; "I trust implicitly to you."

"I will send you a power-of-attorney to sign," said Derville. "Adieu, keep up your courage; if you want money let me know."

Chabert wrung the lawyer's hand, and stood with his back against the wall, unable to follow him except with his eyes. During this conference the face of a man had every now and then looked round one of the gate pillars, behind which its owner was posted waiting for Derville's departure. The man now accosted the young lawyer. He was old, and he wore a blue jacket, a pleated white smock like those worn by brewers, and on his head a cap of otter fur. His face was brown, hollow, and wrinkled, but red at the cheek-bones from hard work and exposure to the weather.

"Excuse me, monsieur, if I take the liberty of speaking to you," he said, touching Derville on the arm. "But I supposed when I saw you that you were the general's friend."

"Well," said Derville, " what interest have you in him? Who are you?" added the distrustful lawyer.

"I am Louis Vergniaud," answered the man, "and I want to have a word with you."

"Then it is you who lodge the Comte Chabert in this way, is it?"

"Pardon it, monsieur. He has the best room in the house. I would have given him mine if I had had one, and slept myself in the stable. A man who has suffered as he has and who is teaching my kids to read, a general, an Egyptian, the first lieutenant under whom I served, — why, all I have is his! I've shared all with him. Unluckily it is so little, — bread and milk and eggs! However, when you 're on a campaign you must live with the mess; and little as it is, it is given with a full heart, monsieur. But he has vexed us."

"He!"

"Yes, monsieur, vexed us; there 's no going behind that. I took this establishment, which is more than I can manage, and he saw that. It troubled him, and he would do my work and take care of the horse! I kept saying to him, 'No, no, my general!' But there! he only answered, 'Am I a lazybones? don't I know how to put my shoulder to the wheel?' So I gave notes for the value of my cow-house to a man named Grados. Do you know him, monsieur?"

" But, my good friend, I have n't the time to listen to all this. Tell me only how Colonel Chabert vexed you."

" He did vex us, monsieur, just as true as my name is Louis Vergniaud, and my wife cried about it. He heard from the neighbors that I couldn't meet that note ; and the old fellow, without a word to us, took all you gave him, and, little by little, paid the note! Wasn't it a trick ! My wife and I knew he went without tobacco all that time, poor old man ! But now, yes, he has the cigars, — I 'd sell my own self sooner ! But it does vex us. Now, I propose to you to lend me on this establishment three hundred francs, so that we may get him some clothes and furnish his room. He thinks he has paid us, does n't he? Well, the truth is, he has made us his debtors. Yes, he has vexed us ; he shouldn't have played us such a trick, — wasn't it almost an insult? Such friends as we are ! As true as my name is Louis Vergniaud, I will mortgage myself rather than not return you that money."

Derville looked at the cow-keeper, then he made a step backward and looked at the house, the yard, the the manure, the stable, the rabbits, and the children.

" Faith ! " thought he to himself, "I do believe one of the characteristics of virtue is to own nothing. Yes," he said aloud, " you shall have your three hundred francs, and more too. But it is not I who give them to you, it is the colonel ; he will be rich enough to help you, and I shall not deprive him of that pleasure."

" Will it be soon?"

" Yes, soon."

"Good God! how happy my wife will be." The tanned face of the cow-keeper brightened into joy.

"Now," thought Derville as he jumped into his cabriolet, " to face the enemy. She must not see our game, but we must know hers, and win it at one trick. She is a woman. What are women most afraid of ? Why, of —"

He began to study the countess's position, and fell into one of those deep reveries to which great politicians are prone when they prepare their plans and try to guess the secrets of foreign powers. Lawyers are, in a way, statesmen, to whom the management of individual interests is intrusted. A glance at the situation of Monsieur le Comte Ferraud and his wife is necessary for a full comprehension of the lawyer's genius.

Monsieur le Comte Ferraud was the son of a former councillor of the parliament of Paris, who had emigrated during the Terror, and who, though he saved his head, lost his property. He returned to France under the Consulate, and remained faithful to the interests of Louis XVIII., in whose suite his father had been before the Revolution. His son, therefore, belonged to that section of the faubourg Saint-Germain which nobly resisted the Napoleonic seductions. The young count's reputation for good sense and sagacity when he was called simply "Monsieur Ferraud" made him the object of a few imperial blandishments; for the Emperor took as much satisfaction in his conquests over the aristocracy as he did in winning a battle. The count was promised the restitution of his title, also that of all his property which was not sold, and hopes were held out of a ministry in the future, and a senatorship. The Emperor failed. At the time of Comte Chabert's death Monsieur Ferraud was a young man twenty-six years of age, without fortune, agreeable in appearance and manner, and a social success, whom the faubourg Saint-Germain adopted as one of its distinguished figures.

Madame la Comtesse Chabert had managed the property derived from her late husband so well that after a widowhood of eighteen months she possessed an income of nearly forty thousand francs a year. Her marriage with the young count was not regarded as news by the coteries of the faubourg. Napoleon, who was pleased with an alliance which met his ideas of fusion, returned to Madame Chabert the money derived by the Treasury from her late husband's estate; but here again Napoleon's hopes were foiled. Madame Ferraud not only adored a lover in the young man, but she was attracted by the idea of entering that haughty society which, in spite of its political abasement, was still far above that of the imperial court. Her various vanities as well as her passions were gratified by this marriage. She felt she was about to become "an elegant woman."

When the faubourg Saint-Germain ascertained that the young count's marriage was not a defection from their ranks, all salons were opened to his wife. The Restoration took place. The political fortunes of the Comte Ferraud made no rapid strides. He understood very well the exigencies of Louis XVIII.'s position; he was one of the initiated who waited until "the revolutionary gulf was closed," — a royal phrase which the liberals laughed at, but which, nevertheless, hid a deep political meaning. However, the ordinance with its long-winded clerical phrases quoted by Godeschal in the first pages of this story restored to the Comte Ferraud two forests and an estate which had risen in value during its sequestration. At the period of which we write Comte Ferraud was councillor of State, also a director-general, and he considered his position as no more than the opening of his political career. Absorbed in the pursuit of an eager ambition, he depended much on his secretary, a ruined lawyer named Delbecq, — a man who was more than able, one who knew every possible resource of pettifogging sophistry, to whom the count left the management of all his private affairs.

This clever practitioner understood his position in the
count's household far too well not to be honest out of
policy. He hoped for some place under government
through the influence of his patron, whose property he
took care of to the best of his ability. His conduct so
completely refuted the dark story of his earlier life
that he was now thought to be a calumniated man.

The countess, however, with the shrewd tact of a
woman, fathomed the secretary, watched him carefully,
and knew so well how to manage him, that she had
already largely increased her fortune by his help. She
contrived to convince Delbecq that she ruled Monsieur
Ferraud, and promised that she would get him made
judge of a municipal court in one of the most important cities in France if he devoted himself wholly to
her interests. The promise of an irremovable office,
which would enable him to marry advantageously and
improve his political career until he became in the end
a deputy, made Delbecq Madame Ferraud's abject tool.
His watchfulness enabled her to profit by all those
lucky chances which the fluctuations of the Bourse
and the rise of property in Paris during the first three
years of the Restoration offered to clever manipula-
tors of money. Delbecq had tripled her capital with all
the more ease because his plans commended themselves to the countess as a rapid method of making
her fortune enormous. She spent the emoluments of

the count's various offices on the household expenses, so as to invest every penny of her own income, and Delbecq aided and abetted this avarice without inquiring into its motives. Men of his kind care nothing for the discovery of any secrets that do not affect their own interests. Besides, he accounted for it naturally by that thirst for gold which possesses nearly all Parisian women ; and as he knew how large a fortune Comte Ferraud's ambitions needed to support them, he sometimes fancied that he saw in the countess's greed a sign of her devotion to a man with whom she was still in love.

Madame Ferraud buried the motives of her conduct in the depths of her own heart. There lay the secrets of life and death to her; there is the kernel of our present history.

At the beginning of the year 1818 the Restoration was established on an apparently firm and immovable basis ; its governmental doctrines, as understood by superior minds, seemed likely to lead France into an era of renewed prosperity. Then it was that society changed front. Madame la Comtesse Ferraud found that she had made a marriage of love and wealth and ambition. Still young and beautiful, she played the part of a woman of fashion and lived in the court atmosphere. Rich herself, and rich through her husband, who had the credit of being one of the ablest men of the royalist party, a friend of the king and likely to become a minister, she belonged to the aristocracy and shared its glamour.

In the midst of this triumphant prosperity a moral cancer fastened upon her. Men have feelings which women guess in spite of every effort made by such men to bury them. At the time of the king's first return Comte Ferraud was conscious of some regrets for his marriage. The widow of Colonel Chabert had brought him no useful connections; he was alone and without influence, to make his way in a career full of obstacles and full of enemies. Then, perhaps, after he had coolly judged his wife, he saw certain defects of education which made her unsuitable, and unable, to further his projects. A word he once said about Talleyrand's marriage enlightened the countess and showed her that if the past had to be done over again he would never make her his wife. What woman would forgive that regret, containing as it did, the germs of all insults, nay, of all crimes and all repudiations!

Let us conceive the wound that this discovery made in the heart of a woman who feared the return of her first husband. She knew that he lived; she had repulsed him. Then, for a short time, she heard no more of him, and took comfort in the hope that he was killed at Waterloo together with the imperial eagles and Boutin. She then conceived the idea of binding her second husband to her by the strongest of ties, by a chain of gold; and she determined to be so rich that her great fortune should make that second marriage indissoluble if by chance Comte Chabert reappeared. He had reappeared; and she was unable to understand why the struggle she so much dreaded was not begun. Perhaps the man's sufferings, perhaps an illness had delivered her from him. Perhaps he was half-crazy and Charenton might restore his reason. She was not willing to set Delbecq or the police on his traces, for fear of putting herself in their power, or bringing on a catastrophe. There are many women in Paris who, like the Comtesse Ferraud, are living secretly with moral monsters, or skirting the edges of some abyss; they make for themselves a callus over the region of their wound and still continue to laugh and be amused.

"There is something very singular in Comte Ferrand's situation," said Derville to himself, after long meditation, as the cabriolet stopped before the gate of the hôtel Ferraud in the rue de Varennes. "How is it that he, so wealthy and a favorite of the king, is not already a peer of France? Perhaps Madame de Grandlieu is right in saying that the king's policy is to give higher importance to the peerage by not lavishing it. Besides, the son of a councillor of the old parliament is neither a Crillon nor a Rohan. Comte Ferraud can enter the upper Chamber only, as it were, on sufferance. But if his marriage were ruptured would n't it be a satisfac-

tion to the king if the peerage of some of those old
senators who have daughters only could descend to
him? Certainly that's a pretty good fear to dangle
before the countess," thought Derville, as he went up
the steps of the hôtel Ferraud.

Without knowing it the lawyer had laid his finger on
the secret wound, he had plunged his hand into the cancer that was destroying Madame Ferraud's life. She
received him in a pretty winter dining-room, where she
was breakfasting and playing with a monkey, which was
fastened by a chain to a sort of little post with iron
bars. The countess was wrapped in an elegant morn-
ing-gown; the curls of her pretty hair, carelessly caught
up, escaped from a little cap which gave her a piquant
air. She was fresh and smiling. The table glittered
with the silver-gilt service, the plate, the mother-of-
pearl articles; rare plants were about her, growing in
splendid porcelain vases.

As the lawyer looked at Comte Chabert's wife, rich
with his property, surrounded by luxury, and she herself at the apex of society, while the unhappy husband
lived with the beasts in a cow-house, he said to himself: "The moral of this is that a pretty woman will
never acknowledge a husband, nor even a lover, in a
man with an old topcoat, a shabby wig, and broken
boots." A bitter and satirical smile expressed the
half-philosophic, half-sarcastic ideas that necessarily

come to a man who is so placed that he sees to the bottom of things in spite of the lies under which so many Parisian families hide their existence.

"Good morning, Monsieur Derville," said the countess, continuing to make the monkey drink coffee.

"Madame," he said, abruptly, for he was offended at the careless tone in which the countess greeted him. "I have come to talk to you on a serious matter."

"Oh! I am so very sorry, but the count is absent —"

"I am glad, madame; for he would be out of place at this conference. Besides, I know from Delbecq that you prefer to do business yourself, without troubling Monsieur le comte."

"Very good; then I will send for Delbecq," she said.

"He could do you no good, clever as he is," returned Derville. "Listen to me, madame; one word will suffice to make you serious. Comte Chabert is living."

"Do you expect me to be serious when you talk such nonsense as that?" she said, bursting into a fit of laughter.

But the countess was suddenly subdued by the strange lucidity of the fixed look with which Derville questioned her, seeming to read into the depths of her soul.

" Madame," he replied, with cold and incisive gravity, " you are not aware of the dangers of your position. I do not speak of the undeniable authenticity of the papers in the case, nor of the positive proof that can be brought of Comte Chabert's existence. I am not a man, as you know, to take charge of a hopeless case. If you oppose our steps to prove the falsity of the death-record, you will certainly lose that first suit, and that question once settled in our favor determines all the others."

" Then, what do you wish to speak of ? "

" Not of the colonel, nor of you ; neither shall I remind you of the costs a clever lawyer in possession of all the facts of the case might charge upon you, nor of the game such a man could play with those letters which you received from your first husband before you married your second — "

" It is false ! " she cried, with the violence of a spoilt beauty. " I have never received a letter from Comte Chabert. If any one calls himself the colonel he is a swindler, a galley-slave perhaps, like Cogniard ; it makes me shudder to think of it. How can the colonel come to life again? Bonaparte himself sent me condolences on his death by an aid-de-camp ; and I now draw a pension of three thousand francs granted to his widow by the Chambers. I have every right to reject all Chaberts past, present, and to come."

" Happily we are alone, madame, and we can lie at our ease," he said, coldly, inwardly amused by inciting the anger which shook the countess, for the purpose of forcing her into some betrayal, — a trick familiar to all lawyers, who remain calm and impassible themselves when their clients or their adversaries get angry.

"Now then, to measure swords!" he said to himself, thinking of a trap he could lay to force her to show her weakness. "'The proof that Colonel Chabert's first letter reached you exists, madame," he said aloud. " It contained a draft."

" No, it did not; there was no draft," she said.

" Then the letter did reach you," continued Derville, smiling. " You are caught in the first trap a lawyer lays for you, and yet you think you can fight the law !"

The countess blushed, turned pale, and hid her face in her hands. Then she shook off her shame, and said, with the coolness which belongs to women of her class, " As you are the lawyer of the impostor Chabert, have the goodness to — "

" Madame," said Derville, interrupting her, " I am at this moment your lawyer as well as the colonel's. Do you think I wish to lose a client as valuable to me as you are? But you are not listening to me."

" Go on, monsieur," she said, graciously.

" Your fortune came from Monsieur le Comte Chabert, and you have repudiated him. Your property is colossal, and you let him starve. Madame, lawyers can be very eloquent when their cases are eloquent; here are circumstances which can raise the hue-and-cry of public opinion against you."

" But, Monsieur," said the countess, irritated by the manner in which Derville turned and returned her on his gridiron, " admitting that your Monsieur Chabert exists, the courts will sustain my second marriage on account of my children, and I shall get off by repaying two hundred and fifty thousand francs to Monsieur Chabert."

" Madame, there is no telling how a court of law may view a matter of feeling. If, on the one hand, we have a mother and two children, on the other there is a man overwhelmed by undeserved misfortune, aged by you, left to starve by your rejection. Besides, the judges cannot go against the law. Your marriage with the colonel puts the law on his side ; he has the prior right. But, if you appear in such an odious light you may find an adversary you little expect. That, madame, is the danger I came to warn you of."

" Another adversary ! " she said, " who ? "

" Monsieur le Comte Ferraud, madame."

" Monsieur Ferraud is too deeply attached to me, and respects the mother of his children too — "

" Ah, madame," said Derville, interrupting her, " why

talk such nonsense to a lawyer who can read hearts. At the present moment Monsieur Ferrand has not the slightest desire to annul his marriage, and I have no doubt he adores you. But if some one went to him and told him that his marriage could be annulled, that his wife would be arraigned before the bar of public opinion — "

" He would defend me, monsieur."

" No, madame."

" What reason would he have for deserting me? "

" That of marrying the only daughter of some peer of France, whose title would descend to him by the king's decree."

The countess turned pale.

" I have her! " thought Derville. " Good, the poor colonel's cause is won. Moreover, madame," he said aloud, " Monsieur Ferrand will feel the less regret because a man covered with glory, a general, a count, a grand officer of the Legion of honor, is certainly not a derogation to you, — if such a man asks for his wife — "

" Enough, enough, monsieur," she cried ; " I can have no lawyer but you. What must I do? "

" Compromise."

" Does he still love me? "

" How could it be otherwise? "

At these words the countess threw up her head. A

gleam of hope shone in her eyes; perhaps she thought of speculating on her husband's tenderness and winning her way by some female wile.

" I shall await your orders, madame ; you will let me know whether we are to serve notices of Comte Chabert's suit upon you, or whether you will come to my office and arrange the basis of a compromise," said Derville, bowing as he left the room.

Eight days after these visits paid by Derville, on a fine June morning, the husband and wife, parted by an almost supernatural circumstance, were making their way from the opposite extremes of Paris, to meet again in the office of their mutual lawyer. Certain liberal advances made by Derville to the colonel enabled the latter to clothe himself in accordance with his rank. He came in a clean cab. His head was covered with a suitable wig ; he was dressed in dark-blue cloth and spotlessly white linen, and he wore beneath his waist-coat the broad red ribbon of the grand officers of the Legion of honor. In resuming the dress and the habits of affluence he had also recovered his former martial elegance. He walked erect. His face, grave and mysterious, and bearing the signs of happiness and renewed hope, seemed younger and fuller ; he was no more like the old Chabert in the top-coat than a two-sous piece is like a forty-franc coin just issued. All who passed him knew him at once for a noble relic of our old army, one of those heroic men on whom the light of our national glory shines, who reflect it, as shattered glass illuminated by the sun returns a thousand rays. Such old soldiers are books and pictures too.

The count sprang from the carriage to enter Derville's office with the agility of a young man. The cab had hardly turned away before a pretty coupé with armorial bearings drove up. Madame la Comtesse Ferraud got out of it in a simple dress, but one well suited to display her youthful figure. She wore a pretty drawn bonnet lined with pink, which framed her face delightfully, concealed its exact outline, and restored its freshness.

Though the clients were thus rejuvenated, the office remained its old self, such as we saw it when this history began. Simonnin was eating his breakfast, one shoulder leaning against the window, which was now open; he was gazing at the blue sky above the courtyard formed by four blocks of black buildings.

" Ha ! " cried the gutter-jumper, " who wants to bet a play now that Colonel Chabert is a general and a red-ribbon ? "

" Derville is a downright magician," said Godeschal.

" There's no trick to play him this time," said Desroches.

"His wife will do that, the Comtesse Ferraud," said Boucard.

" Then she 'll have to belong to two — "

" Here she is ! " cried Simounin.

Just then the colonel came in and asked for Derville.

" He is in, Monsieur le Comte," said Simonnin.

" So you are not deaf, you young scamp," said Chabert, catching the gutter-jumper by the ear and twisting it, to the great satisfaction of the other clerks, who laughed and looked at the colonel with the inquisitive interest due to so singular a personage.

Colonel Chabert was in Derville's room when his wife entered the office.

" Say, Boucard, what a queer scene there 's going to be in the master's room ! She can live the even days with Comte Ferraud, and the uneven days with Comte Chabert — "

" Leap-year the colonel will gain," said Godeschal.

" Hold your tongues, gentlemen," said Boucard, severely. " You 'll be overheard. I never knew an office in which the clerks made such fun of the clients as you do here."

Derville had put the colonel into an adjoining room by the time the countess was ushered in.

" Madame," he said to her, " not knowing if it would be agreeable to you to meet Monsieur le Comte Chabert, I have separated you. If, however, you wish — "

" I thank you for that consideration, monsieur."

" I have prepared the draught of an agreement, the conditions of which can be discussed here and now, between you and Monsieur Chabert. I will go from one to the other and convey the remarks of each."

" Begin, monsieur," said the countess, showing signs of impatience.

Derville read: " Between the undersigned, — Monsieur Hyacinthe, called Chabert, count, brigadier-general, and grand officer of the Legion of honor, living in Paris, in the rue du Petit-Banquier, of the first part, and Madame Rose Chapotel, wife of the above-named Monsieur le Comte Chabert, born — "

" That will do," she said ; " skip the preamble and come to the conditions."

" Madame," said the lawyer, " the preamble explains succinctly the position which you hold to each other. Then, in article one, you recognize in presence of three witnesses, namely, two notaries, and the cow-keeper with whom your husband lives, to all of whom I have confided your secret and who will keep it faithfully, — you recognize, I say, that the individual mentioned in the accompanying deeds and whose identity is elsewhere established by affidavits prepared by Alexander Crottat, your notary, is the Comte Chabert, your first husband. In article two Comte Chabert, for the sake of your welfare, agrees to make no use of his rights except under circumstances provided for in the agreement,— and those circumstances," remarked Derville in a parenthesis, " are the non-fulfilment of the clauses of this private agreement. Monsieur Chabert, on his part," he continued, " consents to sue with you for a judgment which shall set aside the record of his death, and also dissolve his marriage. "

" But that will not suit me at all," said the countess, astonished ; " I don't wish a lawsuit, you know why."

" In article three," continued the lawyer, with imperturbable coolness, " you agree to secure to the said Hyacinthe, Comte Chabert, an annuity of twenty-four thousand francs now invested in the public Funds, the capital of which will devolve on you at his death."

" But that is far too dear ! " cried the countess.

" Can you compromise for less ? "

" Perhaps so."

" What is it you want, madame ? "

" I want — I don't want a suit. I want — "

" To keep him dead," said Derville, quickly.

" Monsieur," said the countess, " if he asks twenty-four thousand francs a year, I'll demand justice."

" Yes, justice ! " cried a hollow voice, as the colonel opened the door and appeared suddenly before his wife, with one hand in his waistcoat and the other pointing to the floor, a gesture to which the memory of his great disaster gave a horrible meaning.

"It is he!" said the countess in her own mind.

"Too dear?" continued the old soldier, "I gave you a million and now you trade on my poverty. Well, then, I will have you and my property both; our marriage is not void."

"But monsieur is not Colonel Chabert!" cried the countess, feigning surprise.

"Ah!" said the old man, in a tone of irony, "do you want proofs? Well, did I not take you from the pavements of the Palais-Royal?"

The countess turned pale. Seeing her color fade beneath her rouge, the old soldier, sorry for the suffering he was inflicting on a woman he had once loved ardently, stopped short; but she gave him such a venomous look that he suddenly added, "You were with —"

"For heaven's sake, monsieur," said the countess, appealing to the lawyer, "allow me to leave this place. I did not come here to listen to such insults."

She left the room. Derville sprang into the office after her; but she seemed to have taken wings and was already gone. When he returned to his own room he found the colonel walking up and down in a paroxysm of rage.

"In those days men took their wives where they liked," he said. "But I chose ill; I ought never to have trusted her; she has no heart!"

"Colonel, you will admit I was right in begging you

not to come here!   I am now certain of your identity.
When you came in the countess made a little movement the meaning of which was not to be doubted.
But you have lost your cause.   Your wife now knows
that you are unrecognizable."

" I will kill her."

" Nonsense! then you would be arrested and guil-
lotined as a criminal.   Besides, you might miss your
stroke; it is unpardonable not to kill a wife when you
attempt it.   Leave me to undo your folly, you big
child!   Go away; but take care of yourself, for she
is capable of laying some trap and getting you locked
up at Charenton.   I will see about serving the notices
of the suit on her at once; that will be some protection
to you."

The poor colonel obeyed his young benefactor, and
went away, stammering a few excuses.   He was going
slowly down the dark staircase lost in gloomy thought,
overcome perhaps by the blow he had just received, to
him the worst, the one that went deepest to his heart,
when, as he reached the lower landing, he heard the
rustle of a gown, and his wife appeared.

" Come, monsieur," she said, taking his arm with a
movement like others he once knew so well.

The action, the tones of her voice, now soft and
gentle, calmed the colonel's anger, and he allowed her
to lead him to her carriage.

"Get in," she said, when the footman had let down the steps.

And he suddenly found himself, as if by magic, seated beside his wife in the coupé.

"Where to, madame?" asked the footman.

"To Groslay," she replied.

The horses started, and the carriage crossed the whole city.

"Monsieur!" said the countess, in a tone of voice that seemed to betray one of those rare emotions, few in life, which shake our whole being.

At such moments heart, fibres, nerves, soul, body, countenance, all, even the pores of the skin, quiver. Life seems no longer in us; it gushes out, it conveys itself like a contagion, it transmits itself in a look, in a tone of the voice, in a gesture, in the imposition of our will on others. The old soldier trembled, hearing that word, that first, that expressive "Monsieur!" It was at once a reproach, a prayer, a pardon, a hope, a despair, a question, an answer. That one word included all. A woman must needs be a great comedian to throw such eloquence and so many feelings into one word. Truth is never so complete in its expression; it cannot utter itself wholly, — it leaves something to be seen within. The colonel was filled with remorse for his suspicions, his exactions, his anger, and he lowered his eyes to conceal his feelings.

"Monsieur," continued the countess, after an almost imperceptible pause, "I knew you at once."

"Rosine," said the old soldier, "that word contains the only balm that can make me forget my troubles." ·

Two great tears fell hotly on his wife's hands, which he pressed as if to show her a paternal affection.

"Monsieur," she continued, "how is it you did not see what it cost me to appear before a stranger in a position so false as mine. If I am forced to blush for what I am, at least let it be in my own home. Ought not such a secret to remain buried in our own hearts? You will, I hope, forgive my apparent indifference to the misfortunes of a Chabert in whom I had no reason to believe. I did receive your letters," she said, hastily, seeing a sudden objection on her husband's face; "but they reached me thirteen months after the battle of Eylau; they were open, torn, dirty; the writing was unknown to me; and I, who had just obtained Napoleon's signature to my new marriage contract, supposed that some clever swindler was trying to impose upon me. Not wishing to trouble Monsieur Ferraud's peace of mind, or to bring future trouble into the family, I was right, was I not, to take every precaution against a false Chabert ?"

"Yes, you were right; and I have been a fool, a dolt, a beast, not to have foreseen the consequences of such a situation. But where are we going?" asked the colonel, suddenly noticing that they had reached the Barrière de la Chapelle.

"To my country-place near Groslay, in the valley of Montmorency," she replied. "There, monsieur, we can think over, together, the course we ought to take. I know my duty. Though I am yours legally, I am no longer yours in fact. Surely, you cannot wish that we should be the common talk of Paris. Let us hide from the public a situation which, for me, has a mortifying side, and strive to maintain our dignity. You love me still," she continued, casting a sad and gentle look upon the colonel, "but I, was I not authorized to form other ties? In this strange position a secret voice tells me to hope in your goodness, which I know so well. Am I wrong in taking you, you only, for the sole arbiter of my fate? Be judge and pleader both; I confide in your noble nature. You will forgive the consequences of my innocent fault. I dare avow to you, therefore, that I love Monsieur Ferraud; I thought I had the right to love him. I do not blush for this confession; it may offend you, but it dishonors neither of us. I cannot hide the truth from you. When accident made me a widow, I was not a mother—"

The colonel made a sign with his hand as if to ask silence of his wife; and they remained silent, not saying a word for over a mile. Chabert fancied he saw her little children before him.

" Rosine ! "

" Monsieur ? "

" The dead do wrong to reappear."

" Oh, monsieur, no, no ! Do not think me ungrateful. But you find a mother, a woman who loves another man, where you left a wife. If it is no longer in my power to love you, I know what I owe to you, and I offer you still the devotion of a daughter."

" Rosine," said the old man, gently, " I feel no resentment towards you. We will forget all that once was," he said, with one of those smiles whose charm is the reflection of a noble soul. " I am not so lost to delicacy as to ask a show of love from a woman who no longer loves me."

The countess gave him such a grateful glance that poor Chabert wished in his heart he could return to that grave at Eylau. Certain men have souls capable of vast sacrifices, whose recompense to them is the certainty of the happiness of one they love.

" My friend, we will talk of all this later, with a quiet mind," said the countess.

The conversation took another turn, for it was impossible to continue it long in this strain. Though husband and wife constantly touched upon their strange position, either by vague allusions, or grave remarks, they nevertheless made a charming journey, recalling many of the events of their union, and of the Empire.

The countess knew how to impart a tender charm to these memories, and to cast a tinge of melancholy upon the conversation, enough at least to keep it serious. She revived love without exciting desire, and showed her first husband the mental graces and knowledge she had acquired, — trying to let him taste the happiness of a father beside a cherished daughter. The colonel had known the countess of the Empire, he now saw a countess of the Restoration.

They at last arrived, through a cross-road, at a fine park in the little valley which separates the heights of Margency from the pretty village of Groslay. The house was a delightful one, and the colonel saw on arriving that all was prepared for their stay. Misfortune is a sort of talisman, the power of which lies in strengthening and fulfilling our natural man; it increases the distrust and evil tendencies of certain natures just as it increases the goodness of those whose heart is sound. Misfortune had made the colonel more helpful and better than he had ever been; he was therefore able to enter into those secrets of woman's suffering which are usually unknown to men. And yet, in spite of his great lack of distrust, he could not help saying to his wife : —

" You seem to have been sure of bringing me here?"

" Yes," she answered, " if I found Colonel Chabert in the petitioner."

The tone of truth which she gave to that answer dispersed the few doubts which the colonel already felt ashamed of admitting.

For three days the countess was truly admirable in her conduct to her first husband. By tender care and constant gentleness she seemed to try to efface even the memory of the sufferings he had endured, and to win pardon for the misfortunes she had, as she admitted, innocently caused. She took pleasure in displaying for his benefit, though always with a sort of melancholy, the particular charms under the influence of which she knew him to be feeble, — for men are more particularly susceptible to certain ways, to certain graces of heart and mind; and those they are unable to resist. She wanted to interest him in her situation, to move his feelings enough to control his mind and so bend him absolutely to her will. Resolved to take any means to reach her ends, she was still uncertain what to do with the man, though she meant, undoubtedly, to destroy him socially.

On the evening of the third day she began to feel that in spite of all her efforts she could no longer conceal the anxiety she felt as to the result of her manœuvres. To obtain a moment's relief she went up to her own room, sat down at her writing-table, and took off the mask of tranquillity she had worn before the colonel, like an actress returning weary to her room after a trying fifth act and falling half-dead upon a couch, while the audience retains an image of her to which she bears not the slightest resemblance. She began to finish a letter already begun to Delbecq, telling him to go to Derville and ask in her name for a sight of the papers which concerned Colonel Chabert, to copy them, and come immediately to Groslay. She had hardly finished before she heard the colonel's step in the corridor; for he was coming, full of anxiety, to find her.

"Oh!" she said aloud, "I wish I were dead! my position is intolerable — "

"What is it? is anything the matter?" said the worthy man.

"Nothing, nothing," she said.

She rose, left the colonel where he was, and went to speak to her maid without witnesses, telling her to go at once to Paris and deliver the letter, which she gave her, into Delbecq's own hands, and to bring it back to her as soon as he read it. Then she went out and seated herself on a bench in the garden, where she was in full view of the colonel if he wished to find her. He was already searching for her and he soon came.

" Rosine," he said, " tell me what is the matter."

She did not answer. It was one of those glorious calm evenings of the month of June, when all secret harmonies diffuse such peace, such sweetness in the sunsets. The air was pure, the silence deep, and a distant murmur of children's voices added a sort of melody to the consecrated scene.

" You do not answer me," said the colonel.

"My husband — " began the countess, then she stopped, made a movement, and said, appealingly, with a blush, " What ought I to say in speaking of Monsieur le Comte Ferraud?"

" Call him your husband, my poor child," answered the colonel, in a kind tone; " he is the father of your children."

"Well, then," she continued, " if he asks me what I am doing here, if he learns that I have shut myself up with an unknown man, what am I to say?　Hear me, monsieur," she went on, taking an attitude that was full of dignity, " decide my fate; I feel I am resigned to everything — "

" Dear," said the colonel, grasping his wife's hands, " I have resolved to sacrifice myself wholly to your happiness — "

" That is impossible," she cried, with a convulsive movement.　" Remember that in that case you must renounce your own identity — and do so legally."

" What! " exclaimed the colonel, " does not my word satisfy you? "

The term " legally " fell like lead upon the old man's heart and roused an involuntary distrust.　He cast a look upon his wife which made her blush; she lowered her eyes, and for a moment he feared he should be forced to despise her. The countess was alarmed lest she had startled the honest shame, the stern upright-ness of a man whose generous nature and whose primi-tive virtues were well-known to her. Though these ideas brought a cloud to each brow they were suddenly dispelled, harmony was restored, — and thus: A child's cry resounded in the distance.

" Jules, let your sister alone ! " cried the countess.

" What ! are your children here? " exclaimed the colonel.

" Yes, but I forbade them to come in your way."

The old soldier understood the delicacy and the womanly tact shown in that graceful consideration, and he took her hand to kiss it.

" Let them come ! " he said.

The little girl ran up to complain of her brother.

" Mamma ! he plagued me — "

" Mamma ! "

" It was his fault — "

" It was hers — "

The hands were stretched out to the mother, and the two voices mingled. It was a sudden, delightful picture.

" My poor children ! " exclaimed the countess, not restraining her tears, " must I lose them? To whom will the court give them? A mother's heart cannot be shared. I will have them ! yes, I — "

“ You are making mamma cry,” said Jules, the elder, with an angry look at the colonel.

“ Hush, Jules ! ” cried his mother, peremptorily.

The two children examined their mother and the stranger with an indescribable curiosity.

“ Yes,” continued the countess, “ if I am parted from Monsieur Ferraud, they must leave me my children ; if I have them, I can bear all.”

Those words brought the success she expected.

“ Yes,” cried the colonel, as if completing a sentence he had begun mentally. “ I must return to the grave ; I have thought so already.”

“ How can I accept such a sacrifice ? ” replied the countess. “ If men have died to save the honor of their mistresses, they gave their lives but once. But this would be giving your daily life, your lifetime ! No, no, it is impossible ; if it were only your existence perhaps it might be nothing, but to sign a record that you are not Colonel Chabert, to admit yourself an impostor, to sacrifice your honor, to live a lie for all the days of your life, — no ; human devotion cannot go to such a length ! No, no ! if it were not for my poor children I would fly with you to the ends of the earth.”

“ But,” said Chabert, “ why can I not live here, in that little cottage, as a friend and relative. I am as useless as an old cannon ; all I need is a little tobacco and the ‘ Constitutionnel.’ ”

The countess burst into tears. Then followed a struggle of generosity between them, from which Colonel Chabert came forth a conqueror. One evening, watching the mother in the midst of her children, deeply moved by that picture of a home, influenced, too, by the silence and the quiet of the country, he came to the resolution of remaining dead; no longer resisting the thought of a legal instrument, he asked his wife what steps he should take to secure, irrevocably, the happiness of that home.

"Do what you will," replied the countess; "I declare positively that I will have nothing to do with it, — I ought not."

Delbecq had then been in the house a few days, and, in accordance with the countess's verbal instructions, he had wormed himself into the confidence of the old soldier. The morning after this little scene Colonel Chabert accompanied the former lawyer to Saint-Leu-Taverny, where Delbecq had already had an agreement drawn up by a notary, in terms so crude and brutal that on hearing them the colonel abruptly left the office.

"Good God! would you make me infamous! why, I should be called a forger!"

"Monsieur," said Delbecq, "I advise you not to sign too quickly. You could get at least thirty thousand francs a year out of this affair; Madame would give them."

Blasting that scoundrel emeritus with the luminous glance of an indignant honest man, the colonel rushed from the place driven by a thousand conflicting feelings. He was again distrustful, indignant, and merciful by turns. After a time he re-entered the park of Groslay by a breach in the wall, and went, with slow steps, to rest and think at his ease, in a little study built beneath a raised kiosk which commanded a view of the road from Saint-Leu.

The path was made of that yellow earth which now takes the place of river-gravel, and the countess, who was sitting in the kiosk above, did not hear the slight noise of the colonel's footstep, being preoccupied with anxious thoughts as to the success of her plot. Neither did the old soldier become aware of the presence of his wife in the kiosk above him.

"Well, Monsieur Delbecq, did he sign?" asked the countess, when she saw the secretary, over the sunk-fence, alone upon the road.

"No, Madame; and I don't even know what has become of him. The old horse reared."

"We shall have to put him in Charenton," she said; "we can do it."

The colonel, recovering the elasticity of his youth, jumped the ha-ha, and in the twinkling of an eye applied the hardest pair of slaps that ever two cheeks received. "Old horses kick!" he said.

His anger once over, the colonel had no strength left to jump the ditch again. The truth lay before him in its nakedness. His wife's words and Delbecq's answer had shown him the plot to which he had so nearly been a victim. The tender attentions he had received were the bait of the trap. That thought was like a sudden poison, and it brought back to the old hero his past sufferings, physical and mental. He returned to the kiosk through a gate of the park, walking slowly like a broken man. So, then, there was no peace, no truce for him! Must he enter upon that odious struggle with a woman which Derville had explained to him? must he live a life of legal suits? must he feed on gall, and drink each morning the cup of bitterness. Then, dreadful thought! where was the money for such suits to come from. So deep a disgust of life came over him, that had a pistol been at hand he would have blown out his brains. Then he fell back into the confusion of ideas which, ever since his interview with Derville in the cow-yard, had changed his moral being. At last, reaching the kiosk, he went up the stairs to the upper chamber, whose oriel windows looked out on all the enchanting perspectives of that well-known valley, and where he found his wife sitting on a chair. The countess was looking at the landscape, with a calm and quiet demeanor, and that impenetrable countenance which certain determined women know so well how to assume. She dried her eyes, as though she had shed tears, and played, as if abstractedly, with the ribbons of her sash. Nevertheless, in spite of this apparent composure, she could not prevent herself from trembling when she saw her noble benefactor before her, — standing, his arms crossed, his face pale, his brow stern.

" Madame," he said, looking at her so fixedly for a moment that he forced her to blush; "Madame, I do not curse you, but I despise you. I now thank the fate which has parted us. I have no desire for vengeance; I have ceased to love you. I want nothing from you. Live in peace upon the faith of my word; it is worth more than the legal papers of all the notaries in Paris. I shall never take the name I made, perhaps, illustrious. Henceforth, I am but a poor devil named Hyacinthe, who asks no more than a place in God's sunlight. Farewell — "

The countess flung herself at his feet and tried to hold him by catching his hands, but he repulsed her with disgust, saying, " Do not touch me ! "

The countess made a gesture which no description can portray when she heard the sound of her husband's departing steps. Then, with that profound sagacity which comes of great wickedness, or of the savage, material selfishness of this world, she felt she might live in peace, relying on the promise and the contempt of that loyal soldier.

Chabert disappeared. The cow-keeper failed and became a cab-driver. Perhaps the colonel at first found some such occupation. Perhaps, like a stone flung into the rapids, he went from fall to fall until he sank engulfed in that great pool of filth and penury which welters in the streets of Paris.

Six months after these events Derville, who had heard nothing of Colonel Chabert or of the Comtesse Ferraud, thought that they had probably settled on a compromise, and that the countess, out of spite, had employed some other lawyer to draw the papers. Accordingly, one morning he summed up the amounts advanced to the said Chabert, added the costs, and requested the Comtesse Ferraud to obtain from Monsieur le Comte Chabert the full amount, presuming that she knew the whereabouts of her first husband.

The next day Comte Ferraud's secretary sent the following answer: —

Monsieur, — I am directed by Madame la Comtesse Ferraud to inform you that your client totally deceived you, and that the individual calling himself the Comte Chabert admitted having falsely taken that name.

Receive the assurance, etc., etc.

Delbecq.

" Well, some people are, upon my honor, as devoid of sense as the beasts of the field, — they 've stolen their baptism!" cried Derville. "Be human, be generous, be philanthropic, and you'll find yourself in the lurch! Here's a business that has cost me over two thousand francs."

Not long after the reception of this letter Derville was at the Palais, looking for a lawyer with whom he wished to speak, and who was in the habit of practising in the criminal courts. It so chanced that Derville entered the sixth court-room as the judge was sentencing a vagrant named Hyacinthe to two months' imprisonment, the said vagrant to be conveyed at the expiration of the sentence to the mendicity office of the Saint-Denis quarter, — a sentence which was equivalent to perpetual imprisonment. The name, Hyacinthe, caught Derville's ear, and he looked at the delinquent sitting between two gendarmes on the prisoner's bench, and recognized at once his false Colonel Chabert. The old soldier was calm, motionless, almost absent-minded. In spite of his rags, in spite of the poverty marked on every feature of the face, his countenance was instinct with noble pride. His glance had an expression of stoicism which a magistrate ought not to have overlooked; but when a man falls into the hands of justice, he is no longer anything but an entity, a question of law and facts; in the eyes of statisticians, he is a numeral.

When the soldier was taken from the court-room to wait until the whole batch of vagabonds who were then being sentenced were ready for removal, Derville used his privilege as a lawyer to follow him into the room adjoining the sheriff's office, where he watched him for a few moments, together with the curious collection of beggars who surrounded him. The ante-chamber of a sheriff's office presents at such times a sight which, unfortunately, neither legislators, nor philanthropists, nor painters, nor writers, ever study. Like all the laboratories of the law this antechamber is dark and ill-smelling; the walls are protected by a bench, blackened by the incessant presence of the poor wretches who come to this central rendezvous from all quarters of social wretchedness, — not one of which is unrepresented there. A poet would say that the daylight was ashamed to lighten that terrible sink-hole of all miseries. There is not one spot within it where crime, planned or committed, has not stood ; not a spot where some man, rendered desperate by the stigma which justice lays upon him for his first fault, has not begun a career leading to the scaffold or to suicide. All those who fall in Paris rebound against these yellow walls, on which a philanthropist could decipher the meaning of many a suicide about which hypocritical writers, incapable of taking one step to prevent them, rail ; written on those walls he will find a preface to the dramas of the Morgue and those of the place de Grève. Colonel Chabert was now sitting in the midst of this crowd of men with nervous faces, clothed in the horrible liveries of poverty, silent at times or talking in a low voice, for three gendarmes paced the room as sentries, their sabres clanging against the floor.

"Do you recognize me?" said Derville to the old soldier.

"Yes, Monsieur," said Chabert, rising.

"If you are an honest man," continued Derville, in a low voice, "how is it that you have remained my debtor?"

The old soldier colored like a young girl accused by her mother of a clandestine love.

"Is it possible," he cried in a loud voice, "that Madame Ferraud has not paid you?"

"Paid me!" said Derville, "she wrote me you were an impostor."

The colonel raised his eyes with a majestic look of horror and invocation as if to appeal to heaven against this new treachery. "Monsieur," he said, in a voice that was calm though it faltered, "ask the gendarmes to be so kind as to let me go into the sheriff's office ; I will there write you an order which will certainly be paid."

Derville spoke to the corporal, and was allowed to take his client into the office, where the colonel wrote a few lines and addressed them to the Comtesse Ferraud.

"Send that to her," he said, "and you will be paid for your loans and all costs. Believe me, Monsieur, if

I have not shown the gratitude I owe you for your kind acts it is none the less *there*," he said, laying his hand upon his heart; "yes it is there, full, complete. But the unfortunate ones can do nothing, — they love, that is all."

" Can it be," said Derville, " that you did not stipulate for an income?"

" Don't speak of that," said the old man. " You can never know how utterly I despise this external life to which the majority of men cling so tenaciously. I was taken suddenly with an illness, — a disgust for humanity. When I think that Napoleon is at Saint-Helena all things here below are nothing to me. I can no longer be a soldier, that is my only sorrow. Ah, well," he added, with a gesture that was full of childlike playfulness, " it is better to have luxury in our feelings than in our clothes. I fear no man's contempt."

He went back to the bench and sat down. Derville went away. When he reached his office, he sent Godeschal, then advanced to be second clerk, to the Comtesse Ferraud, who had no sooner read the missive he carried than she paid the money owing to Comte Chabert's lawyer.

In 1840, towards the close of the month of June, Godeschal, then a lawyer on his own account, was on his way to Ris, in company with Derville. When they reached the avenue which leads into the mail road to Bicêtre, they saw beneath an elm by the roadside one of those hoary, broken-down old paupers who rule the beggars about them, and live at Bicêtre just as pauper women live at La Salpêtrière. This man, one of the two thousand inmates of the "Almshouse for Old Age," was sitting on a stone and seemed to be giving all his mind to an operation well-known to the dwellers in charitable institutions; that of drying the tobacco in their handkerchiefs in the sun, — possibly to escape washing them. The old man had an interesting face. He was dressed in that gown of dark, reddish cloth which the Almshouse provides for its inmates, a dreadful sort of livery.

"Derville," said Godeschal to his companion, "do look at that old fellow. Is n't he like those grotesque figures that are made in Germany. But I suppose he lives, and perhaps he is happy!"

Derville raised his glass, looked at the pauper, and gave vent to an exclamation of surprise; then he said: "That old man, my dear fellow, is a poem, or, as the romanticists say, a drama. Did you ever meet the Comtesse Ferraud?"

"Yes, a clever woman and very agreeable, but too pious."

"That old man is her legitimate husband, Comte Chabert, formerly colonel. No doubt she has had him placed here. If he lives in an almshouse instead of a mansion, it is because he reminded the pretty countess that he took her, like a cab, from the streets. I can still see the tigerish look she gave him when he said it."

These words so excited Godeschal's curiosity that Derville told him the whole story. Two days later, on the following Monday morning, as they were returning to Paris, the two friends glanced at Bicêtre, and Derville proposed that they should go and see Colonel Chabert. Half-way up the avenue they found the old man sitting on the trunk of a fallen tree, and amusing himself by drawing lines on the gravel with a stick which he held in his hand. When they looked at him attentively they saw that he had been breakfasting elsewhere than at the almshouse.

"Good-morning, Colonel Chabert," said Derville.

"Not Chabert! not Chabert! my name is Hyacinthe," answered the old man. "I'm no longer a man; I'm number 164, seventh room," he added, looking at Derville with timid anxiety, — the fear of old age or of childhood. "You can see the condemned prisoner," he said, after a moment's silence; "he's not married, no! he's happy — "

"Poor man!" said Godeschal; "don't you want some money for tobacco?"

The colonel extended his hand with all the naïveté

of a street boy to the two strangers, who each gave him a twenty-franc gold piece. He thanked them both, with a stupid look, and said, " Brave troopers ! " Then he pretended to shoulder arms and take aim at them, calling out with a laugh, " Fire the two pieces, and long live Napoleon ! " after which he described an imaginary arabesque in the air, with a flourish of his cane.

" The nature of his wound must have made him childish," said Derville.

" He childish ! " cried another old pauper who was watching them. " Ha ! there are days when it won't do to step on his toes. He 's a knowing one, full of philosophy and imagination. But to-day, don't you see, he 's been keeping Monday. Why, Monsieur, he was here in 1820. Just about that time a Prussian officer, whose carriage was going over the Villejuif hill, walked by on foot. Hyacinthe and I were sitting by the roadside. The officer was talking with another, I think it was a Russian or some animal of that kind, and when they saw the old fellow, the Prussian, just to tease him, says he : ' Here 's an old voltigeur who must have been at Rosbach —' ' I was too young to be at Rosbach,' says Hyacinthe, but I 'm old enough to have been at Jena ! ' Ha, ha ! that Prussian cleared off — and no more questions —"

" What a fate ! " cried Derville ; " born in the Foundling, he returns to die in the asylum of old age, having in the interval helped Napoleon to conquer Egypt and Europe! —   Do you know, my dear fellow," continued Derville, after a long pause, " that there are three men in our social system who cannot respect or value the world, — the priest, the physician, and the lawyer. They wear black gowns, perhaps because they mourn for all virtues, all illusions. The most unhappy among them is the lawyer. When a man seeks a priest he is forced to it by repentance, by remorse, by beliefs which make him interesting, which ennoble him and comfort the soul of his mediator, whose duty is not without a certain sort of joy; the priest purifies, heals, reconciles. But we lawyers! we see forever the same evil feelings, never corrected; our offices are sink-holes which nothing can cleanse.

"How many things have I not seen and known and learned in my practice! I have seen a father die in a garret, penniless, abandoned by daughters, to each of whom he had given an income of forty thousand francs. I have seen wills burned. I have seen mothers robbing their children, husbands stealing from their wives, wives killing their husbands by the very love they inspired, so as to live in peace with their lovers. I have seen women giving to the children of a first marriage tastes which led them to their death, so that the child of love might be enriched. I could not tell you what I have seen, for I have seen crimes against which justice is powerless. All the horrors that romance-writers think they invent are forever below the truth. You are about to make acquaintance with such things ; as for me, I shall live in the country with my wife ; I have a horror of Paris."

1832.

THE ATHEIST'S MASS.

This is dedicated to Auguste Borget, by his friend,

De Balzac.

A PHYSICIAN to whom science owes a masterly physiological theory, and who, though still young, has taken his place among the celebrities of the School of Paris, that centre of medical intelligence to which the physicians of Europe pay just homage, Doctor Horace Bianchon practised surgery for some time before he devoted himself to medicine. His studies were directed by one of the greatest of French surgeons, the illustrious Desplein, who passed like a meteor through the skies of science. Even his enemies admit that he carried with him to the grave an incommunicable method. Like all men of genius, he had no heirs of his faculty; he held all within him, and he carried all away with him.

The fame of surgeons is something like that of actors: it lives during their lifetime only, and is not fully appreciable after they are gone. Actors and surgeons, also great singers, and all virtuosi who by execution increase the power of music tenfold, are the heroes of a moment. Desplein is a proof of the universal fate of these transitory geniuses. His name, so celebrated yesterday, to-day almost forgotten, remains within the limits of his specialty, and will never reach beyond them.

But, let us ask, must there not exist some extraordinary circumstances to bring the name of a great worker from the domain of science into the general history of humanity? Had Desplein that universality of knowledge which makes a man the Word and the Form of an era? Desplein possessed an almost divine insight; he penetrated both patient and disease with an intuition, natural or acquired, which enabled him to seize the idiosyncrasies of the individual, and so determine the exact moment, to the hour and the minute, when it was right to operate, — taking note of atmospheric conditions, and peculiarities of temperament. Was he guided in this by that power of deduction and analogy to which is due the genius of Cuvier? However that may have been, this man certainly made himself the confidant of flesh; he knew its secrets of the past, and of the future, as he dealt with its present. But did he sum up the whole of science in his own person, like Galen, Hippocrates, Aristotle? Has he led a school to new and unknown worlds? No.

Though it is impossible to deny to this perpetual observer of human chemistry some faculty of the ancient science of magic, — that is to say, a perception of principles in fusion, the causes of life, the life before the life, and what the life becomes through its preparations before being, — we must admit, speaking justly, that unfortunately all with Desplein was Self; he was isolated in life through egoism, and egoism has killed his fame. No speaking statue surmounts his tomb, and tells the future of the mysteries that genius wrested from her. But perhaps Desplein's talent was one with his beliefs, and therefore mortal. To him, the terrestrial atmosphere was a generating pouch; he saw the earth like an egg in its shell; unable to discover whether the egg or the hen were the beginning, he denied both the cock and the egg. He believed neither in the anterior animal nor in the posterior spirit of man.

Desplein was not a doubter; he affirmed his beliefs. His clear-cut atheism was like that of a great many men of science, who are the best people in the world, but invincible atheists, atheists like those religious folk who will not admit that there can be atheists. It could not be otherwise with a man accustomed from his earliest youth to dissect the human being before, during, and after life; to pry into all its apparatus and never find that soul-germ so essential to religious theories. Finding in the human body a brain centre, a nervous centre, a centre of the blood circulation (the first two of which so complement each other that during the last two days of Desplein's life he came to a conviction that the sense of hearing was not absolutely necessary in order to hear, nor the sense of sight absolutely necessary in order to see, and that, beyond all doubt, the solar plexus did replace them), — Desplein, we say, finding thus two souls in man, corroborated his atheism by this very fact, though he asserted nothing in relation to God. The man died, the world said, in the impenitence in which so many men of noblest genius unhappily leave this life, — men whom it may, perhaps, please God to pardon.

The life of this man presented, to use the expression of his enemies, who were jealous of his fame and sought to belittle it, many pettinesses which it is more just to call apparent contradictions. Fools and detractors, having no knowledge of the influences that act upon superior minds, make the most of superficial inconsistencies, to bring accusations on which they sit in judgment. If, later, success attends the labors of a man thus attacked, showing the correlation of preparations and results, a few of the past calumnies are sure to remain fixed upon him. In our day Napoleon was condemned by contemporaries when his eagles threatened England; it needed 1822 to explain 1804 and the flat-boats of Boulogne.

Desplein's fame and science were invulnerable; his enemies therefore found fault with his odd temper, his peculiar character, — the fact being that he merely possessed that quality which the English call "eccentricity." At times gorgeously dressed, like the tragic Crébillon, he would change suddenly to a singular indifference in the matter of clothes; sometimes he drove in his carriage, sometimes he went about on foot. By turns rough and kind, apparently crabbed and stingy, he was capable of offering his whole fortune to his exiled masters, who did him the honor to accept it for a few days; no man was therefore more liable to contradictory judgments. Though capable, in order to win that black ribbon which physicians ought never to have solicited, of dropping a prayer-book from his pocket in some room at the palace, it was more because in his heart he sneered at all things. He had the deepest contempt for men, having examined them from head to foot, having detected their veritable being through all the acts of existence, the most solemn and the most insignificant. In great men great qualities often support and require each other. Though some among these Colossi may have more faculty than mind, their minds are nevertheless more enlightened than that of others of whom the world says simply, "They are men of mind." All genius presupposes a moral insight; that insight may be applied to some specialty, but whoso

can see a flower can see the sun. The story is told of
Desplein that when he heard a diplomate, whose life he
had saved, asking " How is the Emperor?" he replied,
" The courtier returns, the man will follow," — proving
that he was not only a great surgeon and a great physician, but wonderfully wise and witty. So the patient
and assiduous student of humanity will admit the ex-
orbitant claims of Desplein, and will think him, as he
thought himself, fit to be as great a statesman as he
was a surgeon.

Among the enigmas offered to the eyes of contemporaries by Desplein's life we have chosen one of the most
interesting, because of its final word, which may, perhaps, vindicate his memory from certain accusations.

Of all the pupils whom the great surgeon had taught
in his hospital, Horace Bianchon was the one to whom
he was most attached. Before becoming a house pupil
at the Hôtel-Dieu, Horace Bianchon was a medical student living in a miserable *pension* in the Latin quarter,
known under the name of the Maison Vauquer. There
the poor young fellow felt the assaults of bitter poverty,
that species of crucible from which great talents issue
pure and incorruptible as diamonds which can bear all
blows and never break. From the strong fires of their
vehement passions such natures acquire an uncompro-
mising rectitude ; they gain the habit of those struggles
which are the lot of genius through constant toil, in

the dull round of which they are forced to keep their balked appetites.

Horace was an honorable young man, incapable of paltering with his sense of duty; given to deeds, not words; ready to pawn his cloak for a friend, or to give him his time and his nights in watching. Horace was, indeed, one of those friends who care nothing for what they receive in exchange for what they give, sure of finding a return in their hearts far greater than the value of their gift. Most of his friends felt that inward respect for him which virtue without assumption inspires, and many among them feared his censure. Horace displayed his fine qualities without conceit. Neither a puritan nor a sermonizer, he gave advice with an oath, and was ready enough for a " tronçon de chière lie" when occasion offered. A jolly comrade, no more prudish than a cuirassier, frank and open, — not as a sailor, for sailors now-a-days are wily diplomates, — but like a brave young fellow with nothing to conceal in his life, he walked the earth with his head up and his thoughts happy. To express him in one sentence, Horace was the Pylades of more than one Orestes, creditors being in these days the nearest approach to the ancient Furies. He carried his poverty with an easy gayety which is perhaps one of the greatest elements of courage, and like all those who have nothing he contracted few debts. Sober as a camel, agile as a deer, he was firm in his ideas, and in his conduct. Bianchon's successful life may be said to have begun on the day when the illustrious surgeon became fully aware of the virtues and the defects which made Doctor Horace Bianchon so doubly dear to his friends.

When a clinical chief takes a young man into his rounds that young man has, as they say, his foot in the stirrup. Desplein always took Bianchon with him for the sake of his assistance when he went among his opulent patients, where many a fee dropped into the pupil's pouch, and where, little by little, the mysteries of Parisian life revealed themselves to his provincial eyes. Desplein kept him in his study during consultations and employed him there; sometimes he sent him travelling with a rich patient to baths; in short, he provided him with a practice. The result was that, after a time, the autocrat of surgery had an *alter ego*. These two men — one at the summit of science and of all honors, enjoying a large fortune and a great fame; the other, the modest omega, without either fame or fortune — became intimates. The great Desplein told his pupil everything; the pupil knew what woman had been seated in a chair beside the master, or on the famous sofa which was in the study and on which Desplein slept; Bianchon knew the mysteries of that temperament, half-lion, half-bull, which finally expanded and amplified beyond all reason the great man's chest, and caused his death by enlargement of the heart. He studied the eccentricities of that busy life, the schemes of that sordid avarice, the hopes of the politic man hidden in the scientific man; he was therefore fitted to detect the deceptions, had any existed, in the sole sentiment buried in a heart that was less hard than hardened.

One day Bianchon told Desplein that a poor water-carrier in the quartier Saint-Jacques had a horrible disease caused by over-work and poverty; this poor Auvergnat had eaten nothing but potatoes during the severe winter of 1821. Desplein left all his patients and rushed off, followed by Bianchon, and took the poor man himself to a private hospital established by the famous Dubois, in the faubourg Saint-Denis. He attended the man personally, and when he recovered gave him enough money to buy a horse and a water-cart. This Auvergnat was remarkable for an original act. One of his friends fell ill, and he took him at once to Desplein, saying to his benefactor, " I would n't hear of his going to any one else." Gruff as he was, Desplein pressed the water-carrier's hand. " Bring them all to me," he said; and he put the friend in the Hôtel-Dieu, where he took extreme care of him. Bianchon had already noticed several times the evident predilection his chief felt for an Auvergnat, and especially for a water-carrier, but as Desplein's pride was in the management of his hospital cases the pupil saw nothing really strange in the incident.

One day, crossing the place Saint-Sulpice, Bianchon caught sight of his master entering the church about nine o'clock in the morning. Desplein, who at that time of his life went everywhere in his cabriolet, was on foot, and was slipping along by the rue du Petit-Lion as if in quest of some questionable resort. Naturally seized with curiosity, the pupil, who knew the opinions of his master, slipped into Saint-Sulpice himself, and was not a little amazed to see the great Desplein, that atheist without pity even for the angels who so little require a scalpel and cannot have stomach-aches or fistulas, in short, that bold scoffer, humbly kneeling — where? in the chapel of the Virgin, before whom he was hearing a mass, paying for the service, giving money for the poor, and as serious in demeanor as if preparing for an operation.

"Heavens!" thought Bianchon, whose amazement was beyond all bounds. "If I had seen him holding one of the ropes of the canopy at the Fête-Dieu I should have known it was all a joke; but here, at this hour, alone, without witnesses! Certainly it is something to think about."

Not wishing to seem to spy upon the great surgeon of the Hôtel-Dieu, Bianchon went away. It so chanced

that Desplein asked him to dine with him that day,
away from home, at a restaurant. By the time the
dessert appeared Bianchon had reached by clever stages
the topic of religious services, and called the mass a
a farce and a mummery.

"A farce," said Desplein, "which has cost Christianity more blood than all the battles of Napoleon and
all the leeches of Broussais. The mass is a papal
invention based on the *Hoc est corpus*, and dates back
to the sixth century only. What torrents of blood had
to flow to establish the Fête-Dieu, by the institution of
which the court of Rome sought to confirm its victory
in the matter of the Real Presence, — a schism which
kept the church in hot water for three centuries! The
wars of the Comte de Toulouse and the Albigenses were
the sequel of it. The Vaudois and the Albigenses both
refused to accept that innovation — "

And Desplein launched with all an atheist's ardor into
a flux of Voltairean sarcasm, or, to be more exact, into
a wretched imitation of the "Citateur."

"Whew!" thought Bianchon; "where's the man
who was on his knees this morning?"

He was silent, for he began to doubt whether he had
really seen his chief at Saint-Sulpice after all. Desplein
would surely never have troubled himself to deceive
him. They knew each other too well, had exchanged
thoughts or questions fully as serious, and discussed

systems *de natura rerum*, probing them or dissecting them with the knife and scalpel of unbelief.

Six months went by. Bianchon took no outward notice of this circumstance, though it remained stamped in his memory. One day a doctor belonging to the Hôtel-Dieu took Desplein by the arm in Bianchon's presence as if to question him, and said, —

" Why did you go to Saint-Sulpice to-day, my dear master? "

" To see a priest with caries of the knee whom Madame la Duchesse d'Angoulême did me the honor to recommend to me," replied Desplein.

The doctor was satisfied, but not so Bianchon.

" Ha! he went to see a stiff knee in a church, did he? " thought the pupil. " He went to hear his mass."

Bianchon resolved to watch Desplein. He recollected the day and hour at which he had seen him entering Saint-Sulpice, and he determined to return the next year at the same time and see if he should surprise him in the same place. If so, then the periodicity of his devotion would warrant scientific investigation ; for it was impossible to expect in such a man a positive contradiction between thought and action.

The following year, at the time named, Bianchon, who was now no longer Desplein's pupil, saw the surgeon's cabriolet stop at the corner of the rue de

Tournon and the rue du Petit-Lion, from which point his friend slipped jesuitically along the wall of the church, where he again entered and heard mass before the altar of the Virgin. Yes, it assuredly was Desplein, the surgeon-in-chief, the atheist *in petto*, the pietist by chance. The plot thickened. The persistency of the illustrious surgeon added a complication.

When Desplein had left the church, Bianchon went up to the verger, who was rearranging the altar, and asked him if that gentleman were in the habit of coming there.

"It is twenty years since I came here," said the verger, "and ever since then Monsieur Desplein comes four times a year to hear this mass. He founded it."

"A mass founded by him!" thought Bianchon as he walked away. "It is a greater mystery than the Immaculate Conception, — a thing, in itself, which would make any doctor an unbeliever."

Some time went by before Doctor Bianchon, though Desplein's friend, was in a position to speak to him of this singularity of his life. When they met in consultation or in society it was difficult to find that moment of confidence and solitude in which they could sit with their feet on the andirons, and their heads on the back of their chairs, and tell their secrets as two men do at such times. At last, however, after the revolution of 1830, when the populace attacked the Archbishop's

palace, when republican instigations drove the crowd
to destroy the gilded crosses which gleamed like flashes
of lightning among the many roofs of that ocean of
houses, when unbelief, keeping pace with the riot,
strutted openly in the streets, Bianchon again saw
Desplein entering Saint-Sulpice. He followed him and
knelt beside him, but his friend made no sign and
showed not the least surprise. Together they heard
the mass.

"Will you tell me, my dear friend," said Bianchon,
when they had left the church, "the reason for this
pious performance? This is the third time I have
caught you going to mass, you! You must tell me
what this mystery means, and explain the discrepancy
between your opinions and your conduct. You don't
believe, but you go to mass! My dear master, I hold
you bound to answer me."

"I am like a great many pious people, — men who
are deeply religious to all appearance, but who are
really as much atheists at heart as you or I — "

And he went on with a torrent of sarcasms on certain
political personages, the best known of whom presents
to this century a new and living edition of the Tartufe
of Molière.

"I am not talking to you about that," said Bianchon;
"I want to know the reason for what you have just
done; and why you founded that mass?"

" Ah, well ! my dear friend," replied Desplein, " I am on the verge of my grave, and I can afford to tell you the events of my early life."

Just then Bianchon and the great surgeon were passing through the rue des Quatre-Vents, one of the most horrible streets in Paris. Desplein pointed to the sixth story of a house that looked like an obelisk, the gate of which opened upon a passage-way at the end of which was a winding stair lighted by holes in the planked side of it. It was a greenish-looking house, occupied on the ground-floor by a furniture-dealer, and seeming to harbor on each story some different form of poverty. Desplein threw up his arm with an energetic action and said to Bianchon, " I once lived up there for two years."

" I know the house ; d'Arthez lived in it. I went there nearly every day in my early youth ; we used to call it the ' harbor of great men.' Well, what next?"

" The mass I have just heard is connected with events which happened when I lived in the garret where you say d'Arthez lived, — that one, where you see the clothes-line and the linen above the flower-pots. My beginnings were so hard, my dear Bianchon, that I can bear away the palm of Parisian sufferings from every one, no matter who. I have endured all, — hunger, thirst, the want of a penny, of linen, boots, all, even the worst that poverty can bring. I have blown upon my frozen fingers in that harbor of great men, which I should like now to see again with you. I have worked there a whole winter and seen the vapor issuing from my head just as you see horses smoking in frosty weather.

"I don't know where a man can take his stand and find support against a life like that. I was alone, without help, without a sou to buy books, or to pay the costs of my medical education; having no friend to understand me, my irascible temper, uneasy and touchy as it is, did me harm. No one saw in my irritable ways the evidence of the anxiety and toil of a man who from the lowest social state is struggling to reach the surface. But I had, — and this I can say to you before whom there is no need that I should drape myself, — I had that understratum of right feelings and keen sensibility which will always be the attribute of men who are strong enough to mount a height, no matter what it is, after paddling long in the swamps of misery. I could ask nothing of my family, nor of my native town, beyond the insufficient allowance that they made me.

"Well, at this time of my life, I made my breakfast of a roll sold to me by the baker of the rue du Petit-Lion at half-price, because it was a day or two days old, and I crumbled it into some milk. So my morning repast cost me exactly two sous. I dined, every other day only, in a pension where the dinner cost sixteen sous. Thus I spent no more than ten sous a day. You know as well as I do what care I had to take of my clothes and my boots! I really can't tell whether we suffer more in after years from the treachery of a tried friend than you and I have suffered from the smiling grin of a crack in our boots, or the threadbare look of a coat-sleeve. I drank nothing but water, and I held the cafés in reverence. Zoppi seemed to me the promised land, where the Luculluses of the Latin quarter alone had the right of entrance. 'Shall I ever,' I used to say to myself, 'drink a cup of coffee there, with cream, and play a game of dominoes?'

"So I let loose upon my work the rage my misery caused me. I tried to possess myself of positive knowledge, so as to have a vast personal value, and thus deserve distinction when the day came that I should issue from my nothingness. I consumed more oil than bread; the lamp which lighted me during those toilsome nights cost me more than all my food. The struggle was long, obstinate, and without alleviation. I awakened no sympathy in any one about me. To have friends we must be friendly with young men, we must have a few sous to tipple with, we must frequent the places where other students go; but I had nothing! Who is there in Paris who realizes that nothing *is nothing?* When I was forced at times to reveal my poverty my throat contracted just as it does with our patients, who then imagine that a ball is rolling up from the œsophagus to the larynx. In later years I have met these people, born rich, who, never having wanted for anything, knew nothing of the problem of this rule of three : A young man *is* to crime what a five-franc piece *is* to *x*. These gilded imbeciles would say to me : ' But why do you run in debt? why do you saddle yourself with obligations?' They remind me of the princess who, when she heard the people were dying for want of bread, remarked : ' Why don't they buy cake?'

"Well, well, I should like to see one of those rich fellows who complain that I charge them too dear for my operations, — yes, I should like to see one of them alone in Paris, without a penny to bless himself with, without a friend, without credit, and forced to work with his five fingers to get food. What would he do? where would he go to appease his hunger ?—Bianchon, if you have sometimes seen me hard and bitter, it was when I was setting my early sufferings against the unfeeling selfishness of which I have had ten thousand proofs in the upper ranks of life ; or else I was thinking of the obstacles which hatred, envy, jealousy, and calumny had raised between success and me. In Paris, when certain persons see you about to put your foot in the stirrup some of them will catch you by the tails of your coat, others will loosen the buckles of the bellyband to give you a fall which will crack your skull; that one will pull the nails out of the horses' shoes, that other will steal your whip; the least treacherous is he whom you see approaching with a pistol to blow out your brains.

"Ah! my dear lad, you have talent enough to be soon plunged into the horrible strife, the incessant warfare which mediocrity wages against superior men. If you lose twenty-five louis some evening the next day you are accused of being a gambler, and your best friends will spread the news that you have lost twenty-five thousand francs. Have a headache, and they'll say you are insane. Get angry, and they'll call you a Timon. If, for the purpose of resisting this battalion of pygmies, you call up within you all the powers you possess, your best friends will cry out that you want to destroy everything, that you want to rule, to tyrannize. In short, your fine qualities are called defects, your defects vices, and your vices crimes. Though you may save a patient you will have the credit of killing him; if he recovers, you have sacrificed his future life to the present; if he does n't die, he soon will. Slip, and you are down! Make an invention, claim your right to it, and you are a quarrelsome knave, a stingy man, who won't let the young ones have a chance.

"And so, my dear fellow, if I don't believe in God, still less do I believe in man. Don't you know that there is in me a Desplein who is totally different from the Desplein whom the world traduces? But don't let us drag that muddy pond.

"Well, to go back, I lived in that house, and I was working to pass my first examination and I had n't a brass farthing. You know!—I had reached that last extremity where a man says, 'I'll pawn!' I had one hope. I expected a trunk of underclothing from my home, a present from some old aunts, who, knowing nothing of Paris, think about your shirts, and imagine that with an allowance of thirty francs a month their nephew must be living on ortolans. The trunk arrived one day when I was at the hospital; the carriage cost forty francs! The porter, a German shoemaker who lived in the loft, paid the money and kept the trunk. I walked about the rue des Fossés-Saint-Germain-des Prés and the rue de L'École-de-Médecine without being able to invent any **stratagem** by which I could get possession of that trunk without paying the forty francs, which I could, of course, pay at once as soon as I had sold the underclothes. My stupidity was enough to prove that I had no other vocation than that of surgery. My dear Bianchon, sensitive souls whose forces work in the higher spheres of thought, lack the spirit of intrigue which is so fertile in resources and schemes : their good genius is chance, — they don't seek, they find.

"That night I entered the house just as my neighbor, a water-carrier named Bourgeat, from Saint-Flour, came home. We knew each other as two tenants must when their rooms are on the same landing, and they hear one another snore, and cough, and dress, and at length become accustomed to one another. My neighbor told me that the proprietor of the house, to whom I owed three months rent, had turned me out; I was warned to quit the next day. He himself was also told to leave on account of his occupation. I passed the most dreadful night of my life. How could I hire a porter to carry away my few poor things, my books? how could I pay him? where could I go? These insoluble questions I said over and over to myself in tears, just as madmen repeat their sing-song. I fell asleep. Ah! poverty alone has the divine slumber full of glorious dreams!

"The next morning, as I was eating my bowlful of bread and milk, Bourgeat came in, and said in his patois, 'Monsieur, I'm a poor man, a foundling from the hospital at Saint-Flour, without father or mother, and I'm not rich enough to marry. You are no better off for friends, and relations, and money, as I judge. Now listen; there is a hand-cart out there which I have hired for two sous an hour; it will hold all our things; if you like, we can go and find some cheap lodging which will hold us both, as we are both

turned out of here. After all, you know, it is n't a
terrestrial paradise.' ' I know that,' I said, ' my good
Bourgeat, but I am in a great quandary; I have a
trunk downstairs which contains at least three hundred francs' worth of linen, with which I could pay
the proprietor if I could only get it from the porter, to
whom I owe forty francs for the carriage.' ' Bah !' he
cried, cheerily, ' I 've got a few pennies tucked away ;'
and he pulled out a dirty old leather purse. ' Keep your
linen ; you 'll want it.'

" Bourgeat paid my three months' rent, and his own,
and the porter. He put all our things and the trunk
into his hand-cart, and dragged it through the streets,
stopping before each house where a sign was up. Then
I went in to see if the place would suit us. At midday we were still wandering round the Latin quarter
without having found what we wanted. The price was
the great obstacle. Bourgeat invited me to breakfast
in a wine-shop, leaving the hand-cart before the door.
Towards evening, I found in the Cour de Rohan, pas-
sage du Commerce, on the top-floor of a house, under
the roof, two rooms, separated by the staircase. For a
yearly rent of sixty francs each, we were able to take
them. So there we were, housed, my humble friend and
I. We dined together. Bourgeat, who earned about
fifty sous a day, possessed something like three hundred francs. He was close upon realizing his great

ambition, which was to buy a horse and a water-cart. Learning my situation, for he wormed my secrets out of me, with a depth of cunning and an air of good-fellowship the remembrance of which to this day stirs every fibre of my heart, he renounced, for a time, the ambition of his life. Bourgeat never attained it; he sacrificed his three hundred francs to my future."

Desplein clasped the arm he held, violently.

"He gave me the money I needed for my examinations. That man — my friend — felt that I had a mission; that the needs of my intellect were greater than his own. He busied himself with me; he called me his son; he lent me the money I needed to buy books; he came in sometimes, very softly, to watch me at work; he substituted, with the forethought of a mother, a nourishing and sufficient diet for the poor fare to which I had been so long condemned. Bourgeat, a man then about forty years of age, had a middle-aged burgher face, a prominent forehead, and a head which a painter might have chosen for a model for Lycurgus. The poor soul had a heart full of unplaced affection. He had never been loved except by a dog which had recently died, and of which he often spoke to me, asking whether I thought the Church would be willing to say masses for the repose of its soul. That dog, he said, was a true Christian, who for twelve years had gone with him to church and never barked, listening to the organ without opening his jaws, and crouching by him when he knelt as if he prayed also.

"That man, that Auvergne water-carrier, spent all his affection upon me. He accepted me as a lonely, suffering human being; he became my mother, my delicate benefactor; in short, the ideal of that virtue which delights in its own work. When I met him about his business in the street he flung me a glance of inconceivable generosity; he pretended to walk as if he carried nothing; he showed his happiness in seeing me in good health and well-clothed. His devotion to me was that of the people, — the love of a grisette for one above her. Bourgeat did my errands, woke me at night when I had to be called, cleaned my lamp, polished my floor; as good a servant as a kind father, and as clean as an English girl. He kept house. Like Philopœmen, he sawed our wood, and gave to all his actions the simple dignity of toil; for he seemed to comprehend that the object ennobled all.

"When I left that noble man to enter the Hôtel-Dieu as an indoor pupil, he suffered dark distress from the thought that he could no longer live with me; but he consoled himself with the idea of laying by the money required for the expenses of my thesis, and he made me promise to come and see him on all my days out. If you will look up my thesis you will find that it is dedicated to him.

"During the last year I was in hospital I earned money enough to return all I owed to that noble Auvergnat, with which I bought him his horse and water-cart. He was very angry when he found out I had deprived myself of my earnings, and yet delighted to see his desires realized ; he laughed and scolded, looked at his cart and at his horse, and wiped his eyes, saying to me : ' It is all wrong. Oh, what a fine cart ! You had no right to do it ; that horse is as strong as an Auvergnat.' Never did I see anything as touching as that scene. Bourgeat positively insisted on buying me that case of instruments mounted in silver which you have seen in my study, and which is to me the most precious of my possessions. Though absolutely intoxicated by my success, he never by word or gesture let the thought escape him, ' It is to me that he owes it.' And yet, without him, misery would have killed me.

"The poor man had wrecked himself for me ; all he ate was a little bread rubbed with garlic, that I might have coffee for my studious nights. He fell ill. You can well believe that I spent nights at his bedside. I pulled him through the first time, but he had a relapse two years later, and, in spite of all my care, he died. No king was ever cared for as he was. Yes, Bianchon, to save that life I tried amazing things. I longed to make him live as the witness of his own work ; to realize his hopes, to satisfy the sole gratitude that ever entered my heart, to extinguish a fire which burns there still.

" Bourgeat," resumed Desplein, with visible emotion, " my second father, died in my arms, leaving all he possessed to me, in a will drawn up by a street writer and dated the year we went to live in the Cour de Rohan. That man had the faith of his kind ; he loved the Blessed Virgin as he would have loved his wife. An ardent Catholic, he never said one word to me about my irreligion. When he was in danger of death he asked me to spare nothing that he might have the succor of the Church. Every day masses were said for him. Often during the night he would tell me of his fears for the future ; he thought he had not lived devoutly enough. Poor man ! he had toiled from morning till night. To whom else does heaven belong, — if indeed there is a heaven ? He received the last offices of religion, like the saint that he was, and his death was worthy of his life. I, alone, followed him to the grave. When the earth covered my sole benefactor I sought a way to pay my debt to him. He had neither family, nor friends, nor wife, nor children, but, he believed ! he had a deep religious belief ; what right had I to dispute it ? He had timidly spoken to me of masses for the repose of the dead, but he never imposed that duty upon me, thinking, no doubt, it would seem like payment for his services. The moment I was able to found a mass I gave Saint-Sulpice the necessary sum for four yearly services. As the sole thing I can offer to Bourgeat is the satisfaction of his pious wishes, I go in his name and recite for him the appointed prayers at the beginning of each season. I say with the sincerity of a doubter: 'My God, if there be a sphere where thou dost place after death the souls of the perfect, think of the good Bourgeat; and if there is anything to be suffered for him, grant me those sufferings that he may the sooner enter what, they say, is heaven.'

"That, my dear friend, is all a man of my opinions can do. God must be a good sort of devil, and he 'll not blame me. I swear to you I would give all I am worth if Bourgeat's belief could enter my brain."

Bianchon, who took care of Desplein in his last illness, dares not affirm that the great surgeon died an atheist. Believers will like to think that the humble water-carrier opened to him the gates of heaven, as he had once opened to him the portals of that terrestial temple on the pediment of which are inscribed the words : —

"To her Great Men, a grateful Country !"

1836.

LA GRANDE BRETÈCHE.

———◆———

"Ah! Madame," replied Doctor Horace Bianchon to the lady at whose house he was supping, "it is true that I have many terrible histories in my repertory; but every tale has its due hour in a conversation, according to the clever saying reported by Chamfort and said to the Duc de Fronsac: "There are ten bottles of champagne between your joke and the present moment."

"But it is past midnight; what better hour could you have?" said the mistress of the house.

"Yes, tell us, Monsieur Bianchon," urged the assembled company.

At a gesture from the complying doctor, silence reigned.

"About a hundred yards from Vendôme," he said, "on the banks of the Loir, is an old brown house, covered with very steep roofs, and so completely isolated that there is not so much as an evil-smelling tannery, nor a shabby inn such as you see at the entrance of all little towns, in its neighborhood. In front of this dwelling is a garden overlooking the river, where the box edgings, once carefully clipped, which bordered the paths, now cross them and straggle as they fancy. A few willows with their roots in the Loir have made a rapid growth, like the enclosing hedge, and together they half hide the house. Plants which we call weeds drape the bank towards the river with their beautiful vegetation. Fruit-trees, neglected for half a score of years, no longer yield a product, and their shoots and suckers have formed an undergrowth. The espaliers are like a hornbeam hedge. The paths, formerly gravelled, are full of purslain ; so that, strictly speaking, there are no paths at all.

"From the crest of the mountain, on which hang the ruins of the old castle of Vendôme (the only spot whence the eye can look down into this enclosure) we say to ourselves that at an earlier period, now difficult to determine, this corner of the earth was the delight of some gentleman devoted to roses and tulips, in a word, to horticulture, but above all possessing a keen taste for good fruits. An arbor is still standing, or rather the remains of one, and beneath it is a table which time has not yet completely demolished.

"From the aspect of this garden, now no more, the negative joys of the peaceful life of the provinces can be inferred, just as we infer the life of some worthy from the epitaph on his tomb. To complete the sad and tender ideas which take possession of the soul, a sundial on the wall bears this inscription, Christian yet bourgeois, 'ULTIMAM COGITA.' The roofs are dilapidated, the blinds always closed, the balconies are filled with swallows' nests, the gates are locked. Tall herbs and grasses trace in green lines the chinks and crevices of the stone portico; the locks are rusty. Sun and moon, summer and winter and snow have rotted the wood, warped the planks, and worn away the paint. The gloomy silence is unbroken save by the birds, the cats, the martens, the rats, the mice, all free to scamper or fly, and to fight, and to eat themselves up.

"An invisible hand has written the word 'MYSTERY' everywhere. If, impelled by curiosity, you wish to look at this house, on the side towards the road you will see a large gate with an arched top, in which the children of the neighborhood have made large holes. This gate, as I heard later, had been disused for ten years. Through these irregular holes you can observe the perfect harmony which exists between the garden side, and the courtyard side of the premises. The same neglect everywhere. Lines of grass surround the paving-stones. Enormous cracks furrow the walls, the blackened caves of which are festooned with pellitory. The steps of the portico are disjointed, the rope of the bell is rotten, the gutters are dropping apart. What fire from heaven has fallen here? What tribunal has ordained that salt be cast upon this dwelling? Has God been mocked here; or France betrayed? These are the questions we ask as we stand there; the reptiles crawl about but they give no answer.

"This empty and deserted house is a profound enigma, whose solution is known to none. It was formerly a small fief, and is called La Grande Bretèche. During my stay at Vendôme, where Desplein had sent me in charge of a rich patient, the sight of this strange dwelling was one of my keenest pleasures. It was better than a ruin. A ruin possesses memories of positive authenticity; but this habitation, still standing, though slowly demolished by an avenging hand, contained some secret, some mysterious thought, — it betrayed at least a strange caprice.

"More than once of an evening I jumped the hedge, now a tangle, which guarded the enclosure. I braved the scratches; I walked that garden without a master, that property which was neither public nor private; for hours I stayed there contemplating its decay. Not even to obtain the history which underlay (and to which no doubt was due) this strange spectacle would I have asked a single question of any gossiping countryman. Standing there I invented enchanting tales; I gave myself up to debauches of melancholy which fascinated me. Had I known the reason, perhaps a common one, for this strange desertion, I should have lost the unwritten poems with which I intoxicated myself. To me this sanctuary evoked the most varied images of human life darkened by sorrows; sometimes it was a cloister without the nuns; sometimes a graveyard and its peace, without the dead who talk to you in epitaphs; to-day the house of the leper, to-morrow that of the Atrides; but above all was it the provinces with their composed ideas, their hour-glass life.

"Often I wept there, but I never smiled. More than once an involuntary terror seized me, as I heard above my head the muffled whirr of a ringdove's wings hurrying past. The soil is damp; care must be taken against the lizards, the vipers, the frogs, which wander about with the wild liberty of nature; above all, it is well not to fear cold, for there are moments when you feel an icy mantle laid upon your shoulders like the hand of the Commander on the shoulder of Don Juan. One evening I shuddered; the wind had caught and turned a rusty vane. Its creak was like a moan issuing from the house; at a moment, too, when I was ending a gloomy drama in which I explained to myself the monumental dolor of that scene.

"That night I returned to my inn, a prey to gloomy thoughts. After I had supped the landlady entered my room with a mysterious air, and said to me, 'Monsieur, Monsieur Regnault is here.'

"'Who is Monsieur Regnault?'

" 'Is it possible that Monsieur does n't know Monsieur Regnault? Ah, how funny!' she said, leaving the room.

"Suddenly I beheld a long, slim man, clothed in black, holding his hat in his hand, who presented himself, much like a ram about to leap on a rival, and showed me a retreating forehead, a small, pointed head and a livid face, in color somewhat like a glass of dirty water. You would have taken him for the usher of a minister. This unknown personage wore an old coat much worn in the folds, but he had a diamond in the frill of his shirt, and gold earrings in his ears.

" 'Monsieur, to whom have I the honor of speaking?' I said.

" He took a chair, sat down before my fire, laid his hat on my table and replied, rubbing his hands: 'Ah! it is very cold.   Monsieur, I am Monsieur Regnault.'

"I bowed, saying to myself: '*Il bondo cani!* seek!'

" 'I am,' he said, ' the notary of Vendôme.'

" 'Delighted, monsieur,' I replied, ' but I am not in the way of making my will, — for reasons, alas, too well-known to me.'

" 'One moment!' he resumed, raising his hand as if to impose silence; 'Permit me, monsieur, permit me! I have learned that you sometimes enter the garden of La Grande Bretèche and walk there —'

"'Yes, monsieur.'

"'One moment!' he said, repeating his gesture. 'That action constitutes a misdemeanor. Monsieur, I come in the name and as testamentary executor of the late Comtesse de Merret to beg you to discontinue your visits. One moment! I am not a Turk; I do not wish to impute a crime to you. Besides, it is quite excusable that you, a stranger, should be ignorant of the circumstances which compel me to let the handsomest house in Vendôme go to ruin. Nevertheless, monsieur, as you seem to be a person of education, you no doubt know that the law forbids trespassers on enclosed property. A hedge is the same as a wall. But the state in which that house is left may well excuse your curiosity. I should be only too glad to leave you free to go and come as you liked there, but charged as I am to execute the wishes of the testatrix, I have the honor, monsieur, to request that you do not again enter that garden. I myself, monsieur, have not, since the reading of the will, set foot in that house, which, as I have already had the honor to tell you, I hold under the will of Madame de Merret. We have only taken account of the number of the doors and windows so as to assess the taxes which I pay annually from the funds left by the late countess for that purpose. Ah, monsieur, that will made a great deal of noise in Vendôme!'

"There the worthy man paused to blow his nose.

I respected his loquacity, understanding perfectly that
the testamentary bequest of Madame de Merret had
been the most important event of his life, the head and
front of his reputation, his glory, his Restoration. So
· then, I must bid adieu to my beautiful reveries, my
romances! I was not so rebellious as to deprive myself of getting the truth, as it were officially, out of the
man of law, so I said, —

"' Monsieur, if it is not indiscreet, may I ask the
reason of this singularity?'

" At these words a look which expressed the pleasure of a man who rides a hobby passed over Monsieur
Regnault's face. He pulled up his shirt-collar with a
certain conceit, took out his snuff-box, opened it,
offered it to me, and on my refusal, took a strong
pinch himself. He was happy. A man who has n't
a hobby does n't know how much can be got out of
life. A hobby is the exact medium between a passion
and a monomania. At that moment I understood
Sterne's fine expression to its fullest extent, and I
formed a complete idea of the joy with which my Uncle
Toby — Trim assisting — bestrode his war-horse.

"' Monsieur,' said Monsieur Regnault, 'I was formerly head-clerk to Maître Roguin in Paris. An excellent lawyer's office of which you have doubtless
heard? No! And yet a most unfortunate failure made
it, I may say, celebrated. Not having the means to

buy a practice in Paris at the price to which they rose in 1816, I came here to Vendôme, where I have relations,—among them a rich aunt, who gave me her daughter in marriage.'

" Here he made a slight pause, and then resumed : —

" ' Three months after my appointment was ratified by Monseigneur the Keeper of the Seals, I was sent for one evening just as I was going to bed (I was not then married) by Madame la Comtesse de Merret, then living in her château at Merret. Her lady's-maid, an excellent girl who is now serving in this inn, was at the door with the countess's carriage. Ah! one moment! I ought to tell you, monsieur, that Monsieur le Comte de Merret had gone to die in Paris about two months before I came here. He died a miserable death from excesses of all kinds, to which he gave himself up. You understand? Well, the day of his departure Madame la Comtesse left La Grande Bretèche, and dismantled it. They do say that she even burned the furniture, and the carpets, and all appurtenances whatsoever and wheresoever contained on the premises leased to the said— Ah! beg pardon; what am I saying? I thought I was dictating a lease. Well, monsieur, she burned everything, they say, in the meadow at Merret. Were you ever at Merret, monsieur?'

" Not waiting for me to speak, he answered for me : 'No. Ah! it is a fine spot? For three months, or thereabouts,' he continued, nodding his head, 'Monsieur le Comte and Madame la Comtesse had been living at La Grande Bretèche in a very singular way. They admitted no one to the house; madame lived on the ground-floor, and monsieur on the first floor. After Madame la Comtesse was left alone she never went to church. Later, in her own château she refused to see the friends who came to visit her. She changed greatly after she left La Grande Bretèche and came to Merret. That dear woman (I say dear, though I never saw her but once, because she gave me this diamond), — that good lady was very ill; no doubt she had given up all hope of recovery, for she died without calling in a doctor; in fact, some of our ladies thought she was not quite right in her mind. Consequently, monsieur, my curiosity was greatly excited when I learned that Madame de Merret needed my services; and I was not the only one deeply interested; that very night, though it was late, the whole town knew I had gone to Merret.'

"The good man paused a moment to arrange his facts, and then continued : 'The lady's maid answered rather vaguely the questions which I put to her as we drove along; she did, however, tell me that her mistress had received the last sacraments that day from the curate of Merret, and that she was not likely to live through the night. I reached the château about eleven o'clock. I went up the grand staircase. After passing through a number of dark and lofty rooms, horribly cold and damp, I entered the state bedroom where Madame la Comtesse was lying. In consequence of the many stories that were told about this lady (really, monsieur, I should never end if I related all of them) I expected to find her a fascinating coquette. Would you believe it, I could scarcely see her at all in the huge bed in which she lay. It is true that the only light in that vast room, with friezes of the old style powdered with dust enough to make you sneeze on merely looking at them, was one Argand lamp. Ah! but you say you have never been at Merret. Well, monsieur, the bed was one of those old-time beds with a high tester covered with flowered chintz. A little night-table stood by the bed, and on it I noticed a copy of the " Imitation of Christ."

" ' Allow me a parenthesis,' he said, interrupting himself. ' I bought that book subsequently, also the lamp, and presented them to my wife. In the room was a large sofa for the woman who was taking care of Madame de Merret, and two chairs. That was all. No fire. The whole would not have made ten lines of an inventory. Ah! my dear monsieur, could you have seen her as I saw her then, in that vast room hung with brown tapestry, you would have imagined you were in the pages of a novel. It was glacial, — better than that, funereal,' added the worthy man, raising his arm theatrically and making a pause. Presently he resumed :

" ' By dint of peering round and coming close to the bed I at length saw Madame de Merret, thanks to the lamp which happened to shine on the pillows. Her face was as yellow as wax, and looked like two hands joined together. Madame la Comtesse wore a lace cap, which, however, allowed me to see her fine hair, white as snow. She was sitting up in the bed, but apparently did so with difficulty. Her large black eyes, sunken no doubt with fever, and almost lifeless, hardly moved beneath the bones where the eyebrows usually grow. Her forehead was damp. Her fleshless hands were like bones covered with thin skin ; the veins and muscles could all be seen. She must once have been very handsome, but now I was seized with—I could n't tell you what feeling, as I looked at her. Those who buried her said afterwards that no living creature had ever been as wasted as she without dying. Well, it was awful to see. Some mortal disease had eaten up that woman till there was nothing left of her but a phantom. Her lips, of a pale violet, seemed not to move when she spoke. Though my profession had familiarized me with such scenes, in bringing me often to the bedside of the dying, to receive their last wishes, I must say that the tears and the anguish of families and friends which I have witnessed were as nothing compared to this solitary woman in that vast building. I did not hear the slightest noise. I did not see the movement which the breathing of the dying woman would naturally give to the sheet that covered her; I myself remained motionless, looking at her in a sort of stupor. Indeed, I fancy I am there still. At last her large eyes moved; she tried to lift her right hand, which fell back upon the bed; then these words issued from her lips like a breath, for her voice was no longer a voice, —

"'"I have awaited you with impatience."

"'Her cheeks colored. The effort to speak was great. The old woman who was watching her here rose and whispered in my ear: "Don't speak; Madame la Comtesse is past hearing the slightest sound; you would only agitate her." I sat down. A few moments later Madame de Merret collected all her remaining strength to move her right arm and put it, not without great difficulty, under her bolster. She paused an instant; then she made a last effort and withdrew her hand which now held a sealed paper. Great drops of sweat rolled from her forehead.

"'"I give you my will," she said. "Oh, my God! Oh!"

"'That was all. She seized a crucifix which lay on her bed, pressed it to her lips and died. The expression of her fixed eyes still makes me shudder when I think of it. I brought away the will. When it was opened

I found that Madame de Merret had appointed me her executor. She bequeathed her whole property to the hospital of Vendôme, save and excepting certain bequests. The following disposition was made of La Grande Bretèche. I was directed to leave it in the state in which it was at the time of her death for a period of fifty years from the date of her decease; I was to forbid all access to it, by any and every one, no matter who; to make no repairs, and to put by from her estate a yearly sum to pay watchers, if they were necessary, to insure the faithful execution of these intentions. At the expiration of that time the estate was, if the testatrix's will had been carried out in all particulars, to belong to my heirs (because, as monsieur is doubtless well aware, notaries are forbidden by law to receive legacies); if otherwise, then La Grande Bretèche was to go to whoever might establish a right to it, but on condition of fulfilling certain orders contained in a codicil annexed to the will and not to be opened until the expiration of the fifty years. The will has never been attacked, consequently — '

"Here the oblong notary, without finishing his sentence, looked at me triumphantly. I made him perfectly happy with a few compliments.

"'Monsieur,' I said, in conclusion, 'you have so deeply impressed that scene upon me that I seem to see the dying woman, whiter than the sheets; those glittering eyes horrify me; I shall dream of her all night. But you must have formed some conjectures as to the motive of that extraordinary will.'

" ' Monsieur,' he replied, with comical reserve, ' I never permit myself to judge of the motives of those who honor me with the gift of a diamond.'

" However, I managed to unloose the tongue of the scrupulous notary so far that he told me, not without long digressions, certain opinions on the matter emanating from the wise-heads of both sexes whose judgments made the social law of Vendôme. But these opinions and observations were so contradictory, so diffuse, that I well-nigh went to sleep in spite of the interest I felt in this authentic story. The heavy manner and monotonous accent of the notary, who was no doubt in the habit of listening to himself and making his clients and compatriots listen to him, triumphed over my curiosity. Happily, he did at last go away.

" ' Ha, ha! monsieur,' he said to me at the head of the stairs, ' many persons would like to live their forty-five years longer, but, one moment ! '—here he laid the forefinger of his right hand on his nose as if he meant to say, Now pay attention to this ! — ' in order to do that, to do *that*, they ought to skip the sixties.'

" I shut my door, the notary's jest, which he thought very witty, having drawn me from my apathy; then I sat down in my armchair and put both feet on the andirons. I was plunged in a romance *à la* Radcliffe, based on the notarial disclosures of Monsieur Regnault, when my door, softly opened by the hand of a woman, turned noiselessly on its hinges.

"I saw my landlady, a jovial, stout woman, with a fine, good-humored face, who had missed her true surroundings ; she was from Flanders, and might have stepped out of a picture by Teniers.

" 'Well, monsieur,' she said, 'Monsieur Regnault has no doubt recited to you his famous tale of La Grande Bretèche ?'

" 'Yes, Madame Lepas.'

" 'What did he tell you ?'

"I repeated in a few words the dark and chilling story of Madame de Merret as imparted to me by the notary. At each sentence my landlady ran out her chin and looked at me with the perspicacity of an innkeeper, which combines the instinct of a policeman, the astuteness of a spy, and the cunning of a shopkeeper.

" 'My dear Madame Lepas,' I added, in conclusion, 'you evidently know more than that. If not, why did you come up here to me ?'

" 'On the word, now, of an honest woman, just as true as my name is Lepas — '

" 'Don't swear, for your eyes are full of the secret. You knew Monsieur de Merret. What sort of man was he ?'

"'Goodness! Monsieur de Merret? well, you see, he was a handsome man, so tall you never could see the top of him, — a very worthy gentleman from Picardy, who had, as you may say, a temper of his own; and he knew it. He paid every one in cash so as to have no quarrels. But, I tell you, he could be quick. Our ladies thought him very pleasant.'

"'Because of his temper?' I asked.

"'Perhaps,' she replied. 'You know, monsieur, a man must have something to the fore, as they say, to marry a lady like Madame de Merret, who, without disparaging others, was the handsomest and the richest woman in Vendôme. She had an income of nearly twenty thousand francs. All the town was at the wedding. The bride was so dainty and captivating, a real little jewel of a woman. Ah! they were a fine couple in those days!'

"'Was their home a happy one?'

"'Hum, hum! yes and no, so far as any one can say; for you know well enough that the like of us don't live hand and glove with the like of them. Madame de Merret was a good woman and very charming, who no doubt had to bear a good deal from her husband's temper; we all liked her though she was rather haughty. Bah! that was her bringing up, and she was born so. When people are noble — don't you see?'

"'Yes, but there must have been some terrible

catastrophe, for Monsieur and Madame de Merret to separate violently.'

"'I never said there was a catastrophe, monsieur; I know nothing about it.'

"'Very good; now I am certain that you know all.'

"'Well, monsieur, I'll tell you all I do know. When I saw Monsieur Regnault coming after you I knew he would tell you about Madame de Merret and La Grande Bretèche; and that gave me the idea of consulting monsieur, who seems to be a gentleman of good sense, incapable of betraying a poor woman like me, who has never done harm to any one, but who is, somehow, troubled in her conscience. I have never dared to say a word to the people about here, for they are all gossips, with tongues like steel blades. And there's never been a traveller who has stayed as long as you have, monsieur, to whom I could tell all about the fifteen thousand francs—'

"'My dear Madame Lepas,' I replied, trying to stop the flow of words, 'if your confidence is of a nature to compromise me, I would n't hear it for worlds.'

"'Oh, don't be afraid,' she said, interrupting me. 'You 'll see—'

"This haste to tell made me quite certain I was not the first to whom my good landlady had communicated the secret of which I was to be the sole repositary, so I listened.

" ' Monsieur,' she said, ' when the Emperor sent the Spanish and other prisoners of war to Vendôme I lodged one of them (at the cost of the government), — a young Spaniard on parole. But in spite of his parole he had to report every day to the sub-prefect. He was a grandee of Spain, with a name that ended in *os* and in *dia*, like all Spaniards — Bagos de Férédia. I wrote his name on the register, and you can see it if you like. Oh, he was a handsome young fellow for a Spaniard, who, they tell me, are all ugly. He was n't more than five feet two or three inches, but he was well made. He had pretty little hands which he took care of — ah, you should just have seen him! He had as many brushes for those hands as a woman has for her head. He had fine black hair, a fiery eye, a rather copper-colored skin, but it was pleasant to look at all the same. He wore the finest linen I ever saw on any one, and I have lodged princesses, and, among others, General Bertrand, the Duc and Duchesse d'Abrantès, Monsieur Decazes and the King of Spain. He did n't eat much ; but he had such polite manners and was always so amiable that I could n't find fault with him. Oh ! I did really love him, though he never said four words a day to me ; if any one spoke to him, he never answered, — that 's an oddity those grandees have, a sort of mania, so I 'm told. He read his breviary like a priest, and he went to mass and to all the services regularly. Where

do you think he sat? close to the chapel of Madame de
Merret. But as he took that place the first time he went
to church nobody attached any importance to the fact,
though it was remembered later. Besides, he never
took his eyes off his prayer-book, poor young man ! '

" My jovial landlady paused a moment, overcome
with her recollections; then she continued her tale :

" ' From that time on, monsieur, he used to walk up
the mountain every evening to the ruins of the castle.
It was his only amusement, poor man ! and I dare say
it recalled his own country ; they say Spain is all
mountains. From the first he was always late at night
in coming in. I used to be uneasy at never seeing him
before the stroke of midnight ; but we got accustomed
to his ways and gave him a key to the door, so that we
did n't have to sit up. It so happened that one of our
grooms told us that one evening when he went to bathe
his horses he thought he saw the grandee in the distance, swimming in the river like a fish. When he
came in I told him he had better take care not to get
entangled in the sedges ; he seemed annoyed that any
one had seen him in the water. Well, monsieur. one
day, or rather, one morning, we did not find him in his
room ; he had not come in. He never returned. I
looked about and into everything, and at last I found
a writing in a table drawer where he had put away fifty
of those Spanish gold coins called " portugaise," which

bring a hundred francs apiece; there were also diamonds worth ten thousand francs sealed up in a little box. The paper said that in case he should not return some day, he bequeathed to us the money and the diamonds, with a request to found masses of thanksgiving to God for his escape and safety. In those days my husband was living, and he did everything he could to find the young man. But, it was the queerest thing! he found only the Spaniard's clothes under a big stone in a sort of shed on the banks of the river, on the castle side, just opposite to La Grande Bretèche. My husband went so early in the morning that no one saw him. He burned the clothes after we had read the letter, and gave out, as Comte Férédia requested, that he had fled. The sub-prefect sent the whole gendarmerie on his traces, but bless your heart! they never caught him. Lepas thought the Spaniard had drowned himself. But, monsieur, I never thought so. I think he was somehow mixed up in Madame de Merret's trouble; and I 'll tell you why. Rosalie has told me that her mistress had a crucifix she valued so much that she was buried with it, and it was made of ebony and silver; now when Monsieur de Férédia first came to lodge with us he had just such a crucifix, but I soon missed it. Now, monsieur, what do you say? is n't it true that I need have no remorse about those fifteen thousand francs? are not they rightfully mine?'

" ' Of course they are. But how is it you have never questioned Rosalie ? ' I said.

" ' Oh, I have, monsieur ; but I can get nothing out of her. That girl is a stone wall. She knows something, but there is no making her talk.'

" After a few more remarks, my landlady left me, a prey to a romantic curiosity, to vague and darkling thoughts, to a religious terror that was something like the awe which comes upon us when we enter by night a gloomy church and see in the distance beneath the arches a feeble light ; a formless figure glides before us, the sweep of a robe — of priest or woman — is heard ; we shudder. La Grande Bretèche, with its tall grasses, its shuttered windows, its rusty railings, its barred gates, its deserted rooms, rose fantastically and suddenly before me. I tried to penetrate that mysterious dwelling and seek the knot of this most solemn history, this drama which had killed three persons.

" Rosalie became to my eyes the most interesting person in Vendôme. Examining her, I discovered the traces of an ever-present inward thought. In spite of the health which bloomed upon her dimpled face, there was in her some element of remorse, or of hope ; her attitude bespoke a secret, like that of devotees who pray with ardor, or that of a girl who has killed her child and forever after hears its cry. And yet her postures were naïve, and even vulgar; her silly smile was surely not criminal; you would have judged her innocent if only by the large neckerchief of blue and red squares which covered her vigorous bust, clothed, confined, and set off by a gown of purple and white stripes. 'No,' thought I; 'I will not leave Vendôme without knowing the history of La Grande Bretèche. I'll even make love to Rosalie, if it is absolutely necessary.'

"'Rosalie!' I said to her one day.

"'What is it, monsieur?'

"'You are not married, are you?'
She trembled slightly.

"'Oh! when the fancy takes me to be unhappy there'll be no lack of men,' she said, laughing.

"She recovered instantly from her emotion, whatever it was; for all women, from the great lady to the chambermaid of an inn, have a self-possession of their own.

"'You are fresh enough and taking enough to please a lover,' I said, watching her. 'But tell me, Rosalie, why did you take a place at an inn after you left Madame de Merret? Did n't she leave you an annuity?'

"'Oh, yes, she did. But, monsieur, my place is the best in all Vendôme.'

"This answer was evidently what judges and lawyers call 'dilatory.' Rosalie's position in this romantic history was like that of a square on a checkerboard; she was at the very centre, as it were, of its truth and its interest; she seemed to me to be tied into the knot of it. The last chapter of the tale was in her, and, from the moment that I realized this, Rosalie became to me an object of attraction. By dint of studying the girl I came to find in her, as we do in every woman whom we make a principal object of our attention, that she had a host of good qualities. She was clean, and careful of herself, and therefore handsome. Some two or three weeks after the notary's visit I said to her, suddenly: 'Tell me all you know about Madame de Merret.'

"'Oh, no!' she replied, in a tone of terror, 'don't ask me that, monsieur.'

"I persisted in urging her. Her pretty face darkened, her bright color faded, her eyes lost their innocent, liquid light.

"'Well!' she said, after a pause, 'if you will have it so, I will tell you; but keep the secret.'

"'I'll keep it with the faithfulness of a thief, which is the most loyal to be found anywhere.'

"'If it is the same to you, monsieur, I'd rather you kept it with your own.'

"Thereupon, she adjusted her neckerchief and posed herself to tell the tale; for it is very certain that an attitude of confidence and security is desirable in order to make a narration. The best tales are told at special hours, – like that in which we are now at table. No one ever told a story well, standing or fasting.

"If I were to reproduce faithfully poor Rosalie's diffuse eloquence, a whole volume would scarce suffice. But as the event of which she now gave me a hazy knowledge falls into place between the facts revealed by the garrulity of the notary, and that of Madame Lepas, as precisely as the mean terms of an arithmetical proposition lie between its two extremes, all I have to do is to tell it to you in few words. I therefore give a summary of what I heard from Rosalie.

"The chamber which Madame de Merret occupied at La Grande Bretèche was on the ground-floor. A small closet about four feet in depth was made in the wall, and served as a wardrobe. Three months before the evening when the facts I am about to relate to you happened, Madame de Merret had been so seriously unwell that her husband left her alone in her room and slept himself in a chamber on the first floor. By one of those mere chances which it is impossible to foresee, he returned, on the evening in question, two hours later than usual from the club where he went habitually to read the papers and talk politics with the inhabitants of the town. His wife thought him at home and in bed and asleep. But the invasion of France had been the subject of a lively discussion ; the game of billiards was a heated one ; he had lost forty francs, an enormous sum for Vendôme, where everybody hoards his money, and where manners and customs are restrained within modest limits worthy of all praise, — which may, perhaps, be the source of a certain true happiness which no Parisian cares anything at all about.

" For some time past Monsieur de Merret had been in the habit of asking Rosalie, when he came in, if his wife were in bed. Being told, invariably, that she was, he at once went to his own room with the contentment that comes of confidence and custom. This evening, on returning home, he took it into his head to go to Madame de Merret's room and tell her his ill-luck, perhaps to be consoled for it. During dinner he had noticed that his wife was coquettishly dressed; and as he came from the club the thought crossed his mind that she was no longer ill, that her convalescence had made her lovelier than ever, — a fact he perceived, as husbands are wont to perceive things, too late.

" Instead of calling Rosalie, who at that moment was in the kitchen watching a complicated game of ' brisque,' at which the cook and the coachman were playing, Monsieur de Merret went straight to his wife's room by the light of his lantern, which he had placed on the first step of the stairway. His step, which was easily recognized, resounded under the arches of the corridor. Just as he turned the handle of his wife's door he fancied he heard the door of the closet, which I mentioned to you, shut; but when he entered, Madame de Merret was alone, standing before the fireplace. The husband thought to himself that Rosalie must be in the closet; and yet a suspicion, which sounded in his ears like the ringing of bells, made him distrustful. He looked at his wife, and fancied he saw something wild and troubled in her eyes.

" ' You are late in coming home,' she said. That voice, usually so pure and gracious, seemed to him slightly changed.

" Monsieur de Merret made no answer, for at that moment Rosalie entered the room. Her appearance was a thunderbolt to him. He walked up and down the room with his arms crossed, going from one window to another with a uniform movement.

" ' Have you heard anything to trouble you?' asked his wife, timidly, while Rosalie was undressing her. He made no answer.

" ' You can leave the room,' said Madame de Merret to the maid. ' I will arrange my hair myself.'

" She guessed some misfortune at the mere sight of her husband's face, and wished to be alone with him.

" When Rosalie was gone, or supposed to be gone, for she went no further than the corridor, Monsieur de Merret came to his wife and stood before her. Then he said, coldly:

" ' Madame, there is some one in your closet.'

" She looked at her husband with a calm air, and answered, ' No, monsieur.'

" That ' no ' agonized Monsieur de Merret, for he did not believe it. And yet his wife had never seemed purer nor more saintly than she did at that moment. He rose and went towards the closet to open the door; Madame de Merret took him by the hand and stopped him; she looked at him with a sad air and said, in a voice that was strangely shaken : ' If you find no one, remember that all is over between us.'

" The infinite dignity of his wife's demeanor restored her husband's respect for her, and suddenly inspired him with one of those resolutions which need some wider field to become immortal.

" ' No, Josephine,' he said, ' I will not look there. In either case we should be separated forever. Listen to me : I know the purity of your soul, I know that you lead a saintly life ; you would not commit a mortal sin to save yourself from death.'

" At these words, Madame de Merret looked at her husband with a haggard eye.

" ' Here is your crucifix,' he went on. ' Swear to me before God that there is no one in that closet and I will believe you ; I will not open that door.'

" Madame de Merret took the crucifix and said ' I swear it.'

"'Louder!' said her husband; 'repeat after me, — I swear before God that there is no person in that closet.'

"She repeated the words composedly.

"'That is well,' said Monsieur de Merret, coldly. After a moment's silence he added, examining the ebony crucifix inlaid with silver, 'That is a beautiful thing; I did not know you possessed it; it is very artistically wrought.'

"'I found it at Duvivier's,' she replied; 'he bought it of a Spanish monk when those prisoners-of-war passed through Vendôme last year.'

"'Ah!' said Monsieur de Merret, replacing the crucifix on the wall. He rang the bell. Rosalie was not long in answering it. Monsieur de Merret went quickly up to her, took her into the recess of a window on the garden side, and said to her in a low voice: —

"'I am told that Gorenflot wants to marry you, and that poverty alone prevents it, for you have told him you will not be his wife until he is a master-mason. Is that so?'

"'Yes, monsieur.'

"'Well, go and find him; tell him to come here at once and bring his trowel and other tools. Take care not to wake any one at his house but himself; he will soon have enough money to satisfy you. No talking to any one when you leave this room, mind, or—'

"He frowned. Rosalie left the room. He called her back; 'Here, take my pass-key,' he said.

"Monsieur de Merret, who had kept his wife in view while giving these orders, now sat down beside her before the fire and began to tell her of his game of billiards, and the political discussions at the club. When Rosalie returned she found Monsieur and Madame de Merret talking amicably.

"The master had lately had the ceilings of all the reception rooms on the lower floor restored. Plaster is very scarce at Vendôme, and the carriage of it makes it expensive. Monsieur de Merret had therefore ordered an ample quantity for his own wants, knowing that he could readily finds buyers for what was left. This circumstance inspired the idea that now possessed him.

"'Monsieur, Gorenflot has come,' said Rosalie.

"'Bring him in,' said her master.

"Madame de Merret turned slightly pale when she saw the mason.

"'Gorenflot,' said her husband, 'fetch some bricks from the coach-house,—enough to wall up that door; use the plaster that was left over, to cover the wall.'

"Then he called Rosalie and the mason to the end of the room, and, speaking in a low voice, added, 'Listen to me, Gorenflot; after you have done this work you will sleep in the house; and to-morrow morning

I will give you a passport into a foreign country, and six thousand francs for the journey. Go through Paris where I will meet you. There, I will secure to you legally another six thousand francs, to be paid to you at the end of ten years if you still remain out of France. For this sum, I demand absolute silence on what you see and do this night. As for you, Rosalie, I give you a dowry of ten thousand francs, on condition that you marry Gorenflot, and keep silence, if not —'

" 'Rosalie,' said Madame de Merret, 'come and brush my hair.'

" The husband walked up and down the room, watching the door, the mason, and his wife, but without allowing the least distrust or misgiving to appear in his manner. Gorenflot's work made some noise; under cover of it Madame de Merret said hastily to Rosalie, while her husband was at the farther end of the room. 'A thousand francs annuity if you tell Gorenflot to leave a crevice at the bottom;' then aloud she added, composedly, 'Go and help the mason.'

" Monsieur and Madame de Merret remained silent during the whole time it took Gorenflot to wall up the door. The silence was intentional on the part of the husband to deprive his wife of all chance of saying words with a double meaning which might be heard within the closet; with Madame de Merret it was either prudence or pride.

"When the wall was more than half up, the mason's tool broke one of the panes of glass in the closet door; Monsieur de Merret's back was at that moment turned away. The action proved to Madame de Merret that Rosalie had spoken to the mason. In that one instant she saw the dark face of a man with black hair and fiery eyes. Before her husband turned the poor creature had time to make a sign with her head which meant 'Hope.'

"By four o'clock, just at dawn, for it was in the month of September, the work was done. Monsieur de Merret remained that night in his wife's room. The next morning, on rising, he said, carelessly: 'Ah! I forgot, I must go to the mayor's office about that passport.'

"He put on his hat, made three steps to the door, then checked himself, turned back, and took the crucifix.

"His wife trembled with joy; 'He will go to Duvivier's,' she thought.

"The moment her husband had left the house she rang for Rosalie. 'The pick-axe!' she cried, 'the pick-axe! I watched how Gorenflot did it; we shall have time to make a hole and close it again.'

"In an instant Rosalie had brought a sort of cleaver, and her mistress, with a fury no words can describe, began to demolish the wall. She had knocked away a few bricks, and was drawing back to strike a still more vigorous blow with all her strength, when she saw her husband behind her. She fainted.

"'Put madame on her bed,' said her husband, coldly.

"Foreseeing what would happen, he had laid this trap for his wife; he had written to the mayor, and sent for Duvivier. The jeweller arrived just as the room had been again put in order.

"'Duvivier,' said Monsieur de Merret, 'I think you bought some crucifixes of those Spaniards who were here last year?'

"'No, monsieur, I did not.'

"'Very good; thank you,' he said, with a tigerish glance at his wife. 'Jean,' he added to the footman, 'serve my meals in Madame de Merret's bedroom; she is very ill, and I shall not leave her till she recovers.'

"For twenty days that man remained beside his wife. During the first hours, when sounds were heard behind the walled door, and Josephine tried to implore mercy for the dying stranger, he answered, without allowing her to utter a word: —

"'You swore upon the cross that no one was there.'"

As the tale ended the women rose from table, and the spell under which Bianchon had held them was broken. Nevertheless, several of them were conscious of a cold chill as they recalled the last words.

THE PURSE.

———•———

To Sofka:

Have you ever remarked, Mademoiselle, that when the painters and sculptors of the middle ages placed two figures in adoration beside some glorious saint they have always given them a filial resemblance?

When you see your name among those dear to me, under whose protection I place my books, remember this likeness and you will find here not so much a homage as an expression of the fraternal affection felt for you by

Your servant,   De Balzac.

For souls easily moved to joyous feelings there comes a delightful moment when night is not yet and day is no more; the twilight casts its soft tones or its fantastic reflections over everything, and invites to a revery which blends vaguely with the play of light and shadow. The silence that nearly always reigns at such a moment renders it particularly dear to artists, who then gather up their thoughts, stand back a little from their creations, at which they can see to work no longer, and judge them in the intoxication of a subject the esoteric meaning of which then blazes forth to the inner eyes of genius. He who has never stood pensive beside a friend at that dreamy, poetic moment will have difficulty in comprehending its unspeakable benefits. Thanks to the half-light, the *chiaro-scuro*, all the material deceptions employed by art to simulate truth disappear. If a picture is the thing concerned, the persons it represents seem to speak and move; the shadow is really shadow, the light is day, the flesh is living, the eyes turn, the blood flows in the veins, and the silks shimmer. At that hour illusion reigns unchallenged; perhaps it only rises at night-fall! Indeed, illusion is to thought a sort of night which we decorate with dreams. Then it is that she spreads her wings and bears the soul to the world of fantasy, — a world teeming with voluptuous caprices, where the artist forgets the actual world, forgets yesterday, to-day, to-morrow, all, even his distresses, the happy as well as the bitter ones.

At that magic hour a young painter, a man of talent, who saw nought in art but art itself, was perched on a double ladder which he used for the purpose of painting a very large picture, now nearly finished. There, criticising himself and admiring himself in perfect good faith, he was lost in one of those meditations which ravish the soul, enlarge it, caress it, and console it. His revery no doubt lasted long. Night came. Whether he tried to come down his ladder, or whether, thinking he was on the ground, he made some imprudent movement, he was unable to remember, but at any rate he fell, his head struck a stool, he lost consciousness and lay for a time, but how long he did not know, without moving.

A soft voice drew him from the sort of stupor in which he was plunged. When he opened his eyes a bright light made him close them again ; but through the veil that wrapped his senses he heard the murmur of women's voices, and felt two young and timid hands about his head. He soon recovered consciousness and perceived, by the light of one of those old-fashioned lamps called "double air-currents," the head of the loveliest young girl he had ever seen, — one of those heads which are often thought artistic fancies, but which for him suddenly realized the noble ideal which each artist creates for himself, and from which his genius proceeds. The face of the unknown maiden belonged, if we may say so, to the school of Prudhon, and it also possessed the poetic charm which Girodet has given to his imaginary visions. The delightful coolness of the temples, the evenness of the eyebrows, the purity of the outlines, the virginity strongly imprinted on that countenance, made the young girl a perfected being.

Her clothes, though simple and neat, bespoke neither wealth nor poverty. When the painter regained possession of himself, he expressed his admiration in a look of surprise as he stammered his thanks. He felt his forehead pressed by a handkerchief, and he recognized, in spite of the peculiar odor of an atelier, the strong fumes of hartshorn, used, no doubt, to bring him to himself. Next he noticed an old lady, like a countess of the old régime, who held the lamp 'and was advising her companion.

"Monsieur," replied the young girl to one of the painter's questions asked during the moment when he was still half-unconscious, "my mother and I heard the noise of your fall on the floor and we thought we also heard a groan. The silence which succeeded your fall alarmed us and we hastened to come up to you. Finding the key in the door we fortunately ventured to come in. We found you lying on the floor unconscious. My mother obtained what was necessary to bring you to and to stanch the blood. You are hurt in the forehead; there, do you feel it?"

"Yes, now I do," he said.

"It is a mere nothing," said the old mother, "fortunately your fall was broken by that lay-figure."

"I feel much better," said the painter; "all I want is a carriage to take me home. The porter can fetch it."

He tried to reiterate his thanks to the two ladies, but at every sentence the mother interrupted him, saying: "To-morrow, monsieur, put on blisters or apply leeches; drink a few cups of some restorative; take care of yourself, — falls are dangerous."

The young girl glanced shyly at the painter, and around the studio. Her look and demeanor were those of perfect propriety, and her eyes seemed to express, with a spontaneity that was full of grace, the interest that women take in whatever troubles men. These unknown ladies appeared to ignore the works of the painter in presence of the suffering man. When he had reassured them as to his condition they left the room, after examining him with a solicitude that was devoid of either exaggeration or familiarity, and without asking any indiscreet questions, or seeking to inspire him with a wish to know them. Their conduct was marked with every sign of delicacy and good taste. At first their noble and simple manners produced but little effect upon the painter, but later, when he recalled the circumstances, he was greatly struck by them.

Reaching the floor below that on which the studio was situated, the old lady exclaimed, gently, "Adélaïde, you left the door open!"

"It was to succor me," replied the painter, with a smile of gratitude.

"Mamma, you came down just now," said the young girl, blushing.

"Shall we light you down?" said the mother to the painter; "the stairway is dark."

" Oh, thank you, madame, but I feel much better."

" Hold by the baluster."

The two women stood on the landing to light the young man, listening to the sound of his steps.

To explain all that made this scene piquant and unexpected to the painter, we must add that he had only lately removed his studio to the attic of this house, which stood at the darkest and muddiest part of the rue de Suresnes, nearly opposite to the church of the Madeleine, a few steps from his apartments, which were in the rue des Champs Élysées. The celebrity his talent had won for him made him dear to France, and he was just beginning to no longer feel the troubles of want, and to enjoy, as he said, his last miseries. Instead of going to his work in a studio beyond the barrier, the modest price of which had hitherto been in keeping with the modesty of his earnings, he now satisfied a desire, of daily growth, to avoid the long walk and the loss of time which had now become a thing of the utmost value.

No one in the world could have inspired deeper interest that Hippolyte Schinner, if he had only consented to be known; but he was not one of those who readily confide the secrets of their heart. He was the idol of a poor mother who had brought him up at a cost of stern privations. Mademoiselle Schinner, the daughter of an Alsatian farmer, was not married.

Her tender soul had once been cruelly wounded by a wealthy man who boasted of little delicacy in love. The fatal day when, in the glow of youth and beauty, in the glory of her life, she endured at the cost of all her beautiful illusions, and of her heart itself, the disenchantment which comes to us so slowly and yet so fast, — for we will not believe in evil until too late, and then it seems to come too rapidly, — that day was to her a whole century of reflection, and it was also a day of religious thoughts and resignation. She refused the alms of the man who had betrayed her; she renounced the world, and made an honor of her fault. She gave herself up to maternal love, enjoying in exchange for the social enjoyments to which she had bid farewell, its fullest delights. She lived by her labor, and found her wealth in her son; and the day came, the hour came which repaid her for the long, slow sacrifices of her indigence. At the last Exhibition her son had received the cross of the Legion of honor. The newspapers, unanimous in favor of a hitherto ignored talent, rang with praises that were now sincere. Artists themselves recognized Schinner as a master, and the dealers were ready to cover his canvases with gold.

At twenty-five years of age Hippolyte Schinner, to whom his mother had transmitted her woman's soul, fully recognized his position in the world. Wishing to give his mother the pleasures that society had so long withdrawn from her, he lived for her only, — hoping to see her some day, through the power of his fame and fortune, happy, rich, respected, and surrounded by celebrated men.

Schinner had therefore chosen his friends among the most honorable and distinguished men of his own age. Hard to satisfy in his choice, he wished to gain a position even higher than that his talents gave him. By forcing him to live in solitude (that mother of great thoughts) the toil to which he had vowed himself from his youth up had kept him true to the noble beliefs which adorn the earlier years of life. His adolescent soul had lost none of the many forms of chastity which make a young man a being apart, a being whose heart abounds in felicity, in poesy, in virgin hopes, — feeble to the eyes of worn-out men, but deep because they are simple. He was endowed by nature with the gentle, courteous manners, which are those of the heart, and which charm even those who are not able to comprehend them. He was well made. His voice, which echoed his soul, roused noble sentiments in the souls of others, and bore testimony by a certain candor in its tones to his innate modesty. Those who saw him felt drawn to him by one of those moral attractions which, happily, scientific men cannot analyze; if they could they would find some phenomena of galvanism, or the flow of heaven knows what fluid, and formulate our feelings in proportions of oxygen and electricity.

These details may perhaps enlighten persons who are bold by nature, and also men with good cravats, as to why Hippolyte Schinner, in the absence of the porter, whom he had sent to the rue de la Madeleine for a hackney-coach, did not ask the porter's wife any question as to the two ladies whose kindness of heart accident had revealed to him. But though he answered merely yes or no to the questions, natural enough under the circumstances, which the woman put to him on his accident, and on the assistance rendered to him by the occupants of the fourth floor, he could not prevent her from obeying the instincts of her race. She spoke of the two ladies in the interests of her own policy and according to the subterranean judgment of a porter's lodge.

" Ah !" she said, " that must have been Mademoiselle Leseigneur and her mother ; they have lived here the last four years. We can't make out what those ladies do. In the morning (but only till twelve o'clock) an old charwoman, nearly deaf, and who does n't talk any more than a stone wall, comes to help them ; in the evening two or three old gentlemen, decorated, like you, monsieur, — one of them keeps a carriage and servants, and people do say he has sixty thousand francs a year, — well, they spend the evening here and often stay very late.   The ladies are very quiet tenants, like you, monsieur; and economical ! — they live on nothing; as soon as they get a letter they pay their rent.   It is queer, monsieur, but the mother has n't the same name as the daughter.   Ah ! but when they go to walk in the Tuileries mademoiselle is dazzling, and often young gentlemen follow her home, but she has the door shut in their faces, — and she is right; for the proprietor would never allow — "

The coach having arrived, Hippolyte heard no more and went home.   His mother, to whom he related his adventure, dressed his wound and would not let him go back to the studio the next day.   Consultation was had, divers prescriptions were ordered, and Hippolyte was kept at home three days.   During this seclusion, his unoccupied imagination recalled to him in vivid fragments the details of the scene that followed his swoon.   The profile of the young girl was deeply cut upon the shadowy background of his inner sight; again he saw the faded face of the mother and felt Adélaïde's soft hands ; he remembered a gesture he had scarcely noticed at the time, but now its exquisite grace was thrown into relief by memory ; then an attitude or the tones of a melodious voice, made more melodious by recollection, suddenly reappeared, like things that are thrown to the bottom of a river and return to the surface.

So the first day on which he was able to go to work he went early to his studio; but the visit which he had, incontestably, the right to make to his neighbors was the real reason of his haste; his pictures were forgotten. The moment a passion bursts its swaddling-clothes it finds inexplicable pleasures known only to those who love. Thus there are persons who will know why the painter slowly mounted the stairs of the fourth story; they will be in the secret of those rapid pulsations of his heart as he came in sight of the brown door of the humble apartments occupied by Mademoiselle Leseigneur. This young girl, who did not bear the same name as her mother, had awakened a thousand sympathies in the young painter; he longed to find in her certain similarities of position to his own, and he invested her with the misfortunes of his own origin. While he worked, Hippolyte gave himself, complacently, to thoughts of love, and he made as much noise as he could, to induce the ladies to think of him as much as he thought of them. He stayed very late at the studio, and dined there. About seven o'clock he went down to call on his neighbors.

No painter of manners and customs has dared to initiate us — restrained, perhaps, by a sense of propriety — into the truly singular interiors of certain Parisian homes, into the secret of those dwellings whence issue such fresh, such elegant toilets. women so brilliant on the outside who nevertheless betray signs of an equivocal fortune. If the painting of such a home is here too frankly drawn, if you find it tedious, do not blame the description, which forms, as it were, an integral part of the history ; for the aspect of the apartments occupied by his neighbors had a great influence upon the hopes and feelings of Hippolyte Schinner.

The house belonged to one of those proprietors in whom there is a pre-existent horror of repairs or improvements, — one of the men who consider their position as house-owners in Paris as their business in life. In the grand chain of moral species such men hold the middle place between usurers and misers. Optimists from self-interest, they are all faithful to the *statu quo* of Austria. If you mention moving a cupboard or a door, or making the most necessary of ventilators, their eyes glitter, their bile rises, they rear like a frightened horse. When the wind has knocked over a chimney-pot they fall ill of it, and deprive themselves and their families of an evening at the Gymnase or the Porte-Saint-Martin to pay damages. Hippolyte, who, apropos of certain embellishments he wished made to his studio, had enjoyed, gratis, the playing of a comic scene by Monsieur Molineux, the proprietor, was not at all surprised by the blackened, soiled colors, the oily tints, the spots, and other disagreeable accessories which adorned the woodwork. These stigmata of poverty are never without a certain poetry to an artist.

Mademoiselle Leseigneur herself opened the door. Recognizing the young painter she bowed to him; then, at the same moment, with Parisian dexterity, and that presence of mind which pride affords, she turned and shut the door of a glazed partition through which Hippolyte might have seen linen hung to dry on lines above a cheap stove, an old flock bed, coal, charcoal, flatirons, a water-filter, china and glass, and all utensils necessary to a small household. Muslin curtains, that were sufficiently clean, carefully concealed this " capharnaüm,"—a word then familiarly applied to such domestic laboratories, ill-lighted by narrow windows opening on a court.

With the rapid glance of an artist Hippolyte had seen the furnishing, the character, and the condition of this first apartment, which was in fact one room cut in two. The respectable half, which answered the double purpose of ante-chamber and dining-room, was hung with an old yellow paper, and a velvet border, manufactured no doubt by Réveillon, the holes and the spots of which had been carefully concealed under wafers. Engravings representing the battles of Alexander, by Lebrun, in tarnished frames, decorated the walls at equal distances. In the centre of the room was a massive mahogany table, old-fashioned in shape, and a good deal rubbed at the corners. A small stove, with a straight pipe and no elbow, hardly seen, stood before the chimney, the fireplace in which was turned into a closet. By way of an odd contrast, the chairs, which were of carved mahogany, showed the relics of past splendor, but the red leather of the seats, the gilt nails, and the gimps showed as many wounds as an old sergeant of the Imperial Guard. This room served as a museum for a variety of things that are only found in certain amphibious households, unnameable articles, which belong both to luxury and poverty. Among them Hippolyte noticed a spy-glass, handsomely ornamented, which hung above the little greenish mirror on the mantel-shelf. To complete the oddity of this furniture, a shabby sideboard stood between the chimney and the partition, made of common pine painted in mahogany, which of all woods is least successfully imitated. But the red and slippery floor, the shabby bits of carpet before the chairs, and all the furniture, shone with the careful rubbing which gives its own lustre to old things, and brings out all the clearer their dilapidations, their age, and their long service.

The room gave out an indefinable odor resulting from the exhalations of the capharnaüm mingled with the atmosphere of the dining-room and that of the staircase, though the window was open and the breeze from the street stirred the cambric curtains, which were carefully arranged to hide the window-frame where preceding tenants had marked their presence by various carvings, — a sort of domestic frescoing.

Adélaïde quickly opened the door of the next room, into which she ushered the painter with evident pleasure. Hippolyte, who had seen the same signs of poverty in his mother's home, noticed them now with that singular keenness of impression which characterizes the first acquisitions of our memory; and he was able to understand, better perhaps than others could have done, the details of such an existence. Recognizing the things of his childhood, the honest young fellow felt neither contempt for the hidden poverty before him, nor pride in the luxury he had lately achieved for his mother.

"Well, monsieur, I hope you are none the worse for your fall?" said the mother, rising from an old-fashioned sofa at the corner of the fireplace, and offering him a chair.

"No, madame. I have come to thank you for the good care you gave me; and especially mademoiselle, who heard me fall."

While making this speech, full of the adorable stupidity which the first agitations of a true love produce in the soul, Hippolyte looked at the young girl. Adélaïde lighted the lamp with the double current of air, no doubt for the purpose of suppressing a tallow candle placed in a large pewter candlestick that was covered with drippings from an unusual flow of tallow. She bowed slightly, placed the candlestick on the chimney-piece, and sat down near her mother, a little behind the painter, so as to look at him at her ease, while seemingly engaged in making the lamp burn; for the feeble flame of the double current, affected by the dampness of the tarnished chimney, sputtered and struggled with an ill-cut, black wick. Observing the mirror above the mantel-shelf, Hippolyte promptly looked into it to see and admire Adélaïde. The little scheme of the young girl served therefore only to embarrass them both.

While talking with Madame Leseigneur, for Hippolyte at first gave her that name, he examined the salon, but discreetly and with propriety. The Egyptian figures of the andirons (made of iron) could scarcely be seen on the hearth full of ashes, where two small sticks of wood were trying to meet each other in front of an imitation back-log of earthenware. An old Aubusson carpet, well-mended and much faded and worn, hardly covered the tiled floor, which felt cold to the feet. The walls were hung with a reddish paper in the style of a brocade with buff designs. In the centre of the partition opposite to the windows the painter observed an indentation and cracks in the paper, made by the two doors of a folding-bed, where Madame Leseigneur doubtless slept, and which was only partly concealed by a sofa placed in front of it. Opposite to the chimney, and above a chest of drawers in mahogany, the style of which was handsome and in good taste, was the portrait of an officer of high rank, which the poor light hardly enabled the painter to make out; but, from what he could see of it the thought occurred to him that the frightful daub must have been painted in China. The red silk curtains to the windows were faded, like the coverings of the furniture in this salon with two purposes. On the marble top of the chest of drawers was a valuable tray of malachite, holding a dozen coffee-cups, exquisitely painted, and made no doubt at Sèvres. On the mantel-shelf was the inevitable Empire clock, a warrior driving the four horses of a chariot, the twelve spokes of the wheel each telling an hour. The wax tapers in the candelabra were yellow with smoke, and at each end of the shelf was a china vase filled with artificial flowers covered with dust and mixed with mosses.

Hippolyte noticed a card-table in the centre of the room, laid out with new packs of cards. To an observer there was something indescribably sad in this scene of poverty decked out like an old woman who tries to give the lie to her face. Most men of common-sense would have secretly and immediately formulated to their own minds a problem: were these women honor and uprightness itself; or did they live by cards and scheming? But the sight of Adélaïde was to a young man as pure as Schinner the proof of perfect innocence, and it provided the incoherencies of the room with honorable causes.

" My dear," said the old lady to her daughter, " I am cold ; make us a little fire, and give me my shawl."

Adélaïde went into an adjoining room, where no doubt she slept herself, and returned, bringing her mother a cashmere shawl which when new must have been of great value, but being old, faded, and full of darns, it harmonized with the furniture of the room. Madame Lescigneur wrapped it artistically about her with the cleverness of an old woman who wishes to make you believe in the truth of her words. The young girl darted into the capharnaüm, and reappeared with a handful of small wood which she threw into the fire.

It would be difficult to write down the conversation which took place between these three persons. Guided by the tact which deprivations and trials endured in youth nearly always give a man, Hippolyte did not venture on the slightest allusion to the position of his neighbors, though he saw all around him the signs of an ill-disguised indigence. The simplest question would have been indiscreet, and permissible only in the case of an old friend. And yet the painter was deeply preoccupied by this hidden poverty ; his generous heart ached for it ; knowing, however, that all kinds of pity, even the most sympathetic, may be offensive, he grew embarrassed by the conflict that existed between his

thoughts and his words. The two ladies talked first
of painting; for women readily understand the secret
embarrassments of a first visit; perhaps they feel
them, and the nature of their minds gives them the
art of overcoming them. By questioning the young
man on matters of his profession and his studies
Adélaïde and her mother emboldened him to converse.
The little nothings of their courteous and lively conversation soon led him naturally to remarks and reflections
which showed the nature of his habits and his mind.

Sorrows had prematurely withered the face of the old
lady, who must once have been handsome, though
nothing remained of her good looks but the strong
features and outlines, — in other words, the skeleton of
a face which still showed infinite delicacy and much
charm in the play of the eyes, which possessed a certain expression peculiar to the women of the old court,
and which no words can define. These delicate and
subtle points may, however, denote an evil nature;
they may mean feminine guile and cunning raised to
their highest pitch as much as they may, on the other
hand, reveal the delicacy of a noble soul. In fact, the
face of a woman is embarrassing to all commonplace
observers, inasmuch as the difference between frankness
and duplicity, between the genius of intrigue and the
genius of the heart is, to such observers, imperceptible.
A man endowed with a penetrating insight can guess

the meaning of those fleeting tones produced by a line more or less curved, a dimple more or less deep, a feature more or less rounded or prominent. The understanding of such diagnostics lies entirely within the domain of intuition, which alone can discover what others are seeking to hide. The face of this old lady was like the apartment she occupied; it seemed as difficult to know whether the penury of the latter covered vices or integrity as to decide whether Adélaïde's mother was an old coquette accustomed to weigh and to calculate and to sell everything, or a loving woman full of dignity and noble qualities.

But at Schinner's age the first impulse of the heart is to believe in goodness. So, as he looked at Adélaïde's noble and half-disdainful brow, and into her eyes that were full of soul and of thought, he breathed, so to speak, the sweet and modest perfumes of virtue. In the middle of the conversation he took occasion to say something about portraits in general that he might have an opportunity to examine the hideous pastel over the chimney-piece, the colors of which had faded and in some places crumbled off.

"No doubt that portrait is valuable to you, ladies, on account of its resemblance," he said, looking at Adélaïde, "for the drawing is horrible."

"It was done in China, in great haste," said the old lady, with some emotion.

She looked up at the miserable sketch with that surrender to feeling which the memory of happiness brings when it falls upon the heart like a blessed dew, to whose cool refreshment we delight to abandon ourselves. But in that old face thus raised there were also the traces of an eternal grief. At least, that was how the painter chose to interpret the attitude and face of his hostess, beside whom he now seated himself.

"Madame," he said, "before long the colors of that pastel will have faded out. The portrait will then exist only in your memory. You will see there a face that is dear to you, but which no one else will be able to recognize. Will you permit me to copy that picture on canvas? It will be far more durable than what you have there on paper. Grant me, as a neighbor, the pleasure of doing you this service. There come times when an artist is glad to rest from his more important compositions by taking up some other work, and it will really be a relief to me to paint that head."

The old lady quivered as she heard these words, and Adélaïde cast upon the artist a thoughtful glance which seemed like a gush of the soul itself. Hippolyte wished to attach himself to his two neighbors by some tie, and to win the right to mingle his life with theirs. His offer, addressing itself to the deepest affections of the heart, was the only one it was possible for him to make ; it satisfied his artist's pride, and did not wound that of the ladies. Madame Leseigneur accepted it without either eagerness or reluctance, but with that consciousness of generous souls, who know the extent of the obligations such acts fasten on them, and who accept them as proofs of respect, and as testimonials to their honor.

"I think," said the painter, "that that is a naval uniform?"

"Yes," she said, "that of a captain in the navy. Monsieur de Rouville, my husband, died at Batavia, in consequence of wounds received in a fight with an English vessel which he met off the coast of Asia. He commanded a frigate mounting fifty-six guns, but the 'Revenge' was a ninety-gun ship. The battle was unequal, but my husband maintained it bravely until night, under cover of which he was able to escape. When I returned to France, Bonaparte was not yet in power, and I was refused a pension. Lately, when I applied for one again, the minister told me harshly that if the Baron de Rouville had emigrated I should not have lost him, and he would now in all probability be a vice-admiral; his Excellency finally refused my application under some law of forfeiture. I made the attempt, to which certain friends urged me, only for the sake of my poor Adélaïde. I have always felt a repugnance to hold out my hand for money on the ground of a sorrow which deprives a woman of her voice and her strength. I do not like these valuations of blood irreparably shed."

"Dear mother, it always harms you to talk on this subject."

At these words the Baronne Leseigneur de Rouville bowed her head and said no more.

"Monsieur," said the young girl to Hippolyte, "I thought that the occupation of a painter was generally a rather quiet one?"

At this question Schinner blushed, recollecting the noise he had been making overhead. Adélaïde did not finish what she seemed about to say, and perhaps saved him from telling some fib, for she suddenly rose at the sound of a carriage driving up to the door. She went into her room and returned with two gilt candelabra filled with wax tapers which she quickly lighted. Then, without waiting for the bell to ring, she opened the door of the first room and placed the lamp on the table. The sound of a kiss given and received went to the depths of Hippolyte's heart. The impatience of the young man to see who it was that treated Adélaïde so familiarly was not very quickly relieved, for the new arrivals held a murmured conversation with the girl, which he thought very long.

At last, however, Mademoiselle de Rouville reappeared, followed by two men whose dress, physiognomy,

and general appearance were a history in themselves.
The first, who was about sixty years of age, wore one
of those coats invented, I believe, for Louis XVIII.,
then reigning, in which the most difficult of all vestuary
problems was solved by the genius of a tailor who ought
to be immortalized. That artist knew, not a doubt of
it! the art of transitions, which constituted the genius
of that period, politically so fickle. Surely, it was a rare
merit to know how to judge, as that tailor did, of his
epoch! This coat, which the young men of the present
day may consider a myth, was neither civil nor military, but might pass at a pinch for either military or
civil. Embroidered fleurs-de-lis adorned the flaps behind. The gold buttons were also fleur-de-lised. On
the shoulders, two unused eyelet-holes awaited the useless epaulets. These military symptoms were there like
a petition without a backer. The buttonhole of the old
man who wore this coat (of the color called " king's
blue ") was adorned with numberless ribbons. He held,
and no doubt always did hold in his hand his three-
cornered hat with gold tassels, for the snowy wings of his
powdered hair showed no signs of the pressure of that
covering. He looked to be no more than fifty, and
seem to enjoy robust health. While there was in him
every sign of the frank and loyal nature of the old
émigrés, his appearance denoted also easy and liber-
tine habits, — the gay passions and the careless joviality

of the *mousquetaires*, once so celebrated in the annals of gallantry. His gestures, his bearing, his manners, all proclaimed that he did not intend to change his royalism, nor his religion, nor his mode of life.

A truly fantastic figure followed this gay " *voltigeur* of Louis XIV." (that was the nickname given by the Bonapartists to these relics of the old monarchy) ; but to paint it properly the individual himself ought to be the principal figure in a picture in which he is only an accessory. Imagine a thin and withered personage, dressed like the first figure, and yet only the reflection or the shadow of it. The coat was new on the back of the one, and old and faded on that of the other. The powder in the hair of the counterpart seemed less white, the gold of the fleurs-de-lis less dazzling, the eyelets more vacant, the mind weaker, the vital strength nearer its termination, than in the other. In short, he realized that saying of Rivarol about Champcenetz : "He is my moonlight." He was only the echo of the other, a faint, dull echo ; between the two there was all the difference that there is between the first and last proof of a lithograph. The chevalier—for he was a chevalier —said nothing, and no one said anything to him. Was he a friend, a poor relation, a man who stayed by the old beau, as a female companion by an old woman? Was he a mixture of dog, parrot, and friend? Had he saved the fortune, or merely the life of his benefactor?

Was he the Trim of another Uncle Toby? Elsewhere,
as well as at Madame de Rouville's, he excited curiosity.
Who was there under the Restoration who could recollect an attachment before the Revolution on the part of
the Chevalier to his friend's wife, now dead for over
twenty years?

The personage who seemed to be the less ancient
of these two relics, advanced gallantly to the Baronne
de Rouville, kissed her hand, and seated himself beside
her. The other bowed and sat beside his chief, at a
distance represented by two chairs. Adélaïde came up
and put her elbows on the back of the chair occupied
by the old gentleman, imitating unconsciously the attitude which Guérin has given to Dido's sister in his
famous picture. Though the familiarity of the old gentleman was that of a father, it seemed for a moment to
displease her.

"What! do you mean to pout at me?" he said.

Then he cast one of those oblique glances full of
shrewdness and perception at Schinner, — a diplomatic
glance, the expression of which was prudent uneasiness, the polite curiosity of well-bred people who seem
to ask on seeing a stranger, "Is he one of us?"

"This is our neighbor," said the old lady, motioning
to Hippolyte. "Monsieur is the celebrated painter,
whose name you must know very well in spite of your
indifference to art."

The gentleman smiled at his old friend's mischievous omission of the name, and bowed to the young man.

"Yes, indeed," he said, "I have heard a great deal about his pictures in the Salon. Talent has many privileges, monsieur," he added, glancing at the artist's red ribbon. "That distinction which we acquire at the cost of our blood and long services, you obtain young; but all glories are sisters," he added, touching the cross of Saint-Louis which he wore.

Hippolyte stammered a few words of thanks and retired into silence, content to admire with growing enthusiasm the beautiful head of the young girl who charmed him. Soon he forgot in this delightful contemplation the evident poverty of her home. To him, Adélaïde's face detached itself from a luminous background. He answered briefly all questions which were addressed to him, and which he fortunately heard, thanks to that singular faculty of the soul which allows thought to run double at times. Who does not know what it is to continue plunged in a deep meditation, pleasurable or sad, to listen to the inward voice, and yet give attention to a conversation or a reading? Wonderful dualism, which often helps us to endure bores with patience! Hope, fruitful and smiling, brought him a thousand thoughts of happiness; what need for him to dwell on things about him? A child full of trust, he thought it shameful to analyze a pleasure.

After a certain lapse of time he was aware that the old lady and her daughter were playing cards with the old gentleman. As to the satellite, he stood behind his friend, wholly occupied with the latter's game, answering the mute questions the player made to him by little approving grimaces which repeated the interrogative motions of the other's face.

"Du Halga, I always lose," said the gentleman.

"You discard too carelessly," said the baroness.

"It is three months since I have been able to win a single game," said he.

"Monsieur le comte, have you aces?" asked the old lady.

"Yes, mark one," he answered.

"Don't you want me to advise you?" said Adélaïde.

"No, no; stay there in front of me! It would double my losses if I could n't see your face."

At last the game ended. The old gentleman drew out his purse and threw two louis on the table, not without ill-humor. "Forty francs, as true as gold!" said he; "and, the deuce! it is eleven o'clock."

"It is eleven o'clock," repeated the mute personage, looking at the painter.

The young man, hearing those words rather more distinctly than the others, thought it was time to withdraw. Returning to the world of common ideas, he uttered a few ordinary phrases, bowed to the baroness, her daughter, and the two gentlemen, and went home, a prey to the first joys of true love, without trying to analyze the little events of this evening.

The next day the painter was possessed with the most violent desire to see Adélaide again. If he had listened to his passion he would have gone to his neighbors on arriving at his studio at six o'clock in the morning. But he still kept his senses sufficiently to wait till the afternoon. As soon, however, as he thought he could present himself he went down and rang their bell, not without much palpitation of the heart, and then, blushing like a girl, he timidly asked Mademoiselle Leseigneur, who had opened the door, for the portrait of Monsieur de Rouville.

"But come in," said Adélaide, who had no doubt heard his step on the stairway.

The painter followed her, abashed and out of countenance, not knowing what to say, — so stupid did his happiness make him. To see Adélaide, to listen to the rustle of her gown after longing all the morning to be near her, after jumping up a dozen times and saying, "I will go!" and yet not daring to do so, — this, to him, was so rich and full a life that such emotions if too prolonged would have exhausted his soul. The heart has the singular property of giving an extraordinary value to nothings. We know the joy a traveller feels in gathering the twig of a plant or a leaf unknown to him, when he has risked his life in the quest. The nothings of love are precious in the same way.

The old lady was not in the salon. When the young girl found herself alone with the painter she brought a chair and stood on it to take down the portrait; but perceiving that she could not unhook it without stepping on the chest of drawers, she turned to Hippolyte and said to him, blushing : —

"I am not tall enough. Will you take it down?"

A feeling of modesty, shown in the expression of her face and the accent of her voice, was the real motive of her request; and the young man, so understanding it, gave her one of those intelligent glances which are the sweetest language of love. Seeing that the painter had guessed her feeling, Adélaïde lowered her eyes with that impulse of pride which belongs only to virgins. Not finding a word to say and feeling almost intimidated, the painter took down the picture, examined it gravely in the light from the window, and then went away without saying anything more to Mademoiselle Leseigneur than, " I will return it soon."

Each during that rapid moment felt one of those mysterious, violent commotions the effects of which in the soul can be compared only to those produced by a stone when flung into a lake. The soft expansions which then are born and succeed each other, indefinable, multiplying, unending, agitate the heart as the rings in the water widen in the distance from the centre where the stone fell.

Hippolyte returned to his studio, armed with the portrait. His easel was already prepared with a canvas, the palette was set with its colors, the brushes cleaned, the light arranged. Until his dinner-hour he worked at the picture with that eagerness which artists put into their caprices. In the evening he again went to Madame de Rouville's and remained from nine to eleven. Except for the different topics of conversation, this evening was very like its predecessor. The old men arrived at the same hour, the same game of piquet was played, the same phrases were repeated, and the sum lost by Adélaïde's old friend was the same as that lost the night before, — the only change being that Hippolyte, grown a little bolder, ventured to talk to Adélaïde.

Eight days passed in this way, during which the feelings of the painter and those of the young girl underwent those delicious, slow transformations which lead young souls to a perfect understanding. So, day by day, Adélaïde's glance as she welcomed her friend became more intimate, more trustful, gayer, and more frank ; her voice, her manners grew more winning, more familiar. They both laughed and talked and communicated their ideas to each other, talking of themselves with the naïveté of two children, who in the course of one day can make acquaintance as if they had lived

together for three years. Schinner wished to learn
piquet. Totally ignorant of the game he naturally
made blunder after blunder; and, like the old gentleman, he lost nearly every game.

Without having yet told their love, the two lovers
knew very well that they belonged to each other.
Hippolyte delighted in exercising his power over his
timid friend. Many a concession was made to him by
Adélaïde, who, tender and devoted as she was, was
easily the dupe of those pretended sulks which the
least intelligent of lovers, and the most artless of
maidens invent, and constantly employ, just as spoilt
children take advantage of the power their mother's
love has given them. For instance, all familiarity suddenly ceased between the old count and Adélaïde.
The young girl understood the painter's gloom, and
the thoughts hidden beneath the folds of his brow,
from the harsh tone of the exclamations he made as
the old man unceremoniously kissed her hands or
throat. On the other hand, Mademoiselle Leseigneur
soon began to hold her lover to a strict account of
his slightest actions. She was so uneasy and so unhappy if he did not come; she knew so well how to
scold him for his absence, that the painter renounced
seeing his friends, and went no longer into society.
Adélaïde showed a woman's jealousy on discovering
that sometimes, after leaving Madame de Rouville's

at eleven o'clock, the painter made other visits and appeared in several of the gayest salons of Paris. That sort of life, she told him, was very bad for his health, and she asserted, with the profound conviction to which the tones, the gesture, the look of those we love give such immense power, that "a man who was obliged to give his time and the charms of his mind to several women at once, could never be the possessor of a really deep affection."

So the painter was soon led, as much by the despotism of his passion as by the exactions of a young girl, to live almost wholly in the little home where all things pleased him. No love was ever purer or more ardent. On either side the same faith, the same mind, the same delicacy, made their passion grow apace without the help of those sacrifices by which so many persons seek to prove their love. Between these lovers there existed so constant an interchange of tender feelings that they never knew who gave or who received the most. A natural, involuntary inclination made the union of their souls close indeed. The progress of this true feeling was so rapid that two months after the accident through which the painter obtained the happiness of knowing Adélaïde, their lives had become one and the same life. From early morning the young girl, hearing a step above her, said to herself, "He is there!" When Hippolyte returned home to

dine with his mother he never failed to stop on his
way to greet his friends ; and in the evening he rushed
to them, at the usual hour, with a lover's punctuality.
Thus the most tyrannical of loving women, and the
heart most ambitious of love could have found no
fault with the young painter. Adélaïde did indeed
taste an unalloyed and boundless happiness in finding
realized to its fullest extent the ideal of which youth
dreams.

The old gentleman now came less often ; the jealous
Hippolyte took his place in the evening at the green
table, and was equally unlucky at cards. But in the
midst of his happiness, he thought of Madame de
Rouville's disastrous position, — for he had seen more
than one sign of her distress, — and little by little an
importunate thought forced its way into his mind.
Several times, as he returned home, he had said to
himself, " What ! twenty francs every evening ? "
The lover dared not admit a suspicion. He spent
two months on the portrait, and when it was finished,
varnished, and framed, he thought it one of his best
works. Madame de Rouville had never mentioned it
to him ; was it indifference or pride which kept her
silent? The painter could not explain it to himself.
He plotted gayly with Adélaïde to hang the picture
in its right place when Madame de Rouville had gone
out for her usual walk in the Tuileries.

The day came, and Adélaïde went up, for the first time alone, to Hippolyte's studio, under pretence of seeing the portrait favorably in the light in which it was painted. She stood before it silent and motionless, in a delicious contemplation where all the feelings of womanhood were blended into one, — and that one, boundless admiration for the man she loved. When the painter, uneasy at her silence, leaned forward to look at her, she held out her hand to him unable to say a word; but two tears dropped from her eyes. Hippolyte took that hand and kissed it, and for a moment they looked at each other in silence, both wishing to avow their love, neither of them daring to. As the painter held her hand within his own, an equal warmth, an equal throb, told them that their hearts were beating with the same pulse. Too deeply moved, the young girl gently left her lover's side, saying, with a guileless look, " You will make my mother very happy."

" Your mother — only ? " he asked.

" Oh, as for me, I am too happy," she replied.

The painter bent his head and was silent, frightened at the violence of the feeling the tone of those words awakened in his heart. Both understood the danger of their position, and they went downstairs with the portrait and put it in its place. That night Hippolyte dined for the first time with the baroness, who kissed

him with tearful gratitude. In the evening the old
émigré, a former comrade of the Baron de Rouville,
made a special visit to his two friends to announce his
appointment as a vice-admiral. His terrestrial navi-
gations across Germany and Russia had been credited
to him as naval campaigns. When he saw the portrait,
he shook the painter by the hand, exclaiming: "Faith!
though my old carcass is not worth preserving, I'd
gladly give five hundred pistoles for anything as like me
as that is like my friend Rouville."

Hearing the proposal, the baroness looked at her friend
with a smile, and let the signs of a sudden gratitude
appear on her face. Hippolyte fancied that the old
admiral intended to pay the price of the two portraits
in paying for his own; he was offended, and said
stiffly, "Monsieur, if I were a portrait-painter I should
not have painted that one."

The admiral bit his lips and began to play. The
painter sat by Adélaïde, who proposed him six kings
which he accepted. While playing, he noticed in
Madame de Rouville a degree of eagerness for the
game which surprised him. The old lady had never
before manifested such anxiety to win, or looked with
such pleasure at the admiral's gold coins. During that
evening suspicions once more came up in Hippolyte's
mind to trouble his happiness and give him a certain
sense of distrust. Did Madame de Rouville live by

cards? Was she playing at that moment to pay some debt, or was she driven to it by some necessity? Perhaps her rent was due. That old man seemed too worldly-wise to let her win his money for nothing. What interest brought him to that poor house, — he, a rich man? Why, though formerly so familiar with Adélaïde, had he lately renounced all familiarities, — his right perhaps? These involuntary thoughts prompted Schinner to examine the old man and the baroness, whose glances of intelligence and the oblique looks they cast on Adélaïde and himself displeased him greatly.

"Can it be that they deceive me?"

To Hippolyte the thought was horrible, withering; and he believed it just so far as to let it torture him. He resolved to remain after the departure of the two old men, so as to confirm his suspicions or get rid of them. He drew out his purse at the end of the game, intending to pay Adélaïde, but his mind was so filled with these poignant thoughts that he laid it on the table and fell into a revery which lasted several minutes. Then, ashamed of his silence, he rose, answered some commonplace inquiry of Madame de Rouville's, going close up to her to scrutinize that aged face. He left the salon a prey to dreadful uncertainties. After going down a few stairs, he recollected his purse and went back to get it. "I left my purse," he said to Adélaïde.

"No," she answered, coloring.

" I thought I left it there," he said, pointing to tho card-table.

Ashamed for both mother and daughter at not finding it, he stood looking at them with a bewildered air which made them both laugh ; then he turned pale, and felt in his waistcoat pockets, stammering, " I am mistaken, I must have it somewhere."

At one end of the purse were fifteen louis, at the other some small change. The robbery was so flagrant, so impudently denied, that Hippolyte had no doubt as to the character of his neighbors. He stood still on the staircase, for he could hardly go down ; his legs trembled, his head swam, he perspired, his teeth chattered in a cold chill, and he was literally unable to walk in the grasp of that cruel convulsion caused by the overthrow of all his hopes. At that moment, a crowd of apparently trifling circumstances came back into his mind, all corroborating his dreadful suspicions ; taken together with the certainty of this last act, they opened his eyes to the character and the life of the two women. Had they waited till the portrait was done to steal his purse ? Thus combined with profit, the theft seemed more odious than at first. The painter remembered, with anguish, that for the last two or three evenings Adélaide had examined, with what seemed girlish curiosity, the netting of the worn silk, probably to ascertain the sum contained in the purse, — making jests that

seemed innocent, but were no doubt intended to cover
the fact that she was watching for the time when the
purse should be well filled.

"The old admiral must have good reasons for not
marrying her, and the baroness intends that I —"

He stopped, and did not continue the thought, for it
was checked by one more just.

"If," thought he, "the baroness wished me to marry
her daughter they would not have robbed me."

Then, unable to renounce his illusions, or to abandon
a love so deeply rooted in his being, he tried to find
some explanation. "My purse must have fallen on the
ground; perhaps it was under my chair; perhaps I
have it, I am so absent-minded!" He felt in all his
pockets with rapid motions, — but no, that cursed purse
was not in them. His cruel memory recalled every
particular of the fatal facts; he distinctly saw the purse
lying on the table. Unable to doubt the theft, he now
excused Adélaïde, saying to himself that no one ought
to judge the poor and unfortunate too hastily. No
doubt there was some secret in this apparently degrading action. He would not allow himself to believe
that that proud, noble face was a lie. Nevertheless,
that miserable apartment had now lost all those poesies
of love which once embellished it; he saw it as it was,
dirty and faded: it seemed the outward likeness of an
inward life without nobleness, unoccupied and vicious.

Are not our feelings written, so to speak, on the things about us?

The next morning he rose without having slept. The anguish of the heart, that serious moral malady, had made great strides into his being. To lose an imagined happiness, to renounce an expected future, is far more bitter suffering than that caused by the ruin of an experienced joy, however great that joy may have been. Is not hope better than memory? The meditations into which our souls suddenly fall are then like a shoreless sea, on whose bosom we may float for a moment, though nothing can save our love from sinking and perishing. It is a dreadful death. Are not our feelings the most vivid and glorious part of our lives? From such partial death as this come those great ravages seen in certain organizations that are both delicate and strong, when assailed by disillusions or by the balking of hopes and passions. Thus it was with the young painter. He went out early in the morning and walked about in the cool shade of the Tuileries, absorbed in thought, and taking no notice of any one. There, by chance, one of his young friends met him, a college and atelier comrade, with whom he had lived as with a brother.

" Why, Hippolyte, what's the matter?" said François Souchet, a young sculptor who had just obtained the *grand prix* and was soon going to Italy.

"I am very unhappy," replied Hippolyte, gravely.

"Nothing but a love-affair can make you so. Wealth, fame, consideration, — you have everything else!"

Little by little, the confidences began, and finally the painter acknowledged his love. When he spoke of the rue de Suresnes, and of a young girl living on the fourth story, "Halt!" cried Souchet, gayly, "that's a little girl I go to see every morning at the Assumption; I'm courting her. Why, my dear fellow, we all know her. Her mother is a baroness. Do you believe in baronesses who live on a fourth floor? Brrr! Well, well! you belong to the age of gold. The rest of us meet that old mother every day in the Tuileries. That face of hers, and the way she carries herself tells all. Come now, did you never guess what she is, from the way she carries her bag?"

The two friends walked about for some time, and several young men who knew Schinner and Souchet joined them. The painter's love-affair was related by the sculptor, who supposed it of little importance.

Many were the outcries, the laughs, the jests, innocent enough, but full of the familiar gayety of artists, and horribly painful to Hippolyte. A certain chastity of soul made him suffer at the sight of his heart's secret lightly tossed about, his passion torn to shreds, the young girl, whose life had seemed to him so modest, judged, truly or falsely, with such careless indifference.

“But, my dear fellow, have you never seen the baroness’s shawl?” said Souchet.

“Don’t you ever follow the little one when she goes to the Assumption?” said Joseph Bridau, a young art-student in Gros’s atelier.

“Ha! the mother has, among her other virtues, a gray dress which I regard as a type,” said Bixiou, the caricaturist.

“Listen, Hippolyte;” said the sculptor, “come here at four o’clock, and analyze the demeanor of the mother and daughter. If, after that, you have any doubts, I give you up, — nothing can ever be made of you; you ’ll be capable of marrying your porter’s daughter.”

The painter parted from his friends a victim to a contradiction of feelings. Adélaïde and her mother seemed to him above such accusations, and at the bottom of his heart he felt remorse for having ever doubted the purity of that young girl, so beautiful and so simple. He went to his studio, he passed the door of the room where she was sitting, and he felt within his soul the anguish that no man ever misunderstands. He loved Mademoiselle de Rouville so passionately that, in spite of the robbery of his purse, he adored her still. His love was like that of the Chevalier des Grieux, adoring and purifying his mistress in his thoughts as she sat in the cart on her way to the prison for lost women.

"Why should not my love make her the purest of beings? Shall I abandon her to sin and vice, and stretch no friendly hand to her?" That mission pleased him. Love makes profit out of all. Nothing attracts a young man so much as the thought of playing the part of a good genius to a woman. There is something truly chivalrous in such an enterprise which commends itself to lofty souls. Is it not the deepest devotion under the highest form, and the most gracious form? What grandeur in knowing that we love enough to love still where the love of others would be a dead thing!

Hippolyte sat down in his studio, and contemplated his picture without touching it. Night overtook him in that attitude. Wakened from his revery by the darkness, he went downstairs, met the old admiral on the stairway, gave him a gloomy glance and a bow, and fled away. He had meant to go to his neighbors, but the sight of Adélaïde's protector froze his heart and overcame his resolution. He asked himself, for the hundredth time, what interest it could be that brought that old beau, a man worth eighty-thousand francs a year, to that fourth story where he lost forty francs a night; that interest, he fancied, alas, he knew.

The next day and the following days Hippolyte spent on his work, trying to fight his passion by flinging himself into the rush of ideas and the fire of conception. He succeeded only partially. Study comforted him,

but it did not stifle the memory of those dear hours
passed with Adélaïde.   One evening, leaving his studio,
he found the door of the apartments of the two ladies
half-open.   Some one was standing in the recess of the
window.   The position of the door and the stairs was
such that Hippolyte could not pass without seeing
Adélaïde.   He bowed coldly, with a glance of indifference; then, judging of her sufferings by his own, an
inward tremor overcame him, thinking of the bitterness
his cold glance might have carried to a loving heart.
What! end the sweetest joys that ever filled two sacred
hearts, with the scorn of an eight days' absence, with a
contempt too deep for words? — horrible conclusion!
Perhaps that purse was found! he had never inquired;
perhaps Adélaïde had expected him, in vain, every
evening!   This thought, so simple, so natural, filled
the lover with fresh remorse; he asked himself if the
proofs of attachment the young girl had given him, if
those delightful conversations bearing the impress of
love and of a mind which charmed him did not deserve
at least an inquiry, — whether indeed they were not a
pledge of justification.   Ashamed of having resisted
the longings of his heart for one whole week, thinking
himself almost criminal in the struggle, he went that
same evening to Madame de Rouville's.   All his suspicions, all his thoughts of evil vanished at the sight of
the young girl, now pale and thin.

"Good God! what is the matter?" he said to her, after bowing to Madame de Rouville.

Adélaïde made no answer, but she gave him a sad, discouraged look which went to his heart.

"You look as if you had been working too hard," said the old lady. "You are changed. I fear we have been the cause of your seclusion. That portrait must have delayed other work more important for your reputation."

Hippolyte was only too happy to find so good an excuse for his absence. "Yes," he said, "I have been very busy — but I have suffered — "

At these words Adélaïde raised her head; her eyes no longer reproached him.

"You have, then, thought us indifferent to what makes you happy or unhappy?" said the old lady.

"I have done wrong," he said. "And yet there are sufferings which we can tell to no one, no matter who it is, even to a heart that may have known us long."

"The sincerity and the strength of friendship ought not to be measured by time. I have seen old friends who could not shed a tear for each other's misfortune," said the baroness, nodding her head.

"But tell me, what is the matter?" asked Hippolyte of the poor girl.

"Oh, nothing," said the baroness; "Adélaïde insisted on sitting up two or three nights to finish a piece of work; she would not listen to me when I told her that a day more or less could make no difference —"

Hippolyte was not listening. Seeing those two faces, so calm, so noble, he blushed for his suspicions and attributed the loss of the purse to some mysterious accident. That evening was delightful to him, and perhaps to her. There are secrets that young souls understand so well. Adélaïde divined her lover's thoughts. Without intending to reveal his wrong-doing, Hippolyte tacitly admitted it; he returned to his mistress more loving, more affectionate than ever, as if to buy a silent pardon. Adélaïde now tasted joys so sweet, so perfect, that the pangs which had cruelly bruised her spirit seemed but a slight penalty to pay for them. And yet that absolute accord between their hearts, that comprehension which was full of magic, was clouded suddenly by a little speech of Madame de Rouville's. "Let us get ready for our game," she said. "My old Kergarouët insists upon it."

That speech roused all the poor painter's fears; he blushed as he looked at Adélaïde's mother. Yet he could see on that face no other expression than one of a true kind-heartedness without insincerity; no latent thought destroyed its charm; in its shrewdness there was no perfidy; the gentle satire it expressed seemed tender, and no remorse marred its placidity. So he sat down at the card-table. Adélaïde shared his game, pretending that he did not know piquet and needed an adviser. While they played, signs of an understanding passed between the mother and daughter which again made Hippolyte anxious, — all the more because, for once, he was winning. At last, however, a lucky throw put the lovers in Madame de Rouville's debt. Hippolyte withdrew his hands from the table to search for money in his pockets, and suddenly saw lying before him a purse which Adélaïde had slipped there without his noticing her; the poor child held his own purse in her hand, and was hiding her confusion by pretending to look for money to pay her mother. The blood rushed so violently to Hippolyte's heart that he almost lost consciousness. The new purse substituted for the old one had the fifteen louis in it, and was worked with gold beads. The rings, the tassels, all proved the good taste of the maker, who had no doubt spent her little savings on those ornaments of her pretty work. It was impossible to say with greater delicacy that the painter's gift could be acknowledged only by a pledge of tenderness.

When Hippolyte, overcome with happiness, turned his eyes on Adélaïde and her mother he saw them trembling with pleasure, happy in the success of their little fraud. He felt himself small, petty, contemptible; he longed to punish himself, to rend his heart. Tears came into his eyes, and he sprang up with an irresistible

impulse, took Adélaïde in his arms, pressed her to his
heart, snatched a kiss, and cried, with the honest good-
faith of an artist, looking straight at the baroness: —

"I ask you to give her to me for my wife!"

Adélaïde's eyes as she looked at him were half-angry,
and Madame de Rouville, somewhat astonished, was
seeking a reply when the scene was interrupted by a
ring at the bell. The vice-admiral appeared, followed
by Madame Schinner. After guessing the cause of her
son's grief, which he had vainly tried to hide from
her, Hippolyte's mother had made inquiries among her
friends as to Adélaïde. Alarmed by the calumnies
which assailed the young girl, unknown to the old admiral, the Comte de Kergarouët, she went to the latter
and told him what she had heard. In his fury he wanted,
he said, "to cut the ears of those rascals." Excited by
his wrath he told Madame Schinner the secret of his
visits and his intentional losses at cards, that being the
only way in which the baroness's pride gave him a
chance to succor the widow of his old friend.

When Madame Schinner had paid her respects to
Madame de Rouville, the latter looked at the Comte de
Kergarouët, the Chevalier du Halga (the former friend
of the late Comtesse de Kergarouët), then at Hippolyte
and Adélaïde, and said, with the delightful manners of
the heart, "We seem, I think, to be a family party."

LA GRENADIÈRE.

----◆----

TO CAROLINE.

To the poesy of his Journey.
A Grateful Traveller.

La Grenadière is a little habitation on the right bank of the Loire, sloping towards it and about a mile from the bridge of Tours. Just here the river, broad as a lake, is strewn with green islets, and margined by rocky shores, on which are numerous country-houses, all built of white stone and surrounded by vineyards and gardens, in which the finest fruits in the world ripen under a sunny exposure. Industriously terraced by generation after generation, the hollows of the rock reflect the rays of the sun, and the artificial temperature thus produced allows the cultivation of the products of hot climates in the open ground.

From one of the least sunken of these hollows which cut into the hillside, rises the sharp steeple of Saint-Cyr, a little village to which the scattered houses nominally belong. A little beyond, the Choisille falls into the Loire, through a rich valley which runs up among the hills.   La Grenadière [The Pomegranate], standing half-way up the rocky shore, about three hundred feet from the church, is one of those venerable homesteads some two or three hundred years old, which are seen in every lovely situation in Touraine.   A cleft in the rock has facilitated the making of a stairway, which descends by easy steps to the "levée,"—the local name given to the dike built at the base of the slope to keep the Loire to its bed, and along which runs the mail road from Paris to Nantes.

At the top of this flight of steps is a gate opening on a narrow, stony road, cut between two terraces which resemble fortifications, covered with vines and palings to prevent the rolling down of the earth.   This pathway, starting from the foot of the upper terrace, and nearly hidden by the trees that crown it, leads to the house by a steep pitch, giving a view of the river which enlarges at every step.   This sunken path ends at a second gate, gothic in character, arched, and bearing a few simple ornaments, which is now in ruins and overgrown with gilli-flowers, ivy, mosses, and pellitory. These ineradicable plants decorate the walls of all the terraces, hanging from the clefts of the stone courses and designating each season by a garland of its own flowers.

Beyond this mouldy gate a little garden, wrested

from the rock by another terrace, with an old and
blackened balustrade which overlooks the rest, presents a lawn adorned by a few trees, and a multitude
of roses and other flowering plants. Opposite to the
gate, at the other end of the terrace, is a wooden
pavilion resting against a neighboring wall, the posts
of which are hidden under jasmine, honeysuckle, vines,
and clematis. In the middle of the garden stands the
house, beyond a vaulted portico covered with vines, on
which is the gate of a huge cellar hollowed in the rock.
The house is surrounded with vine-clad arbors, and
pomegranate-trees — which give their name to the place,
— are growing in the open ground. The façade has
two large windows separated by a very countrified front-
door, and three attic windows, placed very high up
in the roof relatively to the low height of the ground
floor. This roof has two gables and is covered with
slate. The walls of the main building are painted
yellow, and the door, the shutters on the lower floor,
and the blinds on the roof are green.

When you enter the house, you find a little hall-way
with a winding staircase, the grade of which changes
at every turn; the wood is rotten, and the balusters,
turning like a screw, are discolored by long usage.
To the right of the door is a vast dining-room with
antique panelling, floored in white tiles, manufactured
at Château-Regnault; on the left is the salon, a room

of the same size, but without panels, hung with a gold-colored paper with green bordering. Neither of the two rooms has a plastered ceiling. The joists are of walnut, and the spaces are filled in with a natural white clay mixed with hair. On he first floor are two large chambers with white-washed walls ; the stone chimney-pieces in these rooms are less richly carved than those in the rooms below. All the windows face south. To the north there is only a door opening behind the staircase on a vineyard.

On the left of the house, a building with a wooden front backs against the wall ; the wood being protected from the sun and rain by slates which lie in long blue lines, upright and transversal, upon the walls. The kitchen, consigned as it were to this cottage, communicates with the house, but it has an entrance of its own raised from the ground by a few steps, near to which is a deep well covered with a rustic pump ; its sides overgrown with water-plants and tall grass and juniper. This recent construction proves that La Grenadière was originally a mere *vendangeoir*, where the owners, living in the city (from which it is separated only by the broad bed of the Loire), came only to attend to their vintages, or to bring parties of pleasure. On such occasions they sent provisions for the day, and slept there at night only when the grapes were being gathered.

But the English have fallen like a swarm of grass-hoppers upon Touraine, and La Grenadière was furnished with a kitchen that they might hire it. Fortunately this modern appendage is concealed by the first lindens planted along a path running down a ravine behind the orchard. The vineyard, of about two acres, rises above the house, and overlooks it on a slope so steep that it is very difficult to climb. Between the back of the house and this hill, green with trailing shoots, is a narrow space of not more than five feet, always cold and damp, a sort of ditch full of rampant vegetation, and filled in rainy weather with the drainage from the vineyard, used to enrich the soil of the flower-beds of the terrace with the balustrade.

The little house of the vine-dresser backs against the left gable; it has a thatched roof and makes a sort of pendant to the kitchen. The whole property is enclosed by walls and palings; the orchard is planted with fruit-trees of all kinds; in short, not an inch of the precious soil is lost to cultivation. If man neglects an arid corner of this rock, Nature flings into it a fig-tree perhaps, or wild-flowers, or a few strawberry-vines sheltered among the stones.

Nowhere in the world can you find a home so modest, yet so grand, so rich in products, in fragrance, and in outlook. It is in the heart of Touraine, a little

Touraine in itself, where all the flowers, all the fruits, all the beauties of that region are fully represented. There are the grapes of every clime, the figs, the peaches, the pears of every species, melons growing wild in the open ground, as well as liquorice, the yellow broom of Spain, the oleanders of Italy, the jasmine of the Azores. The Loire flows at your feet. You look down upon it from a terrace raised thirty fathom above its capricious waters. You inhale its breezes coming fresh from the sea and perfumed on their way by the flowers along its shores. A wandering cloud, which changes at every instant its color and its form as it moves in space beneath the cloudless blue of heaven, gives a thousand varied aspects to each detail of that glorious scenery which meets the eye wherever turned. From there, you may see the river shores from Amboise, the fertile plain where rises Tours, its suburbs, its manufactories, and Le Plessis ; also a portion of the left bank, from Vouvray to Saint-Symphorien, describing a half-circle of smiling vineyards. The view here is limited only by the rich slopes of Cher, a blue horizon broken by parks and villas. To the west the soul is lost in contemplation of the broad sheet of waters which bears upon its bosom, at all hours, vessels with white sails filled with the winds which ever sweep its vast basin.

A prince might make La Grenadière his villa ; a poet would make it his home ; lovers would count it their sweetest refuge ; a worthy burgher of Tours might live there, — the spot has poems for all imaginations, for the humblest, for the coldest, as for the highest and the most fervent ; no one ever stayed there without breathing an atmosphere of happiness, without comprehending a tranquil life devoid of ambition, relieved of care. Revery is in the air, in the murmuring flow of waters ; the sands speak, they are sad or gay, golden or sullied : all is in motion around the possessor of this spot, motionless amid its ever-blooming flowers and its toothsome fruits. An Englishman gives a thousand francs merely to live six months in that humble dwelling, and he binds himself to gather no products ; if he wants the fruits, he pays a double rent ; if the wine tempts him, he doubles it again. What, then, is La Grenadière worth, with that flight of steps, the sunken path, the triple terrace, the two acres of vineyard, those balustrades, those roses, the portico, its pump, the wealth of tangled clematis and the cosmopolitan trees? Offer no price. La Grenadière cannot be bought. Sold once in 1690 for forty thousand francs, and left with bitter regret, as the Arab of the desert abandons a favorite horse, it still remains in the same family, of which it is the pride, the patrimonial jewel, the Regent diamond. To see is not to have, saith the poet. From these terraces you see three valleys of Touraine and the cathedral suspended in ether like a delicate filagree.

Can you pay for such treasures? Could you buy the health you will recover beneath those lindens?

In the spring of one of the finest years of the Restoration, a lady, accompanied by a maid and two children, came to Tours in search of a house. She saw La Grenadière and hired it. Perhaps the distance that separated it from the town decided her to take it. The salon was her bed-chamber; she put each child in one of the rooms on the upper floor, and the maid slept in a little chamber above the kitchen. The dining-room became the living-room of the little family. The lady furnished the house very simply, but with taste; there was nothing useless and nothing that conveyed a sense of luxury. The furniture was of walnut, without ornament. The neatness, and the harmony of the interior with the exterior made the charm of the house.

It was difficult to know whether Madame Williamson (that was the name the lady gave) belonged to the rich bourgeoisie, or to the upper nobility, or to certain equivocal classes of the feminine species. Her simplicity of life gave grounds for contradictory suppositions, though her manners seemed to confirm the most favorable. It was, therefore, not long after her arrival at Saint-Cyr that her reserved conduct excited the curiosity of idle persons, who had the provincial habit of remarking upon everything that promised to enliven the narrow sphere in which they lived.

Madame Williamson was rather tall, slight and thin, but delicately made. She had pretty feet, more remarkable for the grace with which they were joined to the ankles than for their narrowness, — a vulgar merit. Her hands were handsome when gloved. A certain redness, that seemed movable and rather dark in tone, disfigured her white skin, which was naturally fair and rosy. Premature wrinkles had aged a brow that was fine in shape and crowned with beautiful auburn hair, always braided in two strands and wound around the head, — a maidenly fashion which became her melancholy face. Her black eyes, sunken in dark circles and full of feverish ardor, assumed a calmness that seemed deceptive ; for at times, if she forgot the expression she imposed upon them, they revealed some secret anguish. Her oval face was rather long, but perhaps in other days happiness and health may have rounded its outlines. A deceptive smile, full of gentle sadness, was ever on her pallid lips, but the eyes grew animated, and the smile expressed the delights of maternal love when the two children, by whom she was always accompanied, looked at her and asked those idle and endless questions which have their meaning to a mother's heart.

Her walk was slow and dignified. She wore but one style of dress, with a constancy that showed a deliberate intention to take no further interest in personal adornment, and to forget the world, by which, no doubt, she wished to be forgot. Her gown was black and very long, fastened round the waist with a watered ribbon, and over it, in guise of a shawl, was a cambric kerchief with a broad hem, the ends passed negligently through her belt. Her shoes and her black silk stockings betrayed the elegance of her former life, and completed the conventional mourning that she always wore. Her bonnet, always of the same English shape, was gray in color and covered with a black veil.

She seemed very weak and ill. The only walk she took was from La Grenadière to the bridge of Tours, where, on a calm evening she would take the two children to breathe the cool air from the river and admire the effects of the setting sun upon a landscape as vast as that of the Bay of Naples or the Lake of Geneva. During the time she lived at La Grenadière she went but twice to Tours, — once to ask the principal of the college to direct her to the best masters of Latin, mathematics, and drawing; and next to arrange with the persons thus designated the price of their instructions, and the hours at which her sons could take their lessons. But it sufficed to show herself once or twice a week on the bridge in the evening, to rouse the interest of nearly all the inhabitants of the town, who made it their habitual promenade.

And yet, in spite of the harmless spying which the dreary leisure and uneasy curiosity of provincial towns forces upon their leading societies, no real information as to the unknown lady, her rank, her fortune, or even her present condition, was obtained. The owner of La Grenadière did, however, tell some of his friends the name (and it was no doubt a true one) under which she had taken the lease. She gave it as "Augusta Williamson, Countess of Brandon." The name was doubtless that of her husband. The later events of her history confirmed this statement; but it was never made public beyond the little world of merchants frequented by the owner.

So Madame Williamson continued a mystery to the leading society of Tours, and all that she allowed them to discover was her simple manners, delightfully natural, her personal distinction, and the tones of an angelic voice. The complete solitude in which she lived, her melancholy, and her beauty so cruelly obscured and even faded, charmed the minds of a few young men, who fell in love with her. But the more sincere they were, the less bold they became; moreover, she was so imposing that it was difficult to address her. When one or two, more courageous than the rest, wrote to her, Madame Williamson put their letters unopened into the fire. She seemed to have come to this enchanting retreat to abandon herself wholly to the pleasure of living there. The three masters who were admitted to La Grenadière spoke with respectful admiration of the close and cloudless union which bound the children and the mother in one.

The children also excited a great deal of interest, and no mother ever looked at them without envy. Both resembled Madame Williamson, who was really their mother. Each had a bright, transparent complexion and high color, clear, limpid eyes, long eyelashes, and the purity of outline which gives such brilliancy to the beauties of childhood. The eldest, named Louis-Gaston, had black hair, and a brave, intrepid eye. Everything about him denoted robust health, just as his broad, high forehead, intelligently rounded, foretold an energetic manhood. He was brisk and agile in his movements, a strapping lad, with nothing assuming about him, not easily surprised, and seeming to reflect on all he saw. His brother, named Marie-Gaston, was very fair, though a few locks of his hair were beginning to show the auburn color of his mother's. He had also the slender figure, the delicate features, and the winning grace so attractive in Madame Williamson. He seemed sickly, his gray eyes had a gentle look, his cheeks were pale; there was a good deal of the woman about him. His mother still kept him to embroidered collars, long curls, and those pretty jackets with frogged fastenings which are worn with so pleasing an effect, and which betray a feminine love of dress.

This dainty attire contrasted with the plain jacket of the elder brother, over which the plain linen collar of his shirt was turned. The trousers, boots, and color of the clothes were the same in the two brothers, and proclaimed their relationship as much as did their physical likeness. Seeing them together, it was impossible not to be struck with the care which Louis took of Marie. The look he gave him was paternal; and Marie, in spite of his childlike heedlessness, seemed full of gratitude to his brother. These two little flowers, scarcely apart on the same twig, were shaken by the same breezes and warmed by the same sun-ray; but while one was vigorous and rosy, the other was half-etiolated. A word, a look, an inflection of the voice sufficed to catch their attention, to make them turn their heads and listen, hear an order, a request, a suggestion, and obey. Madame Williamson made them understand her wishes and her will as though there were but one thought among them.

When they were running or playing before her in their walks, gathering a flower, examining an insect, her eyes rested upon them with such deep and tender emotion that the most indifferent observers were touched; sometimes they even stopped to watch the smiling children, and saluted the mother with a friendly glance. Who, indeed, would not have admired the exquisite nicety of their garments, the pretty tones of their voices, the grace of their movements, their happy faces, and that instinctive nobility which told of careful training from their cradles? Those children seemed never to have wept or screamed. The mother had an almost electric sense of their wishes and their pains, and she calmed them or forestalled them ceaselessly. She seemed to dread a plaint from her children more than eternal condemnation for herself. All things in and about them were to her honor; and the picture of their triple life, seeming one and the same life, gave birth to vague, alluring visions of the joys we dream of tasting in a better world.

The domestic life of these harmonious beings was in keeping with the ideas their outward appearance conveyed; it was orderly, regular, and simple, as became a home where children were educated. The two boys rose early, by daybreak, and said a short prayer, taught them in infancy, — true words said for seven years on their mother's bed, begun and ended by two kisses. Then the brothers, trained to that minute care of the person so essential to health of body and purity of soul, dressed themselves as carefully as a pretty woman might have done. They neglected nothing, so fearful were they of a word of blame, however tenderly their mother might utter it, — as, for instance, when she said at breakfast one morning, "My dear angels, how did you get your nails so black already?"

After dressing, the pair would go down into the garden and shake off the heaviness of the night in its dewy freshness, while waiting for the servant to put in order the dining-room, where they studied their lessons till their mother woke. But from time to time they peeped and listened to find out if she were awake, though forbidden to enter the room before a given hour; and this daily irruption, made in defiance of a compact, was a delightful moment both to them and to their mother. Marie would jump upon the bed and throw his arms about his idol, while Louis, kneeling beside the pillow, held her hand. Then followed tender inquiries like those of a lover, angelic laughter, caresses that were passionate and pure, eloquent silence, words half-uttered, childish stories interrupted by kisses, begun again, always listened to, seldom finished.

"Have you studied your lessons?" the mother would say, in a gentle voice, ready to pity idleness as a misfortune, but readier still with a tearful glance for the one who could say he had done his best. She knew those children desired only to satisfy her; they knew she lived only for them, — that she led them by the wisdom of love and gave them all her thoughts and all her time. A marvellous instinct, which is neither reason nor egotism, which we may perhaps call sentiment in its first sincerity, teaches children whether they are or are not, the object of exclusive care, and whether

others find happiness in caring for them. Do you
truly love them? then the dear creatures, all frankness
and all justice, are delightfully grateful. They love
passionately and jealously; they possess the sweetest
delicacy, they can find the tenderest words; they confide
to you, they trust to you in all things. Perhaps there
are no bad children without bad mothers, for the
affection children feel is always in reply to that they
receive, to the first caress given to them, to the first
words they have heard, to the first looks from which
they have sought for love and life. At that period all
to them is attraction or repulsion. God has put children
in the womb of the mother to teach her that she must
bear them long.

And yet we find some mothers cruelly misunderstood
by their children; we see sublime maternal tenderness
constantly wounded by horrible ingratitude and neglect, — showing how difficult it is to lay down absolute
principles in matters of feeling.

In the heart of this mother and in those of her sons
no one of the thousand ties which could attach them to
one another was missing. Alone on earth they lived a
united life and understood each other. When Madame
Williamson was silent the boys said nothing, respectful
even to the thoughts they could not share. But the
elder, gifted with a mind that was already strong, was
never satisfied with his mother's assurances that her

health was good; he studied her face with silent uneasiness, unaware of danger, yet foreboding it when he noticed the purple tints round the sunken eyes and saw that the hollows deepened and the red patches on the face grew more inflamed. Full of true perception, when he thought that his brother's games were beginning to tire her he would say, " Come, Marie, let's go and breakfast; I 'm hungry."

But when he reached the door he would turn back to catch the expression on his mother's face, which always wore a smile for him, though sometimes tears would start from her eyes as a gesture of her boy revealed his exquisite feeling, his precocious comprehension of her sorrow.

The mother was always present at the lessons which took place from ten to three o'clock, interrupted at midday by the second breakfast, generally taken in the garden pavilion. After this meal came a play-hour, when the happy mother, the unhappy woman, lay on a sofa in the pavilion, whence she could see that sweet Touraine, incessantly changing, ceaselessly rejuvenated by the varying accidents of light and sky and season.

The boys ran about the place, climbing the terraces, chasing the lizards, themselves as agile; they watched the seeds, and studied the insects and the flowers, running constantly to their mother with questions. Children need no playthings in the country; the things about them are amusement and occupation enough.

During the lessons Madame Williamson sat in the room with her work; she was silent and never looked at either masters or pupils, but she listened attentively to catch the meaning of the words and know if Louis were understanding them, and whether his mind were acquiring force. If he interrupted his master with a question, that was surely a sign of progress; then the mother's eyes would brighten, she smiled, and gave the boy a look full of hope. She exacted very little of Marie; all her anxiety was for the elder, to whom she showed a sort of respect, employing her womanly and motherly tact to lift his soul and give him a high sense of what he should become. Behind this course was a hidden purpose which the child was one day to comprehend — and he did comprehend it. After each lesson she inquired carefully of the masters what they thought of Louis's progress. She was so kindly and so winning that the teachers told her the truth and showed her how to make Louis work in directions where they thought him wanting.

Such was their life, uniform but full, — a life where work and play, cheerfully mingled, left no opening for ennui. Discouragement or anger was impossible, the mother's boundless love made all things easy. She had taught her sons discretion by refusing nothing to them; courage, by awarding them just praise; resignation, by showing them its necessity under all circumstances. She developed and strengthened the angelic nature within them with the care of a guardian angel. Sometimes a few tears would moisten her eyes, when, watching them at play, the thought came that they had never caused her a moment's grief. She spent delightful hours lying on her rural couch, enjoying the fine weather, the broad sheet of water, the picturesque country, the voices of her children, their merry laughs rippling into fresh laughter, and their little disputes, which only evidenced their union, and Louis's fatherly care of Marie, and the love of both for her.

They all spoke French and English equally well, and the mother used both languages in conversing with her boys. She ruled them by kindness, — hiding nothing, but explaining all. She allowed no false idea to gain a lodgment in their minds, and no mistaken principle to enter their hearts. When Louis wished to read she gave him books that were interesting and yet sound, true to the facts of life, — lives of famous sailors, biographies of great men, illustrious captains; finding in such books the occasions to explain to him the world and life, to show him the means by which obscure persons who had greatness within their souls, coming from the lower walks of life and without friends, had succeeded in rising to noble destinies.

Such lessons she gave him in the evening, when

Marie, tired with his play, was sleeping on her knees in the cool silence of a beauteous night, when the Loire reflected the heavens. But they increased her secret sadness, and ended often in leaving her exhausted, thoughtful, and with her eyes full of tears.

"Mother, why do you cry?" asked Louis, one rich June evening, just as the half-tints of a softly-lighted night were succeeding a warm day.

"My son," she answered, winding her arm around the neck of the boy, whose concealed emotion touched her deeply, "because the hard lot of Jameray Duval, who reached distinction without help, is the fate I have brought on you and your brother. Soon, my dear child, you will be alone in the world, with no one to lean on, no protector. I am forced to leave you, still mere children; and yet I think that you, my Louis, know enough, and are strong enough to be a guide to Marie. I love you too well not to suffer from such thoughts. God grant you may not some day curse me."

"Why should I curse you, mother?"

"Some day, my child," she answered, kissing his brow, "you will realize that I have done you wrong. I abandon you, here, without means, without fortune, without" — she hesitated — "without a father," she added.

Tears choked her voice; she gently pushed her son away from her, and he, understanding by a sort of intuition that she wished to be alone, carried the sleeping Marie away with him. An hour later, when his brother was in bed, Louis returned with cautious steps to the pavilion where his mother was still lying. He heard her call, in a voice that sounded sweetly on his ear, —

"Louis, come!"

The boy flung himself into his mother's arms, and they kissed each other almost convulsively.

"Dearest," he said, for he often gave her that name, finding even that too feeble to express his tenderness, "dearest, why do you fear that you will die?"

"I am very ill, my poor loved angel," she said. "I grow weaker daily; my disease is incurable, and I know it."

"What disease is it?"

"I must forget; and you, you must never know the cause of my death."

The child was silent for a moment, glancing furtively at his mother whose eyes were raised to heaven, watching the clouds. Moment of tender melancholy! Louis did not believe in his mother's approaching death, but he felt her griefs without understanding them. He respected her long revery. Were he less a child he might have read upon that sacred face thoughts of repentance mingled with happy memories, — the whole of a woman's life; a careless girlhood, a cold marriage, a terrible passion, flowers born of a tempest, hurled by the lightning to the depths of that abyss from which there is no return.

"My precious mother," said Louis at last, "why do you hide your sufferings from me?"

"My son," she answered, "we should always hide our troubles from the eyes of strangers, and show to them a smiling face; we should never speak to others of ourselves, but think only of them. Those things, if we practise them in our homes, will make others happy. Some day you, too, will suffer deeply. Then remember your poor mother, who died before your eyes hiding her griefs, and smiling for you; it will give you courage to bear the woes of life."

Smothering her feelings, she tried to show her boy the mechanism of existence, the just value, the ground-work, and the stability of wealth; the power of social relations; the honorable means of amassing money for the wants of life; and the necessity of education. Then she revealed to him one cause of her sadness and her tears, and told him that on the morrow of her death he and Marie would be destitute, possessing only a trifling sum of money, and with no other protector than God.

"What haste I must make to learn!" cried the boy, glancing at his mother, with a deep, yet plaintive look.

"Ah, I am happy!" she exclaimed, covering her son with tears and kisses. "He has understood me!

Louis," she added, "you will be your brother's guardian, will you not? you promise me? You are no longer a child."

"Yes," he answered, "I promise; but you will not die yet? Say you will not!"

"Poor children!" she said, "my love for you detains me; and this country is so beautiful, the air is so reviving, perhaps — "

"I shall love Touraine more than ever now," said the lad, with emotion.

From that day Madame Williamson, foreseeing her end, talked to her eldest son of his future lot. Louis, who had now completed his fourteenth year, became more thoughtful, applied himself better, and cared less for play. Whether it were that he persuaded Marie to read, instead of caring only for games of play, it is certain that the two boys made much less noise in the sunken paths and in the terraces and gardens of La Grenadière. They conformed their life to the sad condition of their mother, whose face grew paler day by day, with yellow tints, the lines deepening night after night.

In the month of August, six months after the arrival of the little family, all was changed at La Grenadière. The pretty house, once so gay, so lively, had grown sad and silent, and its occupants seldom left the premises. Madame Williamson had scarcely strength to walk to the bridge. Louis, whose imagination had suddenly developed, and who had now identified himself, as it were, with his mother, guessing her weariness, invented pretexts to avoid a walk which he felt was too long for her.　Happy couples passing along the road to Saint-Cyr and the groups of pedestrians below upon the *levée* saw, in the warm evenings, the pale, emaciated woman in deep mourning, near her end yet still brilliant, pacing like a phantom along the terraces.　Great sufferings are divined.　Even the cottage of the vine-dresser became silent.　Sometimes the peasant and his wife and children were grouped about their door, Fanny, the old English servant, would be washing near the well, Madame Williamson and her boys sitting in the pavilion, and yet no sound was heard in the once gay gardens, and all eyes turned, when the dying woman did not see them, to contemplate her.　She was so good, so thoughtful for others, so worthy of respect from all who approached her!

Since the beginning of the autumn, which is always fine and brilliant in Touraine, and which, with its beneficent influences, its fruits, its grapes, did somewhat prolong the mother's life beyond the natural term of her hidden malady, she had thought of nothing but her children, and rejoiced over every hour she had them with her as though it were her last.

From the month of June to the month of September Louis studied at night without his mother's knowledge and made enormous progress ; he was already in the equations of the second degree in algebra, had learned descriptive geometry, and drew admirably well. He was, in fact, prepared to pass an entrance examination to the École Polytechnique. Occasionally in the evenings he went to walk on the bridge of Tours, where he had met a lieutenant of the navy on half-pay ; the manly face, the decorated breast, the hearty bearing of this sailor of the Empire, affected his imagination. The lieutenant, on the other hand, took a fancy to the lad whose eyes sparkled with energy. Louis, eager for military tales and liking to ask questions, walked about with the old salt and listened to him. The lieutenant had a friend and companion in an infantry colonel ; young Gaston could therefore hear of the two lives, military and naval, life in camp and life on seaboard, and he questioned the two officers incessantly.

After a time, entering into their hard lot and their rough experience, he suddenly asked his mother for permission to roam about the canton to amuse himself. As the astonished masters had told Madame Williamson that her son was studying too hard, she acceded to his request with extreme pleasure. The boy took immense walks. Wishing to harden himself to fatigue he climbed the highest trees with agility, he learned to swim, and he sat up working at night. He was no longer the same child ; he was a young man, on whose face the sun had cast its brown tones, bringing out the lines of an already deep purpose.

The month of October came, and Madame Williamson could rise only at midday, when the sun-rays, reflected from the Loire and concentrated on the terraces, produced the same equable warmth at La Grenadière that prevails on warm, moist days around the Bay of Naples, — a circumstance which leads physicians to recommend Touraine. On such days she would sit beneath an evergreen, and her sons no longer left her. Studies ceased, the masters were dismissed. Children and mother wished to live in one another's hearts, without a care, without distractions from the outside. No tears were shed, no happy laughter heard. The elder, lying on the grass beside his mother, was like a lover at her feet, which he sometimes kissed. Marie, restless and uneasy, gathered flowers, which he brought to her with a sad air, rising on tiptoe to take from her lips the kiss of a young girl. That pallid woman with the large black eyes, lying exhausted, slow in all her motions, making no plaint, smiling at her two children so full of health, so living, was indeed a touching spectacle amid the melancholy glories of autumn, with its yellowing leaves, its half-bared trees, the softened light of the sun and the white clouds of a Touraine sky.

The day came when Madame Williamson was ordered by the doctor not to leave her room. Daily it was adorned with the flowers she loved best, and her children stayed there. Early in November she opened her piano for the last time. A Swiss landscape hung above it. Beside the window the brothers, with their arms around each other, showed her their mingled heads. Her eyes moved constantly from her children to the landscape, from the landscape to her children. Her face colored, her fingers ran with passion along the ivory notes. It was her last fête, a fête hidden from others, a fête celebrated in the depths of her soul by the genius of memory.

The doctor came and bade her keep her bed. The sentence was received by her and by her sons in a silence that was almost stupid.

When the physician went away she said: " Louis, take me on the terrace that I may see the country once more."

At these words, simply said, the lad gave her his arm and took her to the centre of the terrace. There her eyes sought, involuntarily perhaps, the heavens rather than the earth; it would have been difficult at that moment to say where was the finer landscape, for the clouds represented vaguely the majestic glaciers of the Alps. Her brow contracted violently, her eyes took an expression of remorse and sorrow, she caught the hands of her children and pressed them to her beating heart.

"Father and mother unknown!" she cried, casting an agonized look upon them. "Poor children! what will become of you? And when you are men, what stern account will you not demand of me for my life and yours?"

She pushed her children from her, placed both elbows on the balustrade, hid her face in her hands, and remained for a few moments alone with her soul, fearing to be seen. When she roused herself from her grief she saw Louis and Marie kneeling beside her like two angels; they watched her looks and both smiled at her.

"Could I but take those smiles with me!" she said, drying her eyes.

She returned to the house and went to her bed, to leave it no more until they placed her in her coffin.

Eight days went by, each day like the rest. The old waiting-woman and Louis took turns to watch that bed at night, their eyes fixed on the patient. It was the same drama, profoundly tragic, which is played at all hours and in all families where they dread that every breath may be the last of some adored member. On the fifth day of this fatal week the doctor proscribed flowers. One by one the illusions of life were taken from her.

After that day Louis and Marie found fire beneath their lips when they kissed their mother's brow. At last, on the Saturday night, she could bear no noise, and her room was left in disorder. That necessary neglect marked the beginning of the death of this woman, once so fastidious, so enamoured of elegance. Louis no longer left her even for a moment.

During the night of Sunday, in the midst of deepest silence, Louis, who thought her dozing, saw by the light of the lamp a white, moist hand put back the curtain.

"My son," she said.

The tones of the dying woman were so solemn that their power, proceeding from her troubled soul, reacted violently on her child; he felt a burning heat in the marrow of his bones.

"What is it, mother?"

"Listen to me. To-morrow all will be over. We shall see each other no more. To-morrow you will be a man, my child. I am obliged to make certain arrangements which must remain a secret between you and me. Take the key of my little table. You have it? Open the drawer. You will find on the left two sealed papers. On one is marked Louis, on the other, Marie."

"I have them, mother."

"My darling son, they are the legal records of your birth, of great importance to you. Give them to my poor old Fanny, who will take care of them for you, and return them to you when needed. Now," she continued, "look again in the same place and see if there is not another paper on which I have written a few lines?"

"Yes, mother."

And Louis began to read : "Marie Augusta William-son, born at — "

"That will do," she said quickly, "Don't go on. My son, when I am dead, give that paper also to Fanny and tell her to take it to the mayor's office at Saint-Cyr, where they will need it to draw up the record of my death. Now bring what you require to write a letter at my dictation."

When she saw that her son was ready and that he turned to her as if to listen, she said, in a calm voice, dictating : "Sir, your wife, Lady Brandon, died at Saint-Cyr, near Tours, department of the Indre-et-Loire. She forgave you. Sign it — "

She stopped, hesitating and agitated.

"Do you feel worse?" asked Louis.

"Sign it, 'Louis Gaston.'"

She sighed, then continued : "Seal the letter and direct it to 'The Earl of Brandon, Brandon Square, Hyde Park, London, England.' Have you written it? Very good," she said. "On the day of my death you must mail that letter from Tours. Now," she continued, after a pause, "bring my little pocket-book — you know it — and come close to me, dear child. In it," she said, when Louis had returned to her, "are twelve thousand

francs. They are rightfully yours, alas! You would
have had far more had your father —"

"My father!" exclaimed the lad, "where is he?"

"Dead," she replied, laying a finger on her lips, —
"dead to save my honor and my life."

She raised her eyes to heaven; she would have wept
had she still had tears for sorrows "Louis," she said,
"swear to me on this pillow that you will forget all that
you have written, and all that I have said to you."

"Yes mother."

"Kiss me, dear angel."

She made a long pause as if to gather courage from
God, and to limit her words to the strength that was
left to her.

"Listen," she said at last. "These twelve thousand
francs are your whole fortune; you must keep them
upon your person, because when I am dead, the legal
authorities will come here and put seals on everything.
Nothing will belong to you, not even your mother.
Poor orphans! all you can do is to go away — God
knows where. I have provided for Fanny; she will
have three hundred francs a year and stay in Tours.
But what will you do with yourself and your brother?"

She raised herself in the bed and looked at the brave
boy, who, with great drops on his forehead, pale from
emotion, his eyes half-veiled in tears, stood erect
before her.

"Mother," he replied in a deep voice, "I have thought of it. I shall take Marie to the college of Tours. I shall give ten thousand francs to old Fanny and tell her to put them in safety, and to watch over my brother. Then, with the rest, I will go to Brest, and enter the navy as an apprentice. While Marie is getting his education I shall be promoted lieutenant. Mother, die easy; I shall be rich; I will put our boy into the École Polytechnique, and he shall follow his bent."

A flash of joy came from the half-quenched eyes of the mother; two tears rolled down her burning cheeks; then a great sigh escaped her lips. She barely escaped dying at that moment from the joy of finding the soul of the father in that of her son, now suddenly transformed into a man.

"Angel from heaven!" she said, weeping, "you have healed my sorrows with those words. Ah! I can die now. He is my son," she added; "I have made, I have trained, a man."

She raised her hands in the air and clasped them, as if to express a boundless joy; then she lay back on the pillows.

"Mother, you are turning white," cried the boy.

"Fetch a priest," she answered, in a dying voice.

Louis woke old Fanny, who ran in terror to the parsonage of Saint-Cyr.

Early in the morning Madame Williamson received the sacraments in presence of her children, with old Fanny, and the family of the vine-dresser, simple folk, now part of the family, kneeling round her. The silver cross borne by a humble choir boy, a village choir boy! was held before the bed; an old priest administered the viaticum to the dying mother. The viaticum! sublime word, idea more sublime than the word, which the apostolic religion of the Roman Church alone employs.

"This woman has suffered much," said the curate in his simple language.

Madame Williamson heard no longer; but her eyes remained fastened on her children. All present, in mortal terror, listened in the deep silence to the breathing of the dying woman as it slackened and grew slower. At intervals, a deep sigh showed that life was still continuing the inward struggle. At last, the mother breathed no longer. Those present wept, excepting Marie, too young, poor child, to be aware of death. Fanny and the vine-dresser's wife closed the eyes of the once exquisite creature, whose beauty reappeared in all its glory. They sent away those present, took the furniture from the room, placed the body of the departed in its shroud, lighted the wax-tapers around the bed, arranged the basin of holy water, the branch of box, and the crucifix, after the manner of that region of country, closed the blinds and drew the curtains. Then the vicar came and passed the night in prayer with Louis, who would not leave his mother.

The funeral took place Tuesday morning ; old Fanny, the children, and the vine-dresser alone followed the body of a woman whose beauty, wit, and grace had given her in other days a European fame ; and whose funeral would have been pompously heralded in the newspapers of London, as an aristocratic solemnity, had she not committed a tender crime, a crime always punished on this earth, perhaps to allow the pardoned angel to enter heaven. When the earth fell on his mother's coffin, Marie wept, comprehending then that he should see her no more.

A simple wooden cross stands above her grave and bears these words, given by the curate of Saint-Cyr.

HERE LIES

A SORROWFUL WOMAN.

SHE DIED AGED THIRTY-SIX,

BEARING THE NAME AUGUSTA IN HEAVEN.

PRAY FOR HER.

When all was over the children returned to La Grenadière to cast a last look upon their home ; then, holding each other by the hand, they prepared to leave it with Fanny, making the vine-dresser responsible to the authorities.

At the last moment the old waiting-woman called Louis to the steps of the well, and said to him apart:

"Monsieur Louis, here is madame's ring."

The boy wept, — moved at the sight of a living memorial of his dead mother. In his strong self-command he had forgotten this last duty. He kissed the old woman. Then all three went down the sunken pathway, and down the flight of steps, and on to Tours without once looking back.

"Mamma used to stand here," said Marie, when they reached the bridge.

Fanny had an old cousin, a retired dressmaker, living in the rue de la Guerche. There she took the lads, thinking they could all live together. But Louis explained his plans, gave her Marie's certificate of birth and the ten thousand francs, and the next day, accompanied by the old woman, he took his brother to the school. He told the principal the facts of the case, but very briefly, and went away, taking his brother with him to the gate. There he tenderly and solemnly told him of their loneliness in the world and gave him counsel for the future, looked at him silently a moment, kissed him, looked at him again, wiped away a tear, and went away, looking back again and again at his brother, left alone at the college gate.

A month later Louis Gaston was an apprentice on board a government ship, leaving the Rochefort roads. Leaning against the shrouds of the corvette " Iris," he watched the coasts of France as they dropped below the blue horizon. Soon he saw himself alone, lost in the midst of ocean, as he was in the midst of life.

" Must n't cry, young fellow ; there 's a God for all the world," said an old seaman, in his gruff voice, both harsh and kind.

The lad thanked him with an intrepid look. Then he bowed his head and resigned himself to a sailor's life, for — was he not a father?

1832.

BALZAC IN ENGLISH.

LOUIS LAMBERT.

"As for Balzac," writes Oscar Wilde, "he was a most remarkable combination of the artistic temperament with the scientific spirit." It is his artistic temperament which reveals itself the most clearly in the novel before us. As we read "Louis Lambert," we feel convinced that it is largely autobiographical. It is a psychical study as delicate as Amiel's Journal, and nearly as spiritual. We follow the life of the sensitive, poetical schoolboy, feeling that it is a true picture of Balzac's own youth. When the literary work on which the hero had written for years in all his spare moments is destroyed, we do not need to be told by Mr. Parsons that this is an episode in Balzac's own experience ; we are sure of this fact already ; and no writer could describe so sympathetically the deep spiritual experiences of an aspiring soul who had not at heart felt them keenly. No materialist could have written "Louis Lambert." — *Boston Transcript.*

Of all of Balzac's works thus far translated by Miss Katharine Prescott Wormeley, the last in the series, "Louis Lambert," is the most difficult of comprehension. It is the second of the author's Philosophical Studies, "The Magic Skin" being the first, and "Seraphita," shortly to be published, being the third and last. In "Louis Lambert" Balzac has presented a study of a noble soul — a spirit of exalted and lofty aspirations which chafes under the fetters of earthly existence, and has no sympathy with the world of materialism. This pure-souled genius is made the medium, moreover, for the enunciation of the outlines of a system of philosophy which goes to the very roots of Oriental occultism and mysticism as its source, and which thus reveals the marvellous scope of Balzac's learning. The scholarly introduction to the book by George Frederic Parsons, in addition to throwing a great deal of valuable light upon other phases of the work, shows how many of the most recent scientific theories are directly in line with the doctrines broadly set forth by Balzac nearly sixty years ago. The book is one to be studied rather than read ; and it is made intelligible by the extremely able introduction and by Miss Wormeley's excellent translation. — *The Book-Buyer.*

"Louis Lambert," with the two other members of the Trilogy, "La Peau de Chagrin" and "Seraphita," is a book which presents many difficulties to the student. It deals with profound and unfamiliar subjects, and the meaning of the author by no means lies on the surface. It is the study of a great, aspiring soul enshrined in a feeble body, the sword wearing out the scabbard, the spirit soaring away from its prison-house of flesh to its more congenial home. It is in marked contrast to the study of the destructive and debasing process which we see in the "Peau de Chagrin." It stands midway between this study of the mean and base and that noble presentation of the final evolution of a soul on the very borders of Divinity which Balzac gives us in "Seraphita."

The reader not accustomed to such high ponderings needs a guide to place him *en rapport* with the Seer. Such a guide and friend he finds in Mr. Parsons, whose introduction of one hundred and fifty pages is by no means the least valuable part of this volume. It is impossible to do more than sketch the analysis of Balzac's philosophy and the demonstration so successfully attempted by Mr. Parsons of the exact correlation between many of Balzac's speculations and the newest scientific theories. The introduction is so closely written that it defies much condensation. It is so intrinsically valuable that it will thoroughly repay careful and minute study. — *From "Light," a London Journal of Psychical and Occult Research, March 9, 1889.*

One handsome 12mo volume, uniform with "Père Goriot," "The Duchesse de Langeais," "César Birotteau," "Eugénie Grandet," "Cousin Pons," "The Country Doctor," "The Two Brothers," "The Alkahest," "Modeste Mignon," "The Magic Skin," "Cousin Bette." Bound in half morocco, French Style. Price, $1.50.

ROBERTS BROTHERS, Publishers,

Boston.